Hen Llywarch, William Owen Pughe

The Heroic Elegies And Other Pieces

Hen Llywarch, William Owen Pughe

The Heroic Elegies And Other Pieces

ISBN/EAN: 9783742893383

Manufactured in Europe, USA, Canada, Australia, Japa

Cover: Foto ©Andreas Hilbeck / pixelio.de

Manufactured and distributed by brebook publishing software
(www.brebook.com)

Hen Llywarch, William Owen Pughe

The Heroic Elegies And Other Pieces

THE

HEROIC ELEGIES

AND

OTHER PIECES

OF

LLYWARÇ HEN,

PRINCE OF THE CUMBRIAN BRITONS:

WITH

A LITERAL TRANSLATION,

BY

' *WILLIAM OWEN.*

Y GWIR YN ERBYN Y BYD.

LONDON:

PRINTED FOR J. OWEN, NO. 168, PICCADILLY,
AND E. WILLIAMS, STRAND.

M DCC XCII.

TO

THOMAS PENNANT

AND

PAUL PANTON, ESQUIRES,

IN TOKEN OF ACKNOWLEDGEMENT,

FROM AN INDIVIDUAL OF A NATION

BENEFITED BY THEIR PATRIOTISM,

THIS COLLECTION OF THE WORKS OF

LLYWARÇ HEN,

IS MOST RESPECTFULLY DEDICATED,

BY THEIR HUMBLE SERVANT,

WILLIAM OWEN.

SOME ACCOUNT

OF

LLÝWARÇ HEṄ,*

WITH A SKETCH OF BRITISH BARDISM.

L LYWARÇ HEṄ, or *Llywarç the Aged*, was one of thofe who fignalized themfelves in an age, remarkable in the hiftory of *Britain* for terrible war and devaftation.

---

* Eight of the Elegies of *Llywarç Hèn*, addreffed to particular perfons, being in fome degree hiftorical, were felected from his other pieces, and the five fhorteft, and part of the three longeft of them tranflated, with notes, and a fketch of the Author's life, by the late *Richard Thomas*, A.B. of *Jefus College*, *Oxford*. Having accefs to the work which Mr. *Thomas* left behind, I was induced, for the fake of a fhort refpite from my long confinement to the compiling of a *Welfh* and *Englifh* Dictionary, to beftow a few days in making a tranflation of the remainder of *Llywarç Hèn's* Poems; but on examining what was already done, I found the Tranflator had been too anxious in aiming at elegance, to preferve that ftrictly literal form which it was my wifh to give; I therefore rendered the whole, line for line, as clofe as the two languages would permit. Indeed the *Englifh* phrafeology has been made fubfervient to the original, as often as it could be done, without becoming unintelligible. This remark I wifh the Reader to remember as an apology for many paffages; but others may be the refult of a want of leifure, and ability. What little account is given of the Author, is for the moft part taken from the fketch by Mr. *Thomas*; whofe premature death, thofe who have a tafte for *Britifh* Antiquities have real caufe to lament.

There were many celebrated Bards amongft the ancient *Britons*, whofe productions have been partly preferved to the prefent time; but it is to be

regretted

tion. As to the exact period wherein he flourished we are
enabled to determine, with a tolerable degree of exactness,
by concurring circumstances, that he was born about the
commencement of the sixth, and lived to the middle of
the seventh century; being about a hundred and fifty
years old at the time of his death.*

He was descended from princes, who had been elective
monarchs of the whole island. His father was *Elidyr
Lydanwyn,*

regretted that a number of most curious relicks have also been lost through
the viciffitudes of destructive warfare; and what remain moulder away
apace. The number of pieces which are now extant, composed anterior .
. to the death of the last *Llywelyn* may be about five hundred; nearly a third
of which are as old as the fifth, sixth and seventh centuries; and written
chiefly by *Aneurin, Myrddin ab Morvryn,* and *Llywarç,* who were northern
Britons, and *Taliesin,* a native of *Wales.* Fearing that a total oblivion
should, at some short period hence, be the fate that awaits these monuments of genius, the Editor, anxious to give the world some notice of their
existence, has it in view to lay them before the public, to give such an idea
of their merits as can be formed from a mere literal version; in the man-
-ner adopted in the present collection.

     * *Arthur* was killed in 542, *Cadwallon* died about the year 646, at both
of which periods *Llywarç* was alive, consequently what is advanced above
cannot be far from the truth. Collateral proofs might be brought from
the old Pedigrees, the Catalogue of *British* Saints, and from the Triades, that
would settle the point with a greater degree of certainty; but perhaps it
will not be thought of such moment as to want farther elucidation.

Lydanwyn, the fon of *Meirçion*, the fon of *Grwſt*, the fon of *Cenau*, the fon of *Coel* king of *Britain*.*

* To gratify the curious in old pedigrees ſtill more, we are enabled to give that of the venerable *Llywarç* here more at large.

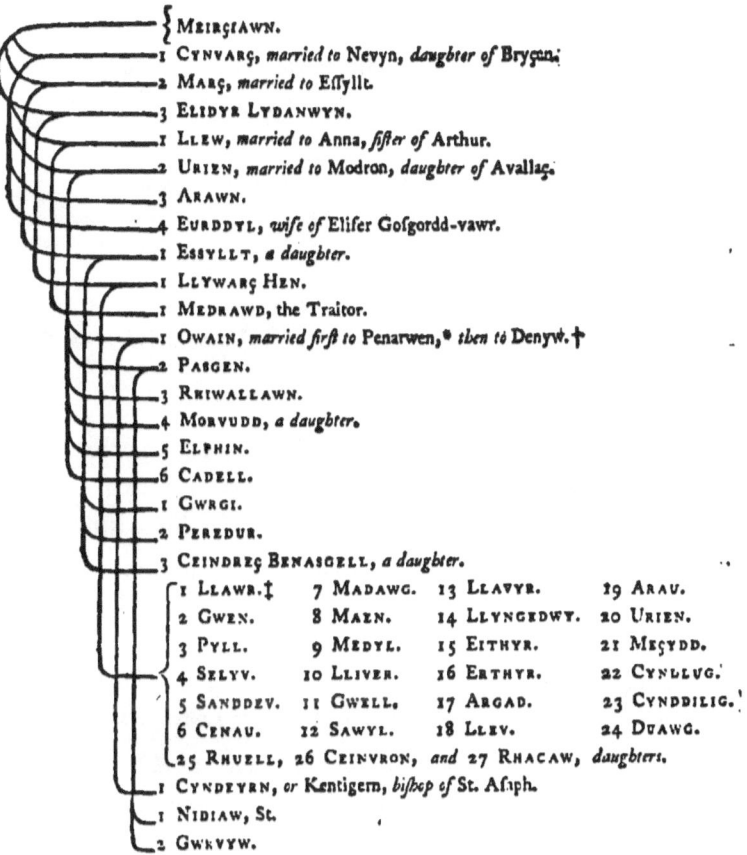

{ MEIRÇIAWN.
1 CYNVARÇ, *married to* Nevyn, *daughter of* Bryçan.
2 MARÇ, *married to* Eſſyllt.
3 ELIDYR LYDANWYN.
1 LLEW, *married to* Anna, *ſiſter of* Arthur.
2 URIEN, *married to* Modron, *daughter of* Avallaç.
3 ARAWN.
4 EURDDYL, *wife of* Elifer Goſgordd-vawr.
1 ESSYLLT, *a daughter.*
1 LLYWARÇ HEN.
1 MEDRAWD, the Traitor.
1 OWAIN, *married firſt to* Penarwen,* *then to* Denyw.†
2 PASGEN.
3 RHIWALLAWN.
4 MORVUDD, *a daughter.*
5 ELPHIN.
6 CADELL.
1 GWRGI.
2 PEREDUR.
3 CEINDREÇ BENASGELL, *a daughter.*

1 LLAWR.‡	7 MADAWG.	13 LLAVYR.	19 ARAU.
2 GWEN.	8 MAEN.	14 LLYNGEDWY.	20 URIEN.
3 PYLL.	9 MEDYL.	15 EITHYR.	21 MEÇYDD.
4 SELYV.	10 LLIVER.	16 ERTHYR.	22 CYNLLUG.
5 SANDDEV.	11 GWELL.	17 ARGAD.	23 CYNDDILIG.
6 CENAU.	12 SAWYL.	18 LLEV.	24 DUAWG.

25 RHUELL, 26 CEINVRON, *and* 27 RHACAW, *daughters.*
1 CYNDEYRN, *or* Kentigern, *biſhop of* St. Aſaph.
1 NIDIAW, St.
2 GWRVYW.

* Daughter of *Cul Vanawyd Prydain.*
† Daughter of *Llewddyn Luyddawg* of Edinburgh.
‡ Variations of the names from different copies—*Gwair, Newydd, Deigyr, Nudd, Rhudd, Heilyn, Llywenydd, Gorwynion, Cain, Llorien, Cyzddelw, Duywg, Erwyr, Rlun.*

What

What has been afferted with refpect to the period wherein *Llywarç* lived, the following detail of the leading incidents that happened to him, will corroborate with a confiderable degree of precifion.

According to the *Hiftorical Triades,** he paffed fome of his younger days in the court of the celebrated *Arthur.* But it feems his continuance there was not long for he departed in difguft; at leaft fo it may be conceived from the following *Triad:*

   " Tri thrwyddedawg, 'ac anvoddawg llŷs Arthur: Llywarç " Hên, a Llwmhunig ab Maon, a Heledd verç Cyndrwyn."

   " The three free and difcontented guefts in the court of *Arthur :* *Llywarç the Aged,* and *Llwmhunig* the fon of *Maon,* and *Heledd* the daughter of *Cyndrwyn.*"

In the fame ancient documents there is a *Triad* that is a very honourable teftimony of the abilities of *Llywarç;* by which it appears he was no lefs efteemed for his wifdom in council, than for his prowefs in the field of battle. Thefe are the words:

   " Tri çyngoriad varçawg llŷs Arthur: Cynon ab Clydno Eiddyn, " Arawn ab Cynvarç, a Llywarç Hên ab Elidyr Lydanwyn."

   " The three counfelling warriors of the court of *Arthur :* *Cynon* " the fon of *Clydno* of *Edinburgh,* *Arawn* the fon of *Cynvarç,* and " *Llywarç Hên* the fon of *Elidyr Lydanwyn.*"

   * The *Triades of the Ifle of Britain,* as they are called, are fome of the moft curious and valuable fragments preferved in the *Wilfh* language. They relate of perfons, and events from the earlieft times to the beginning of the feventh century.

Arthur,

SOME ACCOUNT OF LLYWARÇ HÉN, &c.   ix

Arthur fell in the battle of *Camlan*, in the year 542, at which period *Llywarç* muſt have been nearly forty years old. His ſtay with *Arthur* was not long, the particular time, moſt probably, was when he compoſed the Elegy on *Geraint ab Erbin*, about the year 530, in which *Arthur* is mentioned. *Llywarç* took no part in the civil war that brought on the cataſtrophe at *Camlan,* ſo fatal to the cauſe of the *Britons*; for he was then in his own principality of *Argoed,** in *Cumberland*. Seeing the lowring ſtorm approaching on every ſide, he entered into a confederacy with his relation *Urien,* prince of *Reged,* and his valiant ſon *Owain,†* for the purpoſe of repelling the incroachments of the *Saxons,* on their refpective territories; thoſe perſevering invaders having already obtained poſſeſſion of the countries to the eaſtward, called *Deivyr a Brynaiç,* or *Deira* and *Bernicia.*

The ancient writer of the *Saxon* genealogies, at the end of the Chronicle of *Nennius,* mentions that there were four kings in *Cumbria,* at the ſame time, that is to ſay, *Urien,* who was elected ſovereign; *Rhydderç‡* the Generous;

* The ancient *Cumbria* is not to be underſtood as comprehended within the limits of the province now called *Cumberland*; but it was ſo much of the northern country as the *Cynmry* retained at that period, extending into *Scotland*. However it is pretty certain that *Argoed* was a part of the preſent *Cumberland*; it lay weſt of the Foreſt of *Celyddon,* and was bordered by that wood, to the eaſt, as the name implies.

† " Tri gwyn deyrn Ynys Prydain: Rhun mab Maelgwn, Owain mab " Urien, a Rhuvaon Bevyr mab Deorath Wledig."

" The three bleſſed princes of the iſle of *Britain*: *Rhun* the ſon of *Mael-* " *gwn*; *Owain* the ſon of *Urien*; and *Rhuvaon* the Fair, the ſon of *Deo-* " *rath Wledig.*"   TRIADES.

‡ " Un o dri-ar-ddeg o vreninawl dlyfau Ynys Prydain: Dyrnwyn, ciedd
                                                                          " Rhydderç,

Gwallog the fon of *Llëenog** and *Morgant*.+ Thefe, under the command of *Urien*, defeated *Deoderic* king of *Bernicia*, and obliged him to retreat to the ifland of *Medcant*,
where he was blocked up for three days. Whilft *Urien* was
thus purfuing the advantages over the enemy, he was bafely
murdered by *Llovan Lawddifro*, and *Dyvnaval*, at the in-
ftigation of *Morgant*, who envied his fuperior talents and
military prowefs.‡ This action was included in a *Triad*,
denominated

" Rhydderç Hael; yr hwn pan dynid o'i wain ae'n dân o'i ddwrn hyd ei
" vlaen."

" One of the thirteen princely rarities of *Britain* was *Dyrnwyn*, the fword
" of *Rhydderç* the Generous, which when drawn out of the fheath would
" appear as a gleaming flame from the handle to the point." MSS.

" Tri Hael Ynys Prydain: Rhydderç Hael ab Tudwal Tudglud; Mor-
" dav Hael mab Servan: a Nudd Hael vab Senyllt."

" The three generous chiefs of the ifle of *Britain: Rhydderç Hael*, the fon
" of *Tudwal Tudglud; Mordav Hael*, the fon of *Servan;* and *Nudd Hael*,
" the fon of *Senyllt.*" TRIADES.

* " Tri aerveddawg Ynys Prydain: Selyv mab Cynan Garwyn, ac
" Avaon mab Taliefin, a Gwallawg mab Llëenawg; fev açaws y gelwid
" hwynt, yn aerveddogion, wrth ddial eu cam oc eu bedd."

" The three grave flaughterers of the ifle of *Britain: Selyv* the fon of
" *Cynan Garwyn, Avaon* the fon of *Taliefin*, and *Gwallog* the fon of *Llee-
" nog;* the reafon they were called grave flaughtering chiefs was, that they
" revenged their wrongs even from their graves." TRIADES.

† " Tri Rhuddväawg Ynys Prydain: Arthur, Rhun mab Beli, a Mor-
" gant Mwynvawr."

" The three ruddy chiefs of the ifle of *Britain: Arthur, Rhun* the fon of
" *Beli*, and *Morgant Mwynvawr.*" TRIADES.

‡ *Nennius.* He is confirmed by this *Triad:*

" Tri tharw cåd Ynys Prydain: Cynvawr Cad Cadwg mab Cynwyd
" Cynwydion, Gwenddolau mab Ceidiaw, ac Urien mab Cynvarç."

" The three *Bulls of Conflict* of the ifle of *Britain: Cynvawr Câd Cadwg*
" the

denominated the three villainous deeds of the ifle of *Britain.*

Urien having thus fallen a victim to treachery, his fons *Owain,** *Pafgen,†* *Rhiwallon,‡* *Elphin,* and *Cadell,* in concert

" the fon of *Cynwyd Cynwydion, Gwenddolau* the fon of *Ceidio,* and *Urien*
" the fon of *Cynvarç.*"

* There are feveral poems by *Taliefin* ftill extant recording the battles of *Urien* and his fon *Owain,* who are likewife mentioned in feveral *Triades—*

" Tri gwyn dorllwyth Ynys Prydain : Urien ac Eurddyl, plant Cynvarç
" Hên, a vuant yn un torllwyth y' nghalon Nevyn verç Bryçan eu mam ;
" yr ail Owain ab Urien a Morvudd ei çwaer, a vuant yn un torllwyth
" y' nghalon Modron verç Avallaç ; y trydydd, Gwrgi a Pheredur a Çein-
" dreç Benafgell, plant Elifer Gofgordd vawr, a vuant y' nghalon Eury-
" ddyl verç Cynvarç eu mam."

" The three bleffed burdens of the womb, of the ifle of *Britain : Urien*
" and *Eurddyl,* the children of *Cynvarç,* who were twins in the womb of
" *Nevyn,* daughter of *Bryçan,* their mother ; the fecond was *Owain* ab
" *Urien* and *Morvudd* his fifter that were one burden in the womb of
" *Modron* daughter of *Avallaç;* the third was *Gwrgi, Peredur,* and *Cein-*
" *dreç Benafgell,* the children of *Elifer* with the numerous clan, who were
" one burden in the womb of *Eurddyl* the daughter of *Cynvarç,* their
" mother."

† " Tri thrahawg Ynys Prydain : Sawyl Benuçel, Pafgen mab Urien, a
" Rhun mab Einiawn."

" The three haughty chiefs of the ifle of *Britain : Sawyl Benuçel, Paf-*
" *gen* the fon of *Urien,* and *Rhun* the fon of *Einion.*" TRIADES.

‡ " Tri hualogion deulu Ynys Prydain : teulu Cafwallawn Lawhir, a
" ddodafant hualau eu meirç ar eu traed bob ddau onaddynt, wrth ymladd
" â Serigi Wyddel y' Ngherig y Gwyddyl yn Môn ; a theulu Rhiwallawn
" mab Urien, yn ymladd a'r Saefon ; a theulu Belyn o Leyn, yn ymladd
" ag Edwyn, yn Mryn Cenau yn Rhôs."

" The three fettered clans of the ifle of *Britain:* the clan of *Cafwallzu*
" with the long hand, who put the fetters of their horfes on their legs, two

" by

cert with their relations, but the firſt in particular, ſtrug-
gled hard againſt the *Saxons*, with various ſucceſſes, until
they all eventually fell by the ſword, or were obliged to
quit their country.   Amongſt the latter was the venerable
Llywarç, with his ſurviving ſons, now reduced to a few in
number, who took refuge in *Powys*, where they were
hoſpitably received by *Cynddylan*, prince of a part of that
country.

This *Cynddylan* was the ſon of *Cyndrwyn*, and probably a
relation of *Broçwel*, another *Powyſian* prince, who commanded the army of the *Britons* againſt the *Saxons*, in the
memorable battle of *Bangor*, in the year 603, being then a
very old man.*   *Cyndrwyn*† had four brothers, *Maoddyn*,
Elwydaan, *Eirinwedd*, and *Cynon*; and ſix ſons, *Cynddylan*,
Elvan, *Cynon*, *Gwion*, *Gwyn*, and *Cuawg*.   Moſt of theſe, if
not all, periſhed in their wars with the *Saxons*.

At the time that *Llywarç* came into *Powys*, *Cynddylan*,
and his brother *Elvan*, were at war with the neighbouring
people of *Lloegyr*, probably *Saxons* and *Roman Britons*
united; but whom the Bard calls by the name of *Franks*,
in one paſſage : their commander's name was *Sannier*; who,
in conjunction with one *Twrç*, had ſeized on *Tren*, a town

" by two together, when fighting againſt *Serigi* the *Iriſhman*, at the *Iriſh*
" *Stones* in *Môn*; and the clan of *Rhiwallon* the ſon of *Urien*, fighting
" againſt the *Saxons*; and the clan of *Belyn* of *Llëyn*, fighting againſt *Edwyn*, at *Bryn Cenau* in *Rhôs*."   TRIADES.
    * One of the ſons of *Cyndrwyn* was in that battle.
    † He lived at *Llyſhrawenan* near *Caer Einion*.

that

that was the property of the father of *Cynddylan*, fituate moft likely on the river *Tern*, near the *Wrekin*, where the fcene of the Elegy on *Cynddylan* chiefly lies. *Llywarç*, and his fons, took a very active part in the wars carried on by their protectors. Tradition fays that he was in an engagement at *Rhiw-Waedog*, near *Bala*, in *Meirion*; and which is confirmed by the Poet himfelf, in the following ftanza:

" Cynddelw cadw dithau y rhiw,
" Er à ddêl yma heddyw—
" Cudeb am un mab nid gwiw !"

" *Cynddelw*,* guard thou the cliff,
" Againft whoever may come here this day—
" Fondnefs for one furviving fon fhall not avail !"

This battle probably deprived *Llywarç* of that remaining fon, and it might have been the laft in which he bore a part himfelf.*

Dr. *J. D. Rhys* has preferved the following ftanza, not to be met with in the regular works of *Llywarç*, which he

* There is a ftanza in one of the Elegies that is almoft the fame as this, except the name, confequently one may be only a different reading of the other, the effect of an error in the tranfcript.

* Near the place where it happened, in the middle of the townfhip of *Rhiw-waedog*, there is a deep little valley, where there is generally fome ftagnant water in winter, called at this day *Pwll y Gelanedd*, or the Pool of the Slain; and a few years ago, in a field contiguous to the place, a man found a fpear head, which he believed was brafs, but he had loft it.

made

made on feeing the horfe of his fon *Paen* ftumble under him.

> " Mor fwrth y fyrthioedd març Paen,
> " Yn mariandir, grodir graen
> " Eivionydd, mynyç malaen—
> " Lle ni bo mign e vydd maen."

> " How abruptly fell the horfe of *Paen*,
> " In the fandy, gravelly foil
> " Of *Eivionydd*, teeming with misfortunes—
> " Where there is no bog there a ftone will be. '

An old manufcript furnifhed another fugitive verfe, pre-faced with an anecdote to the following import.* It hap-pened that *Gwen*, the fon of *Llywarç*, had his horfe killed under him in battle; and himfelf was flain fometime after-wards. The fcull of the horfe having been placed, inftead of a ftone, in a bridge over a rivulet, that was contiguous to the fpot where he was killed, *Llywarç* by chance paffed that way, when his fervant told him—" That is the fcull " of the horfe of *Gwen* your fon!" To which he re-plied—

> " Mi a welais ddydd i'r març,
> " Friw hydd, tavledydd tywarç,

---

* Thefe are the original words—Ev a ddamweinioedd lladd març Gwên ab Llywarç mewn brwydyr: Gwedi lladd y març, ev a lâs Gwên; ac yn hir o yfbaid gwedi hỳny y rhoefbwyd penglog y març yn lle càreg mewn farn, dros aber oedd yn ymyl y man lle lladdefid y març. Ac yn ol hỳny damweinioedd i Lywarç Hên dramwyaw ar hyd y fordd hòno; ac yno i dywaid gwâs Llywarç wrtho—" Dacw benglog març Gwên ab Llywarç, " eiç mab çwi."—Ac yno i canoedd Llywarç y pennill hwn ar yr açaws hỳnw.

" Na

" Na fangai neb ar ei én,
" Pan oedd tan Gwên ab Llywarç."

" I faw a day to the horfe,
" With the looks of a ftag, the thrower up of fods,
" That none would have trodden on his jaw,
" When he was under *Gwên* the fon of *Llywarç*."

The whole life of *Llywarç* was almoft an uninterrupted ftate of hoftility, chequered by a feries of uncommon and afflicting viciffitudes. He outlived all his fons, friends and protectors, and being reduced to extreme mifery, he retired to a folitary hut at *Aber Cuawg*,* in *Montgomeryfbire*; but that it feems was not his laft retreat. In the parifh of *Llanvor*, near *Bala*, there is a fecluded place, called *Pabell Llywarç Hen*, or the Cot of Old *Llywarç*. His fituation there is pathetically defcribed in his Elegy on Old Age. There he probably died, but at what particular time cannot be determined; though there is great reafon to fuppofe it was only a little while after the death of *Cadwallon*, which happened about the year 646.† Old traditions agree that *Llywarç* died at the age of one hundred and fifty years; and that he was buried in the church of *Llanvor*. Dr. *Davies* fays, that in his time, there was an in-

* This might have been the patrimony of *Cuawg*, the fon of *Cyndrwyn*, and have taken its name from him.

† Some chronicles place the death of *Cadwallon* as late as the year 676, which certainly is erroneous. There is a confufion in the dates with refpect to the continuance of the reign of *Cadwallon*, and of his fon *Cadwaladyr*; but they agree that the former acceded to the principality of *Wales* about the year 612, and to the nominal fovereignty of *Britain* in 633.

fcription

fcription to be feen in the wall of the church, under which it was faid *Llywarç* was interred; but that is now covered over with the plaifter, or otherwife defaced fo that no remains of it is to be feen.

It may be inferred that *Llywarç* compofed moft of the pieces now extant, after his retreat into *Wales*, to footh his mind, borne down with calamities, and the infirmities of uncommon old age. Cold muft be that breaft that can be unmoved in perufing his artlefs complaint, that death lingered, after he had been bereft of four and twenty fons, wearing the golden chain, the high-prized badge of honour of a *Britifh* warrior.

To the curious, the following documents, relative to *Llywarç*, will be interefting, even for their great antiquity; at the fame time they will fhew, in what high eftimation he was held by his countrymen. He is honourably recorded in the *Triades* of *Britain*, already quoted; and this is one favourable to a trait of his character, little cultivated in his time, and now not much more perhaps—

" Tri lleddyv Unben Ynys Prydain: Manawydan mab Llyr
" Llediaith, Llywarç Hên mab Elidyr Lydanwyn, a Gwgawn
" Gwrawn mab Peredur mab Elifer Gofgordd vawr: Ac yfev açaws
" y gelwyd hwynt yn Lleddyv Unben, wrth na çeifynt gyvoeth; ac
" na allai neb çi luddias iddynt."

" The three difinterefted Princes of the ifle of *Britain*: *Manawydan*
" the fon of *Llyr* with the barbarous language; *Llywarç* the Old, fon
of

" of *Elidyr Lydanwyn* ; and *Gwgon Gwron*, the fon of *Peredur*, the fon
" of *Elifer* with the *numerous clan* : And the reafon they were called
" difinterefted Princes was, becaufe they fought not for dominion,
" when it was out of the power of any to have oppofed them."

Aneurin, the celebrated author of the *Gododin*,[*] a heroic
poem on the Battle of *Cattraeth*, fays that he was releafed
from prifon by a fon of *Llywarç* :

" O garçar anwar daear ym dug;
" O gyvle angau, o anghar dud,
" Cenau vab Llywarç, dihavarç drud."

" From the unpleafant prifon of earth I am releafed ;
" From the haunt of death, and a hateful land,
" By *Cenau* the fon of *Llywarç*, magnanimous and bold."

Nennius, in his fhort lift of bright poetic geniufes, has
Talhaearn, *Tudain Tâd Awen*, *Aneurin*, *Taliefin*, and *Llywarç*.

A compofition of the tenth century, entitled *Ynglynion y
Glywed*, quotes a fentiment there attibuted to *Llywarç* :

" A glyweifti à gânt Llywarç;
" Oedd henwr drud dihavarç :
" Onid cyvarwydd cyvarç."

---

[*] This is the name of a country comprehending the fea-coaft of *North-
umberland*, *Merfe*, and *Lothian*, the inhabitants of which are denominated
Otodini, in *Roman* authors. The above poem is in praife of three hundred and fixty-three chiefs of this country, who were all flain, except three,
in a battle againft the *Saxons*, at *Cattraeth*.

b

" Didft

" Didſt thou hear what *Llywarç* ſang,
" The intriped and brave old man:
" Greet kindly though there be no acquaintance."

Theſe teſtimonials, honourable to the name of *Llywarç*, ſhall conclude with one from the works of *Einion ab Gwgan*, a bard of the twelfth century; who, in complimenting *Llywelyn ab Jorwerth* prince of *Wales*, ſays—

" Llywelyn boed hyn, boed hwy ddyçwain,
" No Llywarç hybarç, hybar gigwain."

" *Llywelyn*, mayeſt thou, in age and good fortune, proſper
" More than *Llywarç* the venerable, with his bloody lance."

It is neceſſary to remark that *Llywarç* was not a member of the regular *Order* of *Bards*, for the whole tenor of his life militated againſt the leading maxims of that ſyſtem; the ground-work of which was univerſal peace, and perfect equality. For a Bard was not to bear arms, nor even to eſpouſe a cauſe, by any other active means; neither was a naked weapon to be held in his preſence, he being deemed the ſacred character of a Herald of Peace. And in any of thoſe caſes, where the rules were tranſgreſſed, whether by his own will, or the act of another againſt him, he was degraded, and no longer deemed one of the order. But inſtances of ſuch tranſgreſſions very ſeldom took place; the *Triades* record three ſuch, as being remarkable, and a more ſatisfactory confirmation of the remark could not well have been procured.*

* " Tri gwaywrudd Veirdd Ynys Prydain: Triſtvardd, bardd Urien ;
" Dygynnelw, bardd Owain; ac Avan Verddig, bardd Cadwallawn mab
" Cadvan."

" The three bards of the iſle of *Britain* who tinged ſpears with blood ;

We muſt here cloſe this ſhort ſketch of the Life of
Llywarç; for hiſtory will aſſiſt us no farther, in any mate-
rial circumſtances, in addition to thoſe already ſtated. As
to any matter that his own works would afford, it is deemed unneceſſary to enlarge upon in this place; but a few
obſervations may be wanting, with reſpect to their general
feature, and comparative merit, as poetical compoſitions.
It firſt ſtrikes our notice that a cloſe copying after nature,
with artleſs ſimplicity, is the prominent outline of the
whole;* and what chiefly contributed to this was the partiality of *Llywarç* for the proverbial maxims of his country; as all his pieces abound with theſe elegant memorials
of the wiſdom, and obſervation of the earlieſt ages; and his
writings are valuable, even conſidered as the vehicle that
brings to our view thoſe maxims, which ſhew the manner
of thinking of our anceſtors at ſo remote a period of antiquity. They have alſo a faithful hiſtorical character; for
whatever particulars are recorded by *Llywarç*, though they

" *Triſtvardd*, the bard of *Urien*; *Dygynnelw*, the bard of *Owain*; and *Avan*
" *Verddig*, the bard of *Cadwallon* the ſon of *Cadvan*."

* The metres uſed by *Llywarç* are of the ſimpleſt kind; for he almoſt
invariably has the *Tribañ Milwr*, or the Warrior's Triplet. He is ſingular
in this reſpect; for his cotemporaries compoſed in a variety of other
metres, admitting more harmonious cadences, and of greater dignity. In
the Poetical Inſtitutes of the Bards there is this obſervation on the Tribañ :
" The moſt ſimple of all the ſtanzas is the Warrior's Triplet; for it has
" ſimplicity of verſe, rhyme, and ſtanza; as the firſt of ſtanzas was the
" triplet, and the firſt kind of rhyme was unirhythm; therefore it is
" judged, that of all the various ſtanzas the Warrior's Triplet is the moſt
" venerable; for ſo is the firſt of all things; and of ſtanzas, the Warrior's
" Triplet is the moſt original."

relate

relate to a confined circle of events, yet, as we may rely on
their authenticity, they must be confidered as a neceffary
link in the chain of our Hiftory; and certainly, in conjunction with all the other productions of contemporary
bards, they fhed a light on the age wherein he lived little
imagined by the world at large.*

. The Odes of *Llywarç* poffefs fome characteriftic peculi-
arities, common to the poetry of the *Cynmry*, not to be
found in that of other nations; and which perhaps, inftead
of being defined here, will appear to the reader with more
fatisfaction, by giving fome account of the fource from

---

* Thofe who have a real wifh to be acquainted with the truths of antiquity, may lament that there has not been fufficient encouragement to pub-
lifh all thefe documents; but on the other hand, what an ample field is
there left for thofe of fertile imagination to form each his own hypothefis, and
to make bold affertions. Within a few years an antiquarian has made his
appearance, well endowed with thofe qualifications. He began very lauda-
bly, to oppofe the abfurdities of thofe who had gone before in the fame
path; but when he conceived he had overturned their fuperftructures, he,
Cromwell-like, affumed unlimited authority to impofe dogmas of his own
invention, to the juftnefs of which all muft affent without appeal. Being
born in that part of *Britain*, which enabled him to make out a fair title to
being a GOTH, he felt, as he thought, the impulfe of fuperior penetration,
and pronounced the inhabitants of other parts, who were made out to be
CELTS, as by nature an inferior race of men; and that they fpoke a jargon
fo rude and confined, as muft be inadequate to exprefs ideas truly *Gothic*.
But, granting he might be able to prove the firft part of the allegation, how
will he maintain that the *Welfh* language, by him deemed *Celtic*, is rude and
confined, when he ought to know of its having above a hundred thoufand
words, regularly formed from monofyllabic roots, upon a rule of combina-
tion that leaves room to double, or even to treble that number, on the fame
ftock, if it were neceffary?

                                                    whence

whence they originate, the Inſtitution of the Bards in *Britain*. Therefore we ſhall, as a matter of ſome curioſity, endeavour to give a very ſhort ſketch of a ſyſtem, of which the world has hitherto unavoidably entertained but a very imperfect notion.

BARDISM.

WHATEVER diſtinguiſhing traits a community may acquire in its early ſtate, conſtituting a national character, muſt be more or leſs preſerved according to the degree of intercourſe it may have, with people of different habits and cuſtoms. From this obſervation we are led to premiſe what ſeems in no want of argument for ſupport, that whatever the advantages, or opportunities might be in favour of a foreign connection, there was a ſtrong principle implanted in the ſocial œconomy of the *Cymmry* militating againſt it.

The name of *Cynmry*, by which the *Welſh* call them-ſelves,* as remarkable for its import, as the length of its continuance, they have preſerved ever ſince they became a ſeparate body of people in the world; and that too amidſt viciſſitudes, which according to common probabilities, muſt have overwhelmed every trace of originality.†

One

---

* It is remarkable there is not an inſtance to be produced of the *Welſh* calling themſelves *Prydeiniaid*, the name that is analagous to *Britons*, as might be ſuppoſed they naturally would, from *Ynys Prydain*, or *the iſle abounding with beauty*, which is the meaning of the iſle of *Britain*.

† There is no particular neceſſity of bringing quotations to ſupport this, as it is very well known that the name is often to be found in Greek and

One caufe which contributed to preferve their diftinction of character was this: whenever any particular tribe of the nation became fo fituated, as to be intermixt with ftrangers, it was confidered by the main body as alienated, and was ftigmatized with a new name. To this muft be attributed the various appellations, which are all confounded together by ftrangers; fuch as *Galatwys, Galwys,* and *Galiaid,* who were the original *Cynmry*; and *Ceiltwys, Ceiltiaid, Belwys, Belgwys, Belgiaid, Peithwys, Yfgodogion, Gwyddyl, Gwyddelod,* and *Celyddon,** who were the borderers of the *Cynmry*; and perfectly of the fame defcription as the *Back-woodmen* are, in the United States of *America*; for all of the laft mentioned clafs of names convey the fame idea, as that we have of thofe *American Settlers.* In like manner the fouth coaft of *Britain* came to be called *Lloegyr,*† from

Roman authors, from the earlieft periods. The found of the name of *Cynmry* is remarkably well preferved in *Kimbros, Coimbri, Cimbri,* and *Cimmerii.* Thofe ancients were more attentive than the moderns in this refpect, for all the *Britifh* names found in their works are lefs corrupted than the names of places in *Wales,* in the maps of the prefent time.

* The exact meaning of *Celt* is a *Covert;* fo *Ceiltwys,* and *Ceiltiaid,* were the *People of the Coverts;* the *Belwys, Belgwys,* and *Belgiaid,* were *thofe who made irruptions out of the borders,* or *Warriors;* and the *Peithwys* were the *Expofed People;* whether becaufe they went naked, or that they dwelt in the *open* or *defert country,* is not certain. The *Welfh* call *Ireland Y Werddon,* or the *Weftern Country;* but the people are denominated *Gwyddyl,* and *Gwyddelod,* the *Inhabitants of the Woods,* or *Wilds.* The name for *Scotland* is *Alban,* the *Higher,* or *Upper Region;* but the people are called *Yfgodogion,* the *Inhabitants of the Shades,* or *Coverts.* It is remarkable that the names for both nations fhould be fynonymous; and alfo that the great foreft, in the north of *Britain,* fhould be called *Coed Celyddon,* the *Wood of Coverts,* or the *Shades.*

† *Lloegyr* feems to be the name by which thofe new comers themfelves
called

its being fettled by later colonies from *Belgic Gaul*; and the name extended, as the *Cynmry* retreated, or coalefced with the new comers; and the *Roman* conqueft carried it much farther ftill; fo that in the time of *Llywarç* it comprehended all *South Britain*, except *Cornwall*, *Wales*, and *Cumbria*; and at this time *Lloegyr* implies *England* in general. The fame may be faid of the *Cynmry* who fettled in *Ireland* and *Scotland*; for they loft their original appellation in both countries, when they became a mixt people.*

The language of the *Cynmry* carries in itfelf the evidence of being free from intermixture; it being fo conftructed, as not to affimilate with foreign words, except fuch as are mere fimple founds; and there could hardly be a cafe where any of this defcription could be wanted; and if words fhould have been adopted, they are very eafily difcriminated.† There are many traits in it, befides its regularity,

called their country; for it has not the appearance of being a *Welfh* word. Compare it with the ancient *Ligurians* on the borders of *Italy*.

* The names of places in *Ireland* and *Scotland*, when thofe that are *Englifh* are left out, are for the moft part *Welfh*; but the *Irifh* and *Erfe* dialects, originally one language, are compounded of fome *Welfh* and more of others, fo as to bear not much greater affinity with the *Welfh*, than it has with the *Latin* or the *Englifh*. The *Welfh*, *Cornifh*, and *Armoric*, are only different dialects of the fame language; and a native of either country can converfe tolerably well with one of either of the other two; but he cannot even perceive the character of his own language when he hears the *Irifh* fpoken.

† All compound words, in the *Welfh*, are regularly formed from thofe that are monofyllables; and thofe again *reducible to claffes of fimilar founds, having a coincidence of import*, one with another; as PEN, a *head*; CEN, the

gularity, that are worthy of inveſtigation; and what is remarkable, we muſt attribute its formation to an age now
deemed, by the learned world, to have been involved in
barbarity. But beyond all doubt, there has been an era
when ſcience diffuſed a light amongſt the *Cynmry*, greater
than will be now readily acknowledged, and that too in a
very early period of the world.

To the period above-mentioned we muſt attribute the
Inſtitution of BARDISM,* amongſt the *Cynmry*, a ſyſtem
embracing all the leading principles which tend to ſpread
liberty, peace and happineſs amongſt mankind; and for that
reaſon, perhaps, too perfect to be generally adopted by any
nation, or body of people.†

---

top, or *firſt*; NEN, the *top*, or what is *over head*; LLEN, a *veil*, or *covering*;
LLEEN, a *teacher*, or a *man of learning*; RHEEN, a *creator*, or *one that gives
a beginning*. None even of this claſs are primitives, but compounded of
PY, CY, NY, LLY, LLE, and RHE, with EN, a *principle*, or *firſt cauſe*:
whence ENAID, the *ſoul*, literally the *principle of life*; from EN, and AID, *life*.

* By this is meant what is generally conceived amongſt the *Engliſh* of
the term *Druidiſm*, which is a miſtake, by giving the appellation of a particular branch to the whole of the order; for as a matter of convenience an
appropriate ſet of Bards were diſtinguiſhed by the name of *Derwyddon*, or
Druids, to give notoriety and diſcriminate viſibility to the religious func-
tionaries. It was difficult for ſtrangers to avoid the miſtake, for the *Druids*
muſt appear to them as prieſts independently of any other order; and as
ſuch they wore the white garment, inſtead of the unicoloured ſky-blue,
which was the general dreſs of the Bards.

† One is tempted to conclude, by comparing the whole together, however difficult it may be to make it appear ſatisfactory, that the principles
are immediately derived from the *Patriarchs*; for it is as rational to ſuppoſe
this, as that the *Cynmry* had in any age the opportunity to arrive *gradually*
at a ſtate of knowledge, which could produce ſuch a ſyſtem.

What

What may be confidered as the foundation of the Order was the doctrine of *Univerfal Peace*, and *Good Will*; for fo entirely was a Bard to be a votary to it, that he was never to bear arms, or in any other manner to become a party in a difpute, either political or religious; nor was a naked weapon even to be held in his prefence, for he was recog-nifed as the facred Herald of Peace, under the title of *Bardd Ynys Prydain*, or Bard of the ifle of *Britain.* * The refult of this was that he could pafs unmolefted, from one hoftile, country to another, where his character was known; and whenever he appeared in his *unicoloured robe,* † by which

---

* The *Beirdd Ynys Prydain* affert that their Inftitution originated in *Bri-tain*; from whence it was introduced into *Gaul, Ireland*, and other coun-tries, but with confiderable deviations from its original fimplicity, and purity. IOLO MORGANWG.

The prefent vulgar acceptation of BARDD, whence the *Englifh Bard*, is fimply a poet. The literal meaning of the word is, *one that maketh confpicu-ous*; and the idea intended to be conveyed is, a *Teacher*, or *Philofopher*; and its import is well defined in *Mafon*'s epithet—*Mafter of Wifdom*. Verfe being the medium by which the Bards conveyed their precepts to the peo-ple, they continued to cultivate Poetry after their power as a body was over-turned, and hence the modern acceptation of their name.

† It was of fky-blue, being their emblem of Peace and Truth. This colour is alfo the emblem of Peace amongft the *Nadoweffes*, a people weft of the *Miffiffippi*, in *America*, as Captain *Carver* fays. This author faw many things amongft thofe *Indians*, furprifing to him, as being of *European* origin; and he was told by them that there was a nation, to the weft of them, " who in fome degree cultivated the arts." The reader may fmile at this relation being introduced here; but I have a collection of evidence which has been fufficient to convert as great fceptics as any that will fee this, that that nation is the *White Padoucas*, known alfo to the *Indian* traders by the name of the *Civilized Indians*, and the *Welfh Indians*; and that they do now actually fpeak the WELSH *Language*. Thefe people are the defcendants of the emigration under the conduct of *Madog ab Owain Guynedd*, in the year 1170.

he

he was known, attention was given to him on all occafions; if it was even between armies in the heat of action, both parties would inftantly defift; * fo that the appearance of a Bard operated as the modern *flag of truce*. His word was to be credited, in preference to that of any other perfon whatever.†

The next important object of the bardic Inftitution, was the free inveftigation of all matters contributing to the attainment of truth and wifdom, grounded upon the apho-rifm—"COELIAW DIM, A ÇOELIAW POB PETH."—*To believe nothing, and to believe every thing*; that is, to believe every thing fupported by reafon and proof, and nothing without. In addition to that the Bard was to be bold in the caufe of Truth; for his motto was—" Y GWIR YN ERBYN Y BYD."—*The Truth in oppofition to the World*.

Another maxim of the order was, the perfect equality of its members, and of three branches, whereof it confifted, one with another. Each order was held in a peculiarity of eftimation, though neither of them were intitled to fuperiority, nor any one deemed more intrinfically excellent than the other. If with refpect to qualification for certain offices one was deemed inferior, it was in other particulars

---

* But we fhall not infift that it was the effect of the harmony of the lyres, or the flowing numbers, that calmed the fierce refentment ftruggling in their breafts, as *Diodorus Siculus* conceived; but it was in confequence of general laws of warfare, common in all ages.

† Gair ei air ev ar bawb.

allowed

allowed to be superior; so that considered in the whole, each of the orders were equally honourable.

The publicity of their actions was also a leading consideration amongst the bards; for all their meetings or *Gorseddau*, were held in the open air, on a conspicuous place, whilst the sun was above the horizon; as they were to perform every thing *in the eye of the light, and in the face of the sun.** The place was set a part, by forming a circle of stones, with a large stone in the middle, beside which the presiding Bard stood. This was termed *Cylç Cyngrair*, or the *Circle of Federation*; and the stones with which it was formed were called *Meini Gwynion, Meini Cyngrair*, or *Meini Crair*; and the middle stone, *Maen Gorfedd, Maen Llôg*, and *Crair Gorfedd*. At these *Gorseddau* it was absolutely necessary to recite the *Bardic Traditions*; and with this whatever came before the meetings was considered and determined upon.

* Yn wyneb haul a llygad goleuni, or, Yn llygad haul ac wyneb goleuni. The influence of this maxim is seen in the poetry of the *Welsh*. Thus *Ll. B. Moç*, a bard of the twelfth century begins one of his poems—

Gwr a wnaeth llewyç o'r gorllewin,
Haul, a lloer addoer, addev iesin,
A'm gwnel radd uçel rwyv cyvyçwin; ·
Cyvlawn Awen, awydd Vyrddin,
I ganu moliant, mal Aneurin gynt,
Dydd i cânt Ododin.

Him that made reflection, blushing from the west,
The sun, and chilling moon, in splendid orbs,
I crave to grant me th' intellectual light ;
That flowing muse which glow'd in *Myrddin*'s lays,
Or like *Aneurin*, when of ancient times
He sang the fam'd *Gododin*.

The

The Bards at thofe places, and on all occafions where they acted officially, wore *unicoloured robes*.

Having exhibited the leading maxims on which Bardifm was eftablifhed, it may be proper, in the next place, to give an infight into the Tenets of its Religion. In this refpect the Bards adhered to, or departed from, their original traditions, only according to the evidence that might be acquired from time to time, in their *fearch after Truth*. During the primitive, or pagan times, if that term may be applied, the opinions of the Bards had a very great affinity with the patriarchal religion; and which, with great probability, we may conclude, was the fountain from whence they flowed. Such being the cafe, they could not be difqualified of being the minifters of the Chriftian difpenfation, or any other appearing to them well founded; for the continuation of the Inftitution did not depend upon the promulgation of certain articles of faith, but upon its own feparate principles of focial compact, that are before mentioned.

The Bards have at all times efpoufed the facred doctrine of a belief in one God, the Creator, and Governor of the Univerfe, and pervading all fpace, of whom the idea of a locality of exiftence was deemed unworthy.* Their conception of his divine nature is fundamentally and comprehenfively explained by the following bold and remarkable

---

* Amongft the names of the Deity, that are older than the introduction of Chriftianity, the following may be reckoned: *Duw, Deon, Dovydd, Yr Hên Ddihenydd, Celi, Jôr, Peryv, Rhëen.*

aphorifm—

aphorifm—Nɪᴅ Dɪᴍ ᴏɴᴅ Dᴜᴡ, ɴɪᴅ Dᴜᴡ ᴏɴᴅ Dɪᴍ.—
Gᴏᴅ *cannot be* Mᴀᴛᴛᴇʀ, *and what is not* Mᴀᴛᴛᴇʀ *muſt be*
Gᴏᴅ.

They taught that this World was to be of permanent du-
ration; but ſubjeƈt to a ſucceſſion of violent revolutions,
which would be produced, ſometimes by the predominat-
ing power of the element of water, and ſometimes of that
of fire.

The bardic doƈtrines concerning the Soul were—that it
pre-exiſted, in a ſtate of gradual advancement by tranſmi-
gration, and that it was immortal. But with reſpeƈt to
ſome of the leading traits of their ideas on this ſubjeƈt
there was a very ſtriking peculiarity; which, conſiſtent
with the brevity that is carefully adopted, we ſhall endeavour to define. The whole animated creation, they ſaid,
originated in the loweſt point of exiſtence, evil in the extreme, and arrived, by a regular train of gradations, at the
probationary ſtate of humanity; and thoſe gradations were
all neceſſarily evil, but more or leſs ſo as they were removed from that firſt ſource. In the ſtate of humanity
good and evil were equally balanced, and conſequently it
was a ſtate of liberty; in which if the aƈtions and conduƈt
of the agent preponderated to evil, death gave but an aw-
ful paſſage, by which he returned to animal life; in a condition below humanity equal to the degree of turpitude he
had debaſed himſelf with in his former ſtate of probation;
and if his life was deſperately wicked, it was poſſible for
him to fall to his original vilenefs, or that loweſt point of
exiſtence, and a renewal of his former progreſſion through
brutal

brutal animation took place; and this was his deftiny, as often as evil had the afcendancy in his ftate of trial. If, on the other hand, good was predominant in the heart of man, death was deemed a welcome meffenger to conduct him to a more exalted condition; where he was ftill progreffive; but he was then removed beyond the influence of evil, or the danger of falling, into a ftate neceffarily good. Eternity being what a finite being could not poffibly endure, there he paffed from one gradation to another by a kind of renovation, without being deprived of the confcioufnefs of his prior conditions, for that would be next to annihilation. He might return to a ftate of fecond manhood, yet without the poffibility of evil having again the afcendancy, confequently the return of fuch a benign foul was confidered a bleffing to the world.

There is hardly a neceffity of obferving that the bardic metempfychofis was an incitement to good morals, and noble actions; but it had a peculiar tendency, that deferves to be noticed. This was, the reftraint, which in a great degree it laid the bards under, of not killing animals; though it did not extend, as with the *Bramins*, to a direct prohibition of depriving any creature of life; on the contrary, it was *allowable* to deftroy thofe which directly, or eventually, might caufe the death of man; confequently moft forts of land animals might be killed; but the whole tribe of fifhes was confidered as not affecting, nor to be affected by the human œconomy.* That ftate of univerfal

---

* The hiftory of the deluge has fomething that feems to fupport this idea; for we find that the fifhes were not deftroyed. To which may be added, they were not allowed in facrifices.

warfare, in which all animated nature feems to be involved, was not looked upon as a curfe; on the contrary the Bards could furvey the fcene with more complacency than others; for in it they perceived the goodnefs of Providence, haftening the changes neceffary to produce a more glorious exiftence.*

Propitiatory facriflce was a part of the bardic religion, as it feems to have been of moft others, whether pure or corrupt, that have been in the world.†

---

* One is induced to think that *Taliefin* entertained this opinion, when he compofed his poem on his tranfmigrations, wherein the following paffage occurs——

  " Mewn boly tywyll i'm tywalltwys,
  " Mewn mor dylan i'm dyçwelwys;
  " Bu goelvain i'm pan ym cain vygwys,
  ⁂ Duw Arglwydd yn rhydd a'm rhyddâwys."

" Into a dark receptacle I was thrown,
" In the laving ocean I was overwhelmed ;
" It was to me tidings of gladnefs when I was happily fuffocated,
" God the Lord from confinement fet me free."

† The human facrifices were criminals, to appeafe divine juftice. Thefe victims are ftill devoted, perhaps in greater numbers, in *London*, and other great towns. But moft authors have always unaccountably added the epithet *borrid* to thofe druidical facrifices, whenever they have had occafion to mention them, feemingly without ever thinking of its propriety or otherwife.

A curious fpecimen of thofe ancient facrifices is ftill practifed in fome parts of *Wales*. When a violent difeafe breaks out amongft the horned cattle, the farmers of the diftrict where it rages join to give up a bullock for a victim, which is carried to the top of a precipice, from whence it is thrown down. This is called——" Bwrw caeth i gythraul."—" Cafting a captive to the devil."

The

The foregoing may fuffice to give an idea of the tendency of the religious eftablifhment of the Bards, with refpect to its more minute precepts, and its confequent influence upon their moral inftitutes; and which, there is great probability, was preferved unpolluted, at leaft, until the ftream of idolatry, following the courfe of the *Roman* arms, bore ftrongly upon them. That the *Britons* had, notwithftanding the purity of the bardic fyftem, many degrading fuperftitions, and abfurd cuftoms, none will think of controverting; but we may fairly infift, that very flight dependance ought to be placed in the relations of foreign authors, with regard to any matters befide mere fimple facts. It was from the oftenfible aggregate of the manners and cuftoms that ftrangers have delineated the community under the influence of bardifm; but undoubtedly they were no more adequate to define that code, in its genuine fimplicity, from fuch a fource, than a perfon ignorant of the Chriftian religion would be able to give the truths of Revelation, from the defultory obfervations he might make on a tour through fome countries of modern *Europe*. It is one of the moft remarkable circumftances in the hiftory of the *Welfh* that, through the long and dark ages of Popifh fuperftition, the Bards retained the Chriftian religion in its original purity and fimplicity, on all occafions expofing the depravity, and abfurdity of the times. Numberlefs inftances of this could be produced from their poetical pieces of all ages, from *Taliefin* in the fixth century, down to the Reformation; and for that reafon they incurred the hatred of the priefts and monks, in the higheft degree, and on whom, in return, *Myrddin*, the *Caledonian* Bard, paffed the following cenfure—

                                    " Mynaiç

" Mynaiç geuawg, bwydiawg, gwydus."
" The lying, gluttonous, and wicked monks."

A report, highly favourable to the ftate of learning amongft the *Welfh*, might be given from the poetry of the feveral Bards who flourifhed in the fixth century; of *Meugant* in the feventh; *Elaeth*, and *Llevoed* in the eighth; and the Laws of *Hywel* in the ninth century. Deftruction of manufcripts leaves a confiderable blank in the hiftory of our poetry afterwards, till the eleventh century; and then we are fortunate to find a *Meilyr*, and his fon *Gwalçmai*; in the twelfth the lift becomes numerous, and amongft thefe we muft diftinguifh *Cynddelw*; to whom the monks of *Yftrad Marçell* fent a deputation, when he was on his death-bed, to inform him he fhould not have Chriftian burial. The report might be continued with great advantage through the thirteenth, and following centuries, becaufe more of the writings of thofe ages are preferved.* The

Bards

---

* There is a paffage of fo much grandeur of expreffion in the works of *Cafnodyn*, who flourifhed about the year 1300, that I cannot avoid tran- fcribing it, as a fpecimen of the powers of the language—

    Pan wnél Duw ddangaws ei varan,
    Dyddwyre dy daerad arnau;
    Dyçryn twryv torvoedd yn ebaq,
    Dyçyrç hynt; dyçre gwynt gwaeddvan;
    Dyçymmriw tòn amliw am làn;
    Dyçymmer uveliar bûr barn,
    Dyçrŷs gwrys gwrês tandde allan.
When Gŏd fhall reveal his countenance,
The houfe of earth will uplift itfelf over us;
A panic of the noife of legions in the conflict,
Will urge on the flight; harfhly the fhrill-voiced wind will call;

The

Bards not only oppofed the ignorance of thofe dark periods, but their works difcover more marks of genius, learning, and elegance, by far, than is to be found in the compofitions of later ages, when the bardic fyftem became neglected.

What now remains to be inveftigated is the difcipline of the Bards, or that practical part of their philofophy which regulated the fociety. The bardic inftitutes, as well as every branch of knowledge appertaining to the fyftem, were retained wholly by tradition, in aphorifms, poems, and adages of a peculiar caft.* There were indeed written memorials, but their authority was not deemed equal to the plan which they adopted, and for that reafon no reference was ever made to them. The firft thing taught to difciples were thofe traditions, comprehending the inftitutes, maxims, rudiments of language, laws of verfe, and fuch kind of knowledge as refpected the organization of the order.† Traditions of perfons fet apart for the ftudy,

and

The motley-tinted wave will lave with foamy rage around the fhore,
The glancing flame will take to itfelf the vengeance of juftice,
Recruited by the heat of contending fires, ever breaking out.

* Thefe were fo far from being any thing like ænigmatical or obfcure, as fome have fuppofed, that they were juft the reverfe; and there is hardly fuch a thing even as a figurative expreffion to be found in any of the traditions.

† It is from thofe traditions that the prefent fketch of bardifm is formed, wherein is given the general fcope of them; and which I have avoided drawing to fuch length as the materials would require, to give a compleat elucidation of them, as not neceffary to the prefent purpofe. With refpect

to

and continuation of them, were preferred to letters, as being *better* guarded againſt impoſition, by coming more immediately under the notice, and cognizance of the people at large. Of the methods of preſerving theſe, the moſt important one was their being recited at every *Gorſedd*, or meeting, by which all became acquainted with them, till they were ſo rooted in the public memory, as never to be liable to undergo any alteration. Oral tradition, according to that plan, is more open to the world at large than written memorials, conſequently more out of the reach of perverſion and innovation. The memory, the more it is exerciſed, becomes proportionably ſtrengthened and improved; whereas thoſe who truſt to books never exert that faculty, and in a ſhort time ſo far forget their ſubjeƈt, as not to be able to ſee when, and where impoſition intrudes. Where a greater dependance is laid on writings than tradition, books of diſtant places, or ages, will be admitted as authorities, when their authenticity has not been proved; and it may be impoſſible to bring any kind of proof for, or againſt them; but this cannot be the caſe with a national tradition, when through all the territories of that nation there are men ſet apart to ſtudy, guard, and continue them, by public, and frequent periodical recital. So very tenacious were the Bards of guarding them from perverſion, impoſition, and oblivion, that no verſes, or poems whatſoever, relative to the ſyſtem, were

to the traditions themſelves, as one of the order I feel a propenſity (a pardonable one I hope) in common with a few remaining members, to preſerve amongſt ourſelves undiſcloſed, except at a *Gorſedd*, thoſe very curious remains, as an inƈitement to preſerve the ſyſtem.

allowed to be spread abroad, without being previously examined, and approved of publicly at a *Gorsedd*, by being recited by the *Dadgeiniaid*, or reciters, in the hearing of all.

The Bards were divided into three essential classes, the BARDD BRAINT, DERWYDD, and OVYDD. But before we proceed to explain the distinctions of these, it is requisite to take' notice of the AWENYDDION, or disciples; whom it may be proper to consider as a fourth class. The *Awenyddion* wore a variegated dress of the bardic colours, blue, green, and white. To be admitted into this class, the first requisite was unimpeached morals; for it was indispensably necessary that the candidate should above all things be a good man. He was seldom initiated into any thing considerable until his understanding, affections, morals, and principles in general had undergone severe trials. His passions and faculties were closely observed, and exercised, when he was least aware of it; at all times, in all places, and on every occasion possible, there was an eye, hid from his observation, continually fixt upon him; and from the knowledge thus obtained of his head and heart, and in short his very soul scrutinized, an estimate was made of his principles and mental abilities; and agreeable to the approbation given, and in the manner, and degree thought, most proper, he was initiated into the mysteries, and instructed in the doctrines of Bardism. During his probationary state of discipline he was to learn such verses and adages as contained the maxims of the institution, and to compose others himself, on any relative subject, doctrinal or moral,

The

The BARDD BRAINT was the title of the corporate degree, or fundamental clafs of the order.* None could be admitted to this degree without having undergone the regular difcipline, amongft the *Awenyddion*. He was, after prefiding at three *Gorfeddau*, denominated one of the *Gorfeddogion*,† and became fully qualified to exercife all the functions of Bardifm; for it was as of this degree, and character, to which was annexed a plenitude of power adequate to all the purpofes of the inftitution, that the chief Bard always prefided. He could proclaim, and hold a *Gorfedd*, admit difciples, and *Ovyddion*; was capable of being employed in embaffies; in the office of herald; and to inftruct youth in the principles of religion and morality. It has been already faid that a Bard could not bear arms, as he was the herald of peace; he was alfo to obferve the moft inviolable fecrefy on all occafions, between fuch parties as engaged him in confidential offices; neither was he to efpoufe any particular party in religion, or in politics, as being inconfiftent with his character. The *Bardd Braint*, on all occafions where he acted officially, wore the unicoloured robe of fky-blue, which was the diftinguifhing drefs of the order, being emblematic of Peace, and alfo of Truth, from having no variety of colours.

The DERWYDDON, or *Druids*,‡ were fuch of the Bards, of either of the orders, of *Bardd Braint*, or of *Ovydd*, that

were

---

* A graduate of this clafs was alfo called *Bardd Trwyddedawg*, and *Trwyddedawg Braint*.

† Or *Beirdd Gorfeddawg*, or fimply *Beirdd Ynys Prydain*.

‡ Called alfo *Derwyddveirdd*, or *Druid Bards*, and in the fingular *Derwydd*,

were fet apart to, or employed peculiarly in the exercife
of religious functions; and long after the converfion of the
Britons to Chriftianity the minifters of religion were called
by this term, notwithftanding they had been for ages the
pagan priefts; but pagans we can hardly call thofe, who
worfhipped the true GOD in fimplicity.*   Therefore let
not the pious be alarmed at the idea of Druidifin being
ftill alive in this ifland; but let him examine it a little,
and he will find that the *Britifh* patriarchal religion is no
more than that of *Noah*, or of *Abraham*, inimical to Chriftianity.   There is in Druidifm, and no lefs in Chriftianity,
what feems extremely repugnant to the manners, and even
the religion of this age—a fevere inflexible morality.
Though the *Derwydd* was more peculiarly, yet he was not
exclufively the minifter of religion, for the *Bardd Braint*,
and even the *Ovydd*, might officiate as fuch, after being

Derwydd, and *Derwyddvardd*. The word *Derwydd* implies, *one fet before*,
or *in prefence*. I am aware fome have rendered it *Oak-man*, but the oak
was called *Derw* for the fame reafon as the prieft was called *Derwydd*, from
its being deemed confecrated wood, and both derived from *Dâr*.

* Amongft the bulk of the people there were certainly many fuperftitious
cuftoms; and on the introduction of Chriftianity not many of them were
exploded, for a great number remain to this day; but if there were any
corrupt principles mixt with the bardic fyftem, they were purged at that
period.

" It is remarkable that fome of thofe places which we call Druidical
" Temples, retain in their names, and other circumftances, evident marks
" of their having been places of Chriftian worfhip. Such is *Carn Moefen*,
" or the *Carnedd of Mofes*, in *Glamorganfhire*; *Carn y Groes*, on the moun-
" tain of *Gelly Onen* in the fame county, where a very ancient crofs ftands;
" *Ty Illtud*, in *Breconfhire*, and many others."

                                            EDWARD WILLIAMS.

                                    confirmed

confirmed by reception into the order, at a *Gorfedd*. There was no fuperiority attached to the order of *Derwydd*; it was only a peculiar officiality, for which the others were deemed equally qualified; and indeed, to be a *Derwydd* it of neceffity implied that he was a *Bardd Braint*; but, as a matter of convenience, the religious eftablifhment was allotted to an appropriate fet of Bards, diftinguifhed by that name, to give notoriety, and difcriminate vifibility to their function. The drefs of the *Derwydd* was white, the emblem of Holinefs, and peculiarly of Truth, as being the colour of light, or the fun. The *Derwydd* was exempted from fome offices, that were incumbent on each of the others. In him fanctity of life, and celebrity for wifdom were recommendatory qualifications always looked for; he was moft immediately the inftructor of youth; and was, from the neceffary obligations of his office, the refiden-ciary Bard of his diftrict, an obligation which the others did not lie under.

The OVYDD was the third order, being an honorary de-gree, to which the candidate could be immediately admit-ted, without being obliged to pafs through the regular dif-cipline. This degree, in every circumftance of its pecu-liar inftitution, appears to be intended to create a power that was capable of acting on emergencies, on a plan dif-ferent from the regular mode of proceeding, as well as of bringing within the fyftem fuch kind of knowledge as was unknown, or foreign to the original inftitution. The re-quifite qualifications were, in general, an acquaintance with valuable difcoveries in fcience; as the ufe of let-

ters,

ters,* medicine, languages, and the like; and it was not
an eafy thing, even in this order, to difpenfe with the
knowledge of, and a genius for, poetry; but this on particular occafions might be done, in confideration of other eminent qualifications; for this order was a provifionary one, for
the purpofe of admitting into the bardic fyftem, in a regular manner, every thing ufeful, and laudable in fcience.
The *Ovydd* was, however, enjoined to acquaint himfelf
with the bardic inftitutes and traditions; for, from feveral
contingencies, it was poffible that the order, or inftitution,
might be perpetuated only by *Ovyddion*; which in its original purity, it could not be done, unlefs they were acquainted with its true principle, nature, and intention. It
was deemed more honourable to be admitted into the orders by having been firft admitted an *Ovydd*, than by going
through a long difcipline, at leaft fuch an idea now prevails. The *Ovydd* could exercife all the functions of Bar-

---

* Some have ignorantly afferted that the Bards, or Druids, were enemies
to the ufe of letters; but there is every reafon to believe that they very
readily admitted, and practifed the ufe of them, as foon as they were
brought fully acquainted with their nature and utility. For the *Ovydd*
was received on no other qualification, but that of having the knowledge of
letters, and the fciences dependant thereon. In addition it may be obferved
that their original alphabet is ftill extant, which may be confidered a very
great curiofity. It contains thirty-fix letters, fixteen of which are radical,
and the reft are mutations of thofe; and it is the only one adequate to convey all the founds of the *Welfb* language without ufing double characters.
It is fingular that the bardic alphabet fhould contain all the *Etrufcan* letters, without the leaft deviation of form, except four or five in the latter,
that are *Roman*. Befides the ufe of letters, the Bards were accuftomed to
record their maxims by means of univerfal fymbols, without any appropriate characters. The *Indian Wampum* feems to be on this principle.

difm;

difm; and by fome particular acts he became intitled, by virtue of having performed them, to other degrees, after fuch acts had been acquiefced in by a *Gorfedd.* It is a received opinion that the Bards, in the character, and being of the order of *Ovydd,* may hold a *Cadair,* or fubordinate provincial meeting, under cover, or within doors. The drefs of the *Ovydd* was green, the fymbol of Learning, and alfo of Truth, from being unicoloured. The candidate for this order was elected at a *Gorfedd,* on the previous recommendation of a graduated Bard of any of the three orders; who might from his own knowledge declare that whom he propofed was duly qualified. If the candidate was not known to a Bard, the recommendation of a judge, or magiftrate, or of twelve reputable men, could conftitute him a candidate, on which he was immediately elected, by *Coelbren,* or ballot. But if it ever happened that the number of Bards was not fufficient to elect, then any one of the order might arbitrarily admit three, who were thereupon deemed finally graduated. No more than three could be admitted in this manner, for that was a fufficient number to proceed by election, in the regular way; becaufe arbitrary proceedings could not be fuffered, but where the number was inadequate to act otherwife, and confequently a matter of neceffity. Proclamation was another way of admiffion to the degree of *Ovydd;* that is, it was proclaimed at a *Gorfedd,* that a perfon of a certain name, place, and qualifications was, on fpecified recommendation, propofed as a candidate; and that at a certain future period, not lefs than a whole year, he was to be admitted to that degree; and if no objection was, during that

time,

time, brought againſt him, he was conſidered to be graduated.

Having taken a ſummary retroſpect of the peculiar regulations affecting the different orders ſeparately, ſome.
obſervations are neceſſary in regard to others that apper-
tain to the ſyſtem in general.

Each of the orders had a peculiarity of eſtimation, yet
neither was held to be more intrinſically excellent than the
other. If with reſpect to qualifications for certain officialities one was deemed inferior, it was in other particulars
allowed to be ſuperior; ſo that conſidered in the whole
they were equally honourable. Thus *Bardd Braint* was
peculiarly the ruling order, *Derwydd* the religious func-
tionary, and the *Ovydd* was the literary, or ſcientific order.
This idea of equality was preſerved with the utmoſt punc-
tuality in all their formulas of diſcipline. In their titles,
the Bards obſerved the order of their graduation, adding
to each the words—" According to the immunities, and
" cuſtoms of the Bards of the iſle of *Britain.*"* By this
means ſuch titles were a hiſtory of their manner of admiſ-
ſion; as—

Bardd Braint,	Bard of Preſidency;
Bardd a Derwydd,	Bard and Druid;
Bardd ac Ovydd,	Bard and Ovate;
Bardd, Ovydd, a Derwydd,	Bard, Ovate, and Druid;

---

* " Wrth vraint (yn mraint) a devawd Beirdd Ynys Prydain."

Bardd,

Bardd, Derwydd, ac Ovydd,	Bard, Druid, and Ovate;
Ovydd, Bardd, a Derwydd,	Ovate, Bard, and Druid;
Ovydd, Derwydd, a Bardd,	Ovate, Druid, and Bard.

The manner of attaining to any particular degree was thus: if an *Ovydd* had been admitted by a Bard, or proclamation had been made of any one being a candidate for this, or any other order, such a candidate was called *Ovydd*, or *Bard Claimant*, or *Presumptive Bard*;* and he was intitled after such proclamation to all passive privileges of the order, but nor to act officially until he had been confirmed in his degrees by a *Gorsedd*. That sanction being obtained, he could perform all the acts and functions of the order; and virtually became intitled to that particular degree incidental to the officialities which he executed: By officiating as *Derwydd*, after a certain time he became of that degree; by presiding at a *Gorsedd* he became, what presidency implies, a *Bardd Braint*; by admitting, and after confirmation of an *Ovydd*, he became intitled to that degree, if he was not so before. Such proceedings are deduced from this general rule—That a graduated Bard executing any of the officialities of the institution, after the acquiescence of a *Gorsedd*, became intitled to the degrees incident to, and implied by such officialities.

The principle on which they acted for perpetuating the institution was—That three, or more Bards could admit by election; but if there should be only one remaining, he could perform arbitrarily all officialities till three had been

* " Ovydd (Bardd) yn mraint hawl ac arddel."

by

by him admitted. The deficiency being fupplied, arbitrary power ceafed, and all was to go on regularly. Two remaining Bards could only act by proclamation; for between two there could be no majority, or cafting voice; and one could not act arbitrarily, becaufe there was another oppofing power of equal authority. The proclamation was therefore an appeal, or reference to public opinion, and to that original authority from which the inftitution was firft derived; and the acquiefcence of the public, in bringing no objections to the propofals of fuch proclamation, conftituted the legality of any act done, in confequence of its having been propofed in the notice. It is allowed that, for moft reafons, it would be beft alfo for one remaining Bard to act by proclamation, rather than arbitrarily; and that this method fhould be preferred even to election, as coming more immediately under the cognizance of the public; but it is evident that, in fome ages, the inftitution could never have been perpetuated by fuch proceedings, and would long ago have become extinct, from oppofition of vulgar prejudice. All thefe modes have been practifed, and each has its propriety under certain circumftances; but when all things will admit, it is deemed beft to recur to that authority which firft eftablifhed the inftitution, the general confent obtained by virtue of a proclamation; the next is the bardic election at a *Gorfedd*; and when occafion calls for it, the arbitrary admiffion is purely confiftent with a provifionary maxim, for creating a neceffary, and for that reafon a legal, power, to effect what is beneficial, at a time when no other authority exifts, to recur to on immediate emergencies. The arbitrary acts of a Bard, fuch as admiffion of an *Ovydd*, or

any

any thing elfe, were done in confequence of a fuppofed, or implied decifion of the Bards at a *Gorfedd*, exifting in a neceffary fiction to fanction an arbitrary act not otherwife allowed. In this fiction they always exift; they may be vifible, but cannot be virtually extinct; for the utility, and principles of their inftitution exift in nature. That being the cafe, the officiating agents of thofe principles are rather dormant than extinct; and to be called into action by proclamation.

The regular manner of qualifying ultimately, or graduating a Bard, is by giving him a *Gorfedd*, or *Cadair*; that is by including him in the number, which muft be three at leaft, of prefiding Bards, at a *Gorfedd*. Amongft the number mentioned in the proclamation, it is not poffible to know, from any thing in the words or form of it, which are the old Bards, and which the newly admitted, as there is nothing in the bardic regulations that can intitle any one to take precedency of another; and to prefide at a *Gorfedd* is only performing the neceffary officialities of the occafion, which might be done by any other Bard prefent with equal propriety. Neither is it neceffary that the prefiding Bards fhould punctually be thofe mentioned in the proclamation, or that they fhould be vifibly prefent, for they are virtually, or reprefentatively fo, as well as all the *Beirdd Ynys Prydain*. Thus to obtain the degree to which one was admitted by giving him prefidency, it was not neceffary he fhould be prefent; for there was nothing implied as an act of his own, in his being, or not being prefent in perfon. The fole intention of giving him prefidency was to announce him to the Bards, all virtually prefent

fent, and to the public, as of the particular order to which
he was admitted.

The regular times of holding a *Gorfedd*, or meeting,*
were the two folftices, and equinoxes; fubordinate meetings might alfo be held every new and full moon, and alfo
at the quarter days, which were chiefly for inftructing difciples. The regular meetings were fuppofed to be well
known, with refpect to time, and place; for there were
appointed places, as well as times.† Irregular meetings
could only be held by proclamation; or if arbitrarily held
on urgent occafions, their acts required the confirmation
of a *Gorfedd*, or public affent by fubfequent proclamation.
The *Gorfeddau*, or meetings, were always held in the open
air, and *in the face of the fun, and eye of the light*. The place
was fet apart by forming a circle of ftones around the
Maen Gorfedd, as already mentioned.‡ At the *Gorfeddau* it
was

* Called alfo *Cadair, Guyddva*, and *Eifteddvod*; but thefe terms are more
particularly for provincial meetings.

† When all *Britain* acknowledged the bardic inftitution the meetings
were held in that part of the ifland moft convenient, and central, which was
Salifbury Plains; and as might be expected, there we find the moft ftupen-
dous monuments that have been left of the former power of the Bards;
Silbury and *Stonehenge* in particular. It is furprizing that *Rowlands*, out of
partiality for his native place perhaps, fhould make the ifle of *Anglefey* the
place of general meeting, when it is confidered how puny the veftiges be,
that are to be found there; befides the inconveniency of the fituation.
That *Suetonius Paulinus* fhould meet with a more than ordinary number in
that ifland is reafonable enough, becaufe there might be many fugitives
from parts where they had been before difturbed by the *Romans*; and who
had fled to that place, fuppofing it to be out of the reach of thofe enemies.

‡ *Maen Gorfedd*, the import of which is *the Stone of the Affembly*, was alfo
called

was abfolutely neceffary to recite the bardic traditions; and with this whatever came before them was confidered, and determined upon. The Bards always ftood bare headed and bare footed, in their unicoloured robes, at the *Gorfedd,* and within the *Cylç Cyngrair,* or Circle of Federation. The ceremony ufed on the opening of a meeting was the fheathing of the fword, on the *Maen Gorfedd,* at which all the prefiding Bards affifted; and this was accompanied with a very fhort pertinent difcourfe. When the bufinefs was finifhed the meeting was clofed by taking up, but not unfheathing, the fword, with a few words on the occafion, when all covered their heads and feet.* There were certain mottos ufed by the Bards; that for the *General Affembly of the Ifle of Britain* † was—Y GWIR YN ERBYN Y BYD, *The Truth in oppofition to the World.* Thofe for the provincial meetings were fuch as had been adopted on the firft eftablifhment, of them refpectively.‡ They were ufed as declaratory

called *Crair Gorfedd,* or *the Covenant Place of the Affembly,* and *Maen Llôg, the Stone of Covenant;* but it never was called *Cromleç,* nor is this name to be found in any old manufcript whatever, it is therefore a name unfairly obtruded upon the public. This altar *might* be called *Cromleç* for the fame reafon as other ftones of the like form and pofition are termed fo in common language, but it has not the leaft allufion to the ufe which the Bards made of it.

* It feems pretty evident that thefe ceremonies of the Bards are the fource from which all thofe who have made pretenfions to be conjurors, and magicians, have borrowed their circles, wands, and other things, to give their fpells an air of greater confequence.

† Gorfedd (*or* Beirdd) Ynys Prydain.

‡ That for *Cadair Gwynedd,* or the chair of Venedotia was—JESU, *Jefus.*

Cadair

claratory of the *Cadair*, or *Talaith*, meeting, or province, whereof the Bard was a member, or of the meeting that enacted any thing refpecting the inftitution. The *Gorfeddau*, and *Cadeiriau*, or the general, and provincial affemblies always virtually exift; and if they do not vifibly appear, they are to be called on to make their appearance, by the proclamation of a *Gorfedd Ynys Prydain*, where three graduated Bards muft prefide; and, as in individuals, fo in collective bodies, thofe *Cadeiriau*, or *Provincial Chairs*, took no precedency one of the other on any occafion, but all were equal in eftimation and dignity. It was requifite that every Bard fhould be known as of fome provincial *Cadair*,* for the fake of vifible diftinction, though the *Beirdd Ynys Prydain*,† (which was their general title) were of every one; for they all exifted in them, as the fountain from whence all are derived ; and fhould any have difappeared, the *Beirdd Ynys Prydain* might call them out by proclamation, or by actually appearing at fuch meetings, and give them immediate vifibility, or by the fame means conftitute new ones. A *Gorfedd* might be fo held as to be a national, and alfo a provincial one at the fame time.‡ It

Cadair Powys, or the chair of Powys—A LADDO A LEDDIR, *He that kills fhall be killed.*

Cadair Dyved, or the chair of Dimetia—CALON WRTH CALON, *Heart united to Heart.*

Cadair Morganwg, or the chair of Glamorgan—DUW A PHOB DAIONI, *God and all Goodnefs.*

* *Cadair*, or *Gorfedd*; as of Gwynedd, Dyved, and others.

† Or *Gorfeddogion Ynys Prydain*, or fimply *Gorfeddogion*, and *Beirdd Gorfeddawg*.

‡ The formula for which ran thus—Gorfedd wrth vraint a devawd Beirdd Ynys Prydain, ac yn mraint Beirdd (*or* Cadair) Powys, &c.

was

was not neceffary that a provincial *Cadair* fhould be actually held within its peculiar territory; for it might be held
any where in *Britain*, or even in a foreign country, as
might alfo a *Gorfedd Ynys Prydain*, retaining on fuch occafion the appropriate titles; which were—*Beirdd Ynys Prydain trwy'r Byd*, and *Twyddedogion Byd*—" The Bards of
the ifle of *Britain* through the world," and " thofe who are
at liberty through the world."

At a meeting there was always one, called the *Dad-
geiniad*, or the reciter, whofe bufinefs was to recite the traditions, and poems; to make proclamations, announce
candidates, open, and clofe the *Gorfedd*, and the like. A
Bard generally executed this office; but it might be done
by one, or as many as were neceffary, of the *Awenyddion*, or
difciples.

A *Gorfedd* was opened, and clofed, as before obferved,
with fhort difcourfes, which were formal with refpect to
the matter, but there was no neceffity for their being fo in
words. The following was the purport of what was faid
at the opening of one *——

" THE

---

* *Y gwir yn erbyn y byd:* ac yn nawdd *Beirdd Ynys Prydain* pawb à gyrç-
ant hyn o le, lle nid noeth arv yn eu herbyn; a phawb a geifiont Urddas a
Thrwyddedogaeth wrth Gerdd a Barddoniaeth, ceifiant gan Iolo Morganwg, W. Meçain, Hywel Eryri, a D. Ddu Eryri, a hwynt oll yn *Veirdd
truyddedawg* yn mraint *Beirdd Ynys Prydain*— *Y Gwir yn erbyn y byd*.

If any were to be graduated the conclufion was altered to this form—
" Yn mraint *Cadair (Beirdd) Cyvoeth Morganwg*, a *Gwent*, ac *Erging*, ac
Yftrad Yw—*Yn enw Duw a phob Daioni*.—This conftituted it a provincial

d *Cadair;*

" THE TRUTH AGAINST THE WORLD: Under the pro-
" tection of the *Bards of the ifle of Britain*, are all who re-
" pair to this place, where there is not a naked weapon
" againſt them; and all who ſeek for the privilege and
" graduation appertaining to Science and Bardiſm, let
" them demand it from *Iolo Morganwg, W. Meçain, Hywel*
" *Eryri*, and *D. Ddu Eryri*, and they being all *graduated*
" *Bards*, according to the privilege of the *Bards of the ifle*
" *of Britain.*—THE TRUTH AGAINST THE WORLD."

In cloſing the *Gorſedd*, the preſiding Bard took up the
ſword, and named the Bards that were mentioned in the
opening; except ſome of them were to be rejected, or
ſuſpended, and then they were noticed thus*——

" *Iolo Morganwg*, and *W. Meçain*, Bards graduated in
" the privilege of the Bards of the ifle of *Britain*; and *D.*

Cadair; and it would be denominated Cadair Morganwg, or the *Chair* of
the *Bards of Glamorgan*. If an Ovydd was to be admitted, the form concluded thus—Ymgeiſiant û *Iolo Morganwg, W. Meçain, Hywel Eryri,* a *D.
Ddu Eryri. Beirdd ac Ovyddion* yn mraint Beirdd Ynys Prydain. *Sev y
dyzved D. Ddu Eryri, ar air, a cyduybod, y gellid Beirdd o honynt; ac yna barn-
aſant y Beirdd yn ngorſedd, y dylid Beirdd o honynt yn ngradd Ovyddion, yn
mraint Beirdd a Çadair Gwynedd—Yn Enw Jeſu!*
And in concluding the *Gorſedd* thus—Iolo Morganwg, W. Meçain, Hywel Eryri, a D. Ddu Eryri, Beirdd ac Ovyddion, *wrth vraint a devawd
Beirdd Gwynedd, yn Ymddal wrth briv ddevawd Beirdd Ynys Prydain: ni
noethant arv yn erbyn neb, ac ni bydd noeth arv yn eu herbyn—Yn Enw, &c.*
* Iolo Morganwg, a W. Meçain Beirdd Trwyddedogion yn mraint
Beirdd Ynys Prydain; a D. *Ddu Eryri*, Bardd wrth hawl ac arddel yn
mraint Cadair Dyved—*Calon wrth Galon.*

Ddu

" *Ddu Eryri, a Bard claimant* under the privilege of the
" *Chair* of *Dimetia*—HEART UNITED TO HEART."*

This alteration, in the manner of naming the Bards from
what was done in the opening of the *Gorſedd*, implies that
D. Ddu Eryri is ſuſpended; and *Hywel Eryri* rejeƈted, or
excepted againſt; and for that reaſon not admitted to
their degrees for which they were candidates.

From the above form it will appear, that ſuch candidates
as are named in a proclamation, and paſſed over in ſilence
at a *Gorſedd*, are rejeƈted; and can never afterwards be admitted; and ſuch as are called, at a *Gorſedd*, after being
named, " *Beirdd wrtb hawl ac arddel*,"—" Bards claimant,
or preſumptive," it implies ſuſpenſion of the deciſion of
the *Gorſedd* concerning them, till a future opportunity.

When it had been proved before a *Gorſedd*, that a Bard
had been guilty of any criminal aƈt, he was ſuſpended, or
degraded, as occaſion required. The firſt was by proclamation, in which he was called *Bard claimant and preſumptive*; as before noticed. Degradation was a particular aƈt
of the *Gorſedd*, before the cloſe of it; and it was called—
" *Dwyn cyrç cyvlavan yn ei erbyn*,"—" To bring the aſſault
of warfare againſt him." After the deciſion all the Bards
covered their heads, and one of them unſheathed the
ſword, named the perſon aloud three times, with the ſword

* A *Gorſedd* might be made a general and a provincial one at the ſame
time, thus—Wrth vraint a devawd Beirdd Ynys Prydain; ac yn mraint
Beirdd Cadair Dyved, &c.

lifted

lifted in his hand, adding when he was laſt named—"*Noeth yw cleddyv yn ei erbyn*,"—" The ſword is naked againſt him." This concluded the ceremony, and he could never after be re-admitted; and he was called—" *Gwr wrth ddivrawd at anraith*."—" A man deprived of privilege and expoſed to warfare." For the purpoſe of degrading a Bard, it is ſometimes deemed moſt proper to hold a particular *Gorſedd* for that purpoſe, by proclamation, in which the occaſion ſhould be ſpecified in this peculiar form of words *—" Where there will not be a naked weapon " againſt any one but *Madog Min*, a man deprived of " privilege, and expoſed to warfare." All beſides in the proclamation to be in the uſual manner. Such having been publiſhed, it is not neceſſary that the *Gorſedd* therein proclaimed ſhould be actually held, for it has a virtual exiſtence, and all that is neceſſary on this occaſion is to announce to the public the degradation of ſuch a Bard.

The proclamation was to this purpoſe †—

" When it was the year of our Lord one thouſand ſeven. " hundred and ninety-two, and *the ſun in the point of the vernal*

---

* " Lle ni bydd noeth arv yn erbyn neb ond Madawg Min, Gwr wrth " ddivrawd ac anraith."

† Rhybydd undydd a blwyddyn—" Pan oedd oed CRIST yn 1792, a'r " haul yn nghyvnod cyhydedd dydd a nôs yn y Gwanwyn, y rhodded " Gwys a Gwahawdd, yn nghlyw Gwlad ac arglwydd, dan ofteg undydd a " blwyddyn, a nawdd i bawb â geiſiont Urddas a Thrwyddedogaeth wrth " Gerdd a Barddoniaeth, gyrçu pen PUMLUMON yn MHOWYS, yn mhen " undydd a blwyddyn, yn oriau'r eçwydd, Lle ni bydd noeth cleddyv yn eu herbyn;

" *vernal equinox*, a fummons and invitation was given, in
" the *hearing of the country and the prince*, under the period
" of a year and a day, with protection for all fuch as might
" feek for *privilege*, *and graduation* appertaining to *Science*,
" *and Bardifm*, to repair to the top of PUMLUMON in,
" Powys, at the expiration of the year and the day, in,
" the hours of noon, where *there will not be a naked weapon*,
" *againft them*; and then, in the prefence of IOLO MOR-
" GANWG, *Bard according to the privilege of the Bards of the*
" *ifle of Britain*; and with him W. MEÇAIN, HYWEL
" ERYRI, and D. DDU ERYRI, and they being all *gradu-*
" *ated Bards under the privilege and cuftom of the Bards of*
" *Britain*,* for the purpofe of pronouncing the judgment
" of a *Gorfedd, in the eye of the fun, and face of the light*, on
" all with refpect to *genius and moral conduct*, who may feek
" for *prefidency and privilege, according to the privilege and*
" *cuftom of the Bards of the ifle of Britain*.—THE TRUTH IN
" OPPOSITION TO THE WORLD."†

" herbyn; acyno'n erwynebawl Iolo Morganwg, Bardd yn mraint Beirdd
" Ynys Prydain, a çydag ev W. Meçain, a Hywel Eryri, a D. Ddu Eryri,
" a hwynt oll yn Drwyddedogion wrth vraint a devawd Beirdd Ynys Pryd-
" ain, er cynnal barn Gorfedd, yn llygad haul ac wyneb goleuni, ar bawb
" o barth, Awen a Buçedd, à geifiont Vraint ac Urddas, herwydd braint a
" devawd Beirdd Ynys Prydain.—Y GWIR YN ERBYN Y BYD."

  * If there are candidates for different degrees they are mentioned thus—
" Iolo Morganwg, *Bardd Trwyddedawg*; W. Meçain, *Bardd ac Oxydd*;
" Hywel Eryri, a D. Ddu Eryri, *Beirdd a Derwyddion*, wrth vraint a
" devawd Beirdd Ynys Prydain, &c. (or Beirdd, or Cadair Gwynedd,) &c."

  † The above is a *Gorfedd* of the ifle of *Britain*; but when the occafion is
local it fhould be a provincial *Cadair*, which is conftituted by concluding
thus, for *Powys*—" Herwydd braint a devawd Beirdd (Cadair) *Powys*—
" A LADDO A LEDDIR."

- Having

Having accompliſhed the foregoing ſketch of Bardiſm, I am tempted to recapitulate the leading articles in the ſyſtem, for the purpoſe of bringing the whole into one point of view, whereby it will be ſeen what a ſurpriſing coincidence there is between it and the principles of a modern ſect that is reſpected through the world.*

PEACE.——There is a neceſſity of reſtoring, eſtabliſhing, and preſerving of peace towards the happineſs of mankind; therefore the Bards give an example by refraining from bearing arms, and from all things that tend to form one party in oppoſition to another. The Bard amid the ſtorms of the moral world muſt aſſume the ſerenity of the unclouded blue ſky.

EQUALITY.——Superiority of individual power is what none but God can poſſibly be intitled to; for the power that gave exiſtence to all is the only power that has a claim of right to rule over all. A man cannot aſſume authority over another; for if he may over one, by the ſame

---

* The ſociety of *Friends*, or the people called Quakers. It is obſervable that they originally appeared under the denomination of *Seekers*; and generally, if not firſt in *South Wales*; and it is known that *George Fox* arranged his ſyſtem, after availing himſelf of the experience and labours of *William Erbury*, and *Walter Cradock*, natives of that part of *Wales* where the bardic inſtitution was preſerved. Doth not this point out ſomething more than mere accidental ſimilarity between the two ſyſtems? Or is it becauſe both have been fortunate in adopting what is congenial with nature? The *Welſh Quakers* have a cuſtom not common to others, which makes the likeneſs ſtill ſtronger: they hold their meetings in the open air, generally in a circular incloſure, called *Monwent*.

reaſon

reafon he may rule over a million, or over a world. All men are neceffarily equal: the FOUR ELEMENTS in their natural ftate, or every thing not manufactured by art, is the common property of all.

TRUTH.——Believe nothing without examination; but where reafon and evidence will warrant the conclufion believe every thing; and let prejudice be unknown. Search for truth on all occafions; and efpoufe it in oppofition to the world.

LIGHT.——The emblem of purity, and holinefs, the fource of good, and by which all truths fhould be illumined. Every act of the Bard muft be done *in the face of the fun, and in the eye of the light.*

MAN.——The laft being that came into exiftence in this world was man. He appeared with the firft rifing fun; before that it was perpetual night. He is deftined to fill a certain place in the creation; but at perfect liberty to act in that character, or able to attach himfelf to either good or evil, as the impulfe of his own inclinations fhall lead him, accountable, rewardable, or punifhable, for all he does. Humanity is therefore a ftate where good and evil are fo equally balanced that it becomes a ftate of liberty, and confequently of probation. In this ftate the foul becomes poffeffed of fuch a perfection of memory, that in what condition foever he may afterwards exift he never lofes the recollection of what ever after befalls him; fo that the reward, or punifhment, is by this means extremely heightened by the comparifon of the prefent with the former, and by ex-

d 4   periencing

periencing the neceffary confequences of good, or evil;
and he cannot attain perfect knowledge until he has gone
through all poffible modes of exiftence.

ANIMALS.——They originated in the loweft point of
exiftence, the meaneft water-worm. Land animals are of
a fuperior order, and rife in their various gradations up to
man. As all modes of exiftence below humanity are neceffarily evil, fo no animal can pafs to a lower ftate when it
dies, but the divine benevolence has fo ordained that it
fhould rife higher; and thus advancing upwards it arrives
at humanity. Animals approach the ftate of humanity in
proportion as they are gentle and harmlefs in their difpofi-
tions; and to haften their progrefs towards happinefs thefe
become, more than any others, liable to be deftroyed un-
timely; which is a regulation of divine benevolence. But
as man has no right to counteract Providence, he is not
permitted to kill any animal, but which would either immediately or eventually kill him; and it is by this law he
muft regulate himfelf, when he deprives any being of life.
We cannot kill an animal, any more than a man, but as a
prevention againft, or a punifhment for killing.

GOOD.——To fuffer with patience, and fortitude, is the
greateft virtue of humanity, and includes all others. Man
muft brave all dangers rather than not act to his duty; for
true valour appears never to fo great advantage as in fuffering unmoved, what cannot be avoided without tranf-
greffing the laws of juftice, and benevolence. If during
human life, or the ftate of probation, the foul attaches itfelf to good, it paffeth in the inftant of death into a higher
                                                    ftate

ftate of exiftence, where good neceffarily prevails, and it is impoffible to fall from fuch a ftate; yet liberty however ftill remains in the exertions of love, and benevolence. Love is the principle which rules every thing in thofe ftates of exiftence that are above humanity; and a man, for that is his condition to all eternity, in fuch a ftate retains the love of his country in particular, though of all the world in general. For this reafon he. may defcend, and again affume the earthly ftate, to reftore the knowledge of truth, and to imprefs the dictates of virtue.*

.Evil.——Pride is that paffion, by which man affumes more than the laws of nature allow him; for all men are equal, though differently ftationed in the ftate of humanity for the common good. Whoever affumes fuch a fuperiority - is an ufurper; and by this affumption of power, derived from pride, a man attaches himfelf to evil, in fuch a degree, that his foul paffes at death into the meaneft worm; or he falls into the loweft point of exiftence. A man by attaching himfelf to evil, becomes in the paffions of his foul depraved, and brutalized; and at death he falls into fuch a ftate as correfponds with the degree of malignity acquired; or his foul paffes into an animal of a difpofition correfponding with what he was at the time of death. From this ftate he again by degrees rifes higher

---

* According to the bardic fcheme the prophets of Ifrael were of this defcription; for none could reveal heavenly things but thofe who had experienced them, and who by returning to this world made them known.—Taliefin is full of this doctrine: he has, he fays, paffed through many tranfmigrations; has afcended to heaven, and returned to earth.

- and

and higher in the fcale of exiftence, until he arrives at the ftate of humanity : from whence he may again fall. Thus let him fall ever fo often, he again returns, as the fame road to ,happinefs lies open to him, and *will* to eternity ; fo that neceffary eternal punifhment, or ftate of mifery, is in itfelf impoffible ; and the infliction of fuch punifhment is the only thing which the Deity cannot do, who is all perfect benevolence.

REWARDS and PUNISHMENTS——Thefe are fo fecured by the eternal laws of creation, that they take place necef-farily, and unavoidably. They may be, and are accele-rated, one as well as the other, by death ; which is the only poffible means ; and this, in a degree, is left in the power of man, and is retained alfo by divine Providence.

PENITENCE and SACRIFICE.——Perfect penitence is intitled to pardon ; and which confifts in making all poffible retribution for the offence, and fubmitting willingly to the punifhment due. A man thus by giving himfelf up voluntarily, to what his confcience tells him is due to his crime, doth all that remains in his power, and fo his foul becomes divefted of its turpitude, and attached to good in the higheft degree poffible. This is the bardic idea of human facrifice; and none were admitted but volun-tary victims ; or thofe condemned of crimes; and to put thefe to death was a coincidence with divine benevolence, in haftening them to that courfe which they muft pafs through, before they could arrive at happinefs.

PROVIDENCE.

PROVIDENCE.——God is benevolence in all his laws of nature; for he has so ordered that the arrival of every being at a state of blifs is by all poffible means accelerated. Thus the vortex of univerfal warfare, in which the whole creation is involved, contributes to forward the victim of its rage to a higher state of exiftence. Even the malignancy of man is rendered fubfervient to the general, and ultimate end of Divine Providence, which is to bring all animated beings to happinefs.

ETERNITY.——No finite beings can poffibly bear the infinite tedium of eternity. They will be relieved from it by continual renovations at proper periods, by paffing into new modes of exiftence; and which will not, like death, be dreaded, but be eagerly wifhed for, and approached with joy. Every exiftence will impart its peculiar stock of knowledge; for confcioufnefs and memory will for ever remain; or there could be no fuch thing as endlefs life.

We fhall now pafs on to give a fhort hiftory of the manner in which Bardifm has been continued to the prefent time. It has been already obferved, that the principles, upon which it was formed, did not in the leaft militate againft the introduction of Chriftianity; for they were, on the contrary, highly ferviceable to facilitate the adoption of the new doctrine; becaufe it was one of the leading maxims, to examine every thing without prejudice, to draw a conclufion from the evidence, and to abide by the refult only, as farther inveftigation fhould fupport it, or otherwife. In confirmation of fuch remark, we have a notable inftance of the influence of that fpirit of inveftigation, re-

corded

corded by the hiftorians of the firft planting of Chriftianity; who teftify that the *Britons* embraced it generally,
and with more opennefs than any other people. Such an
event having taken place, in the manner defcribed, the
functions of the Chriftian priefthood continued to be exer-
cifed exclufively by the different orders of the bards,
amongft the *Cymry*, until nearly about the time of *Germa-
nus* and *Lupus*, about the beginning of the fifth century.
At that period an opening was effected by the intereft of
the clergy of the *Roman* Church; which, in the courfe of
about a century, by depriving the order of the patronage,
totally excluded the Bards from all religious offices; at
leaft with refpect to any pretenfions they might fet up, as
being of fuch order. When thefe changes were beginning
to take place, a prince of the name of *Beli* formed a code
of regulations, which he invited the Bards to adopt;
wherein many deviations from the original inftitution were
difcernible; and, moft probably, their right to the priefthood was amongft the articles omitted *. Such as were
of a complying difpofition acceded to the new laws; but
thofe who had the honour of the ancient inftitution at

* Thefe new laws were afterwards modified in the fixth century, by king
Arthur; and again in the eleventh, by *Grufudd ab Cynan*, king of *Wales*;
and laft of all an incoherent jumble of them were adopted, for want of
proper information, by a congrefs, held at *Caervyrddin* towards the middle
of the fifteenth century. The people who embraced thefe new laws were
called by the primitive Bards, in derifion, *Beirdd Beli*, and *Over-veirdd*,
or the Bards of *Beli*, and pfeudo Bards. However in fome ages they feem
to have been held in greater eftimation than the old Bards; poffibly becaufe
they were not fo inimical to the clergy, and to the popular errors of the
times.

                                          heart,

heart, treated with difdain the propofal of being guided
by any other, than the public Traditions of the *Gorfedd.*
From this period the regular *Beirdd Ynys Prydain* are only
to be confidered a fmall fect, though ftill venerated by the
people, on account of their peaceable principles; and they
ftill poffeffed a confiderable degree of influence, as long as
the *Cymmry* enjoyed their own government; but when that
was loft, by the fall of the laft *Llywelyn,* Bardifm had nearly
been totally annihilated. The Bards were not only deprived
of patronage by this event, but they were even awed by
the terror of a cruel perfecution; the confequence of which
was, that they were obliged to be circumfpect, and to avoid
the regular open *Gorfedd.* This muft have endangered the
lofs of the Traditions, and learning of the Inftitution;
therefore fuch of the Bards as were anxious for its fate began, more than before, to make collections of thofe things
in books *. With a view to confolidate thofe collections
feveral *Gorfeddau* were held from the beginning of the fifteenth century, under the fanction of Sir *Richard Neville*
and others; and a fubfequent one, for the fame purpofe,
was held in 157?, under the aufpices of *William Herbert*
earl of *Pembroke,* the great patron of *Welfh* literature †.
What was done in thofe meetings received confiderable

---

* The Bards who had the principal hand in forming the collections
were——*Einion Ofeiriad, Edeyrn Davawd Aur, Gwrgan ab Rhys, Trabaearn
Brydydd Mawr, Davydd ddu Hiraddug, Sion y Cent, Gwilym Tew, Gwilym
Egwad, Jeuan ab Hywel Swrdwal, Jenan Gethin, Lewys Morganwg,
Meiryg Davydd, Davydd Benwyn, Davydd Llwyd Mathew, Llywelyn b
Langewydd,* and *Edward Davydd,* of *Margam.*

† The great library of Welfh manufcripts, formed by him, at *Rhaglan
Caftle* was deftroyed by *Oliver Cromwell.*

improvement

improvement at one held by Sir *Edward Lewis* of the *Van*, about the year 1580, from the arrangement of the venerable *Llywelyn o Langewydd*; and laftly, a complete revifal of all the former collections was made by *Edward Davydd* of *Margam*, which received the fanction of a *Gorfedd*, held at *Bewpyr*, in the year 1681, under the authority of Sir *Richard Baffet*; when that collection was pronounced to be in every refpect the fulleft illuftration of Bardifm *. From that period to the prefent time a remnant of the Order of the Bards has exifted, obfcurely, in the part of *Wales* where thofe meetings were held, ftill occafionally holding a *Gorfedd* for *Morganwg*, or *Glamorgan*; being the only pro-vincial Chair extant, all the others being difcontinued long ago; and even the members of this were reduced to two before the prefent revival of the inftitution †.

The

---

* Mr. *Edward Williams*, of *Flimfton*, had an opportunity to make a tran-fcript of that book; and from his I made another.

† One of thofe is the Rev. *Edward Evan* of *Aberdar*; and the other is the faid Mr. *Edward Williams*; who has juft at this time given to the world his *Englifh* poetry, in two volumes. It is he who has given a tafte for Bardifm to feveral, which is likely to be the means of reviving the infti-tution; and it is from his communications and affiftance, that I have been enabled to give this account of the Bards.

The following, from a manufcript of the late Mr. *John Bradford*, is a lift of the Bards of the *Chair* of *Glamorgan*, and the order in which they were the *Awenyddion*, or difciples; and it may be confidered as a Bardic pe-digree: the dates denote the times when they prefided——

		His Awenyddion
Trahaearn Brydydd Mawr,	1300	
Hywel Bwr Baç - - - -	1330	Gwilym ab Ieuan Hên.
Davydd ab Gwilym - -	1360	Ieuan Tew Hên.
Ieuan Hên - - - - -	1370	Hywel Swrdwal
		Ieuan Tew Hên - - - 1420
		Awenyddion

The Bardic theology, laws, and principles, have in all ages been referred to infpiration, or afferted to be derived from

Awenyddion
Hywel Swrdwal.
Ieuan ab Hywel Swrdwal.
Ieuan Gethin ab I. ab Lleifion.
Hywel ab Davydd ab I. ab Rhys
Ieuan Gethin ab I. ab Lleifion 1430
    Awenydd
Gwylim Tew, or G. Hendon.
Gwilym Tew - - - - 1460
    Awenyddion.
Huw Cae Llwyd.
Hywel ab Dav. ab I. ab Rhys.
Harri o'r Gareg Lwyd.
Iorwerth Vynglwyd
Meredydd ab Rhoffer - - 1470
    Awenyddion.
Iorwerth Vynglwyd.
Ieuan Deulwyn.
Sir Einion ab Owain.
Ieuan Deulwyn - - - 1480
    Awenyddion.
Iorwerth Vynglwyd.
Lewys Morgahwg.
Harri Hir.
Iorwerth Vynglwyd - - 1500
    Awenyddion.
Lewys Morganwg.
Ieuan Du'r Bilwg.
Lewys Morganwg - - - 1520
    Awenyddion.
Meiryg Davydd.
Davydd Benwyn.
Llywelyn Sion o Langewydd.
Thomas Llywelyn o Regoes.
Meiryg Davydd (died in 1600) 1560
    Awenydd.
Watcin Pywel.
Davydd Benwyn - - - 1560
    Awenyddion.
Llywelyn Sion.
Sion Mawddwy.
Davydd Llwyd Mathew.
Llywelyn Sion (died in 1616) 1580

Awenyddion.
Watcin Pywel.
Ieuan Thomas.
Meilir Mathew.
Davydd ab Davydd Mathew.
Davydd Edward o Vargam.
Edward Davydd o Vargam.
Watcin Pywel - - - - 1620
    Awenyddion.
Davydd Edward.
Edward Davydd.
Davydd ab Davydd Mathew.
Edward Davydd (died in 1690) 1660
    Awenyddion.
Hywel Lewys.
Charles Bwttwn, Efq.
Thomas Roberts Ofeiriad.
S. Jones o Vryn Llywarç, Of⁴.
Evan Sion Meredydd.
Davydd o'r Nant.
Davydd o'r Nant - - - 1680
    Awenyddion.
Hopcin y Gweydd.
Thomas Roberts Ofeiriad.
Davydd Hopcin o'r Coetty.
Samuel Jones Ofeiriad - - 1700
    Awenyddion.
Rhys Prys, Ty'n y Ton. *
William Hain.
Sion Bradford, yn blentyn.
Davydd Hopcin, o'r Coetty 1730
    Awenyddion.
Davydd Thomas
Rhys Morgan, Pencraig Nedd.
Davydd Nicolas.
Sion Bradford.
Sion Bradford (died in 1780) 1760
    Awenyddion.
Lewys Hopcin.
William Hopcin.
Edward Evan.
Edward Williams.

* Father of the late celebrated Dr. Price, of Hackney.

from Heaven, under the denomination of AWEN.   Thus a
Poet of the fixteenth century fays,*

    ——" Dwyn o'r nen
    Deçreuad açau'r Awen."

" We derive from Heaven
The primeval infpiration of Bardifm."

By the term AWEN may be underftood genius, in the general fenfe, though more appropriately a poetical genius,
or the Mufe; but often, in the language of the Bards, it
fignifies infpiration, or the Holy Spirit†.   Thus *Llywarç*

---

 * *Edmund Prys*, the tranflator into Welfh of the Pfalms that are appointed to be fung in churches; and author of many pieces of great merit.
 Taliefin, and moft of the fubfequent Bards, abound with paffages of the
fame idea, refpecting the divine origin of the *Awen*.
 † *Llywelyn o Langewydd*, a writer on Bardifm, who died about the year
1616, fays, that the Awen was firft given to *Enoch*, and that he was the firft
man that praifed God in fong.   He alfo fays that an evil genius appeared in
the world; and that men forfook the ho   for this; and at fome periods this evil one had the afcendancy.   From this we may prefume that
Enoch and his defcendants worfhipped God in purity for fome time; but by
degrees they imbibed the general depravity of the world.   And perhaps this
may be the Bardic explanation of the beginning of the fixth chapter of *Genefis*,
which feems to be an allegory——" It came to pafs, that when men began
" to multiply on the face of the earth, and daughters were born unto them,
" that the fons of God faw the daughters of men that they were fair: and
" they took them wives of all which they chofe."

Rhygorug vy Awen	
I voli vy Rhëen.	TALIESIN.
Da ryw Yfbryd a yrawdd	
Duw o nev, da yw ei nawdd.	E. PRYS.
Cyvarçav ym Rhëen	
Yftyriaw Awen.	TALIESIN.
	B. Moç,

B. Moç, a poet of the twelfth century, invokes to be inspired, to fing the praife of *Llywelyn* I.——

> Crift Greawdyr, llywiawdyr llu daear a nev,
> A'm' noddwy rhag avar ;
> Crift Celi, bwyv celvydd, a gwâr,
> Cyn diwedd gyvyngwedd gyvar l
> Crift Vab Duw a'm rhydd arlavar,
> I voli vy Rhwyv rwyſg oddyar ;
> Ac——a'm pair o'r pedwar devnydd,
> Dovyn Awen ddiarçar !

May Chrift, who form'd and governs earth, and heav'n,
Protect me from misfortune's gloomy way;
That Chrift myfterious make me wife and mild,
Ere to the narrow houfe of death I go!
May He with eloquence attune my tongue,
To praife my chief, whofe courfe is noify war ;
And may He grant me, from pure nature's ftore,
A penetrating Genius, unreftrain'd.

It may not be amifs to conclude this head with the introduction of thofe aphorifms that are relative to it, from the Poetic Triades——

1. The three foundations of Genius: the gift of God, man's exertion, and the events of life.
2. The three primary requifites of Genius: an eye that can fee nature, a heart that can feel nature, and boldnefs that dares follow nature.

3. The

1. Tair fail Awen: rhodd Duw, ymgais dyn, a damwain bywyd.
2. Tri phriv anhepgor Awen: llygad yn gweled anian, calon yn teimlaw, anian, a glewder à vaidd gydvyned ag anian.

e   3. Tri

3. The three indifpenfables of Genius: underftanding, feel-
ing, and perfeverance.

4. The three properties of Genius: fine thought, appropriate thought, and a luxuriantly diverfified thought.

5. The three things that ennoble Genius: vigour, fancy,
and knowledge.

6. The three fupports of Genius: ftrong mental endow-
ments, memory, and learning.

7. The three minifters of Genius: memory, vigour, and
learning.

8. The three marks of Genius: extraordinary underftanding, extraordinary conduct, and extraordinary exertion.

9. The three friends of Genius: vigour, difcretion, and
pleafantry.

10. The three things that improve Genius: proper exertion, frequent exertion, and profperity in its exertion.

11. The three effects of Genius: generofity, gentlenefs,
and complacency.

12. The

---

3. Tri anhepgor Awen: deall, yftyriaeth, ac amynedd.

4. Tair cynneddyv Awen: hardd veddwl, priodawl veddwl, ac amrywedd
veddwl.

5. Tri bonedd Awen: nwyv, pwyll, a gwybodaeth.

6. Tri çadernyd Awen: athrylith, còv, a dyfg.

7. Tri gweinidogion Awen: còv, nwyv, a dyfg.

8. Tri nód Awen: anghyfredin ddeall, anghyfredin ymddwyn, ac anghyfredin ymgais.

9. Tri çyvaill Awen: nwyv, callineb, a digrivwç.

10. Tri pheth à gynnydd Awen: iawn arver, a mynyç arver, a llwyddiant
o'i harver.

11. Tair efaith Awen: haelioni, gwarineb, a çaredigrwydd.

12. Tri

12. The three things that enrich Genius: contentment of mind, the cherishing of good thoughts, and exercising the memory.

13. The three things that exalt Genius: learning, exertion, and reverence.

14. The three supports of Genius: prosperity, social acquaintance, and praise.

15. The three things that will insure Prosperity: appropriate exertion, feasible exertion, and uncommon exertion.

16. The three things that will insure Acquaintance: complacency, ingenuity, and originality.

17. The three things that will insure Praise: amiable conduct, learned in science, and pure morals.

The Bards bestowed great attention to the formation of their Poetical Institutes, which they brought to a high state of perfection at a very early period ; because verse was generally the medium by which they preserved historical events, and taught the moral, and religious duties to the people. The peculiar character of the Poetry of the *Bri-*

---

12. Tri pheth a frwythlona'r Awen : diddanwç meddwl, coledd daionus veddwl, a phorthi côv.

13. Tri pheth à dderçaiv Awen : dyfg, ymgais, a pharç.

14. Tri çynnaliaeth Awen : llwyddiant, cydnabyddiaeth, a çanmoliaeth.

15. Tri pheth à ddybryn Lwyddiant : priodawl ymgais, hywaith ymgais, ac anghyfredin ymgais.

16. Tri pheth à ddybryn Gydnabyddiaeth : caredigrwydd, celvyddgarwç, a çynnevinder.

17. Tri pheth à ddybryn Ganmoliaeth : hygar ymddwyn, hyddyfg gelvyddyd, a glân gampau.

tons was to avoid fable; for, agreeable to the radical prin‑
ciples of Bardifm, it was confecrated to be the organ of
Truth.*

With refpect to what relates to the rules of poetical cri‑
ticifm and profody, they are extremely curious, and ori‑
ginal ; and there is no hazard in afferting that they are as
juft as can be produced in any language; becaufe there
are none that follow nature with more clofenefs.   Thefe
are comprehended under the ten following heads†—

The Welfh Language.
Fancy and Invention.
The defign and intention of Poetry.
The nature and principle of juft Thinking.
Rules with refpect to Arrangement.
Rules of juft Defcription.
Variety of Matter and Invention.

Rules

---

* It is not here intended to infinuate, that there was no fuch thing
amongft the Welfh, in later ages, as any productions on the model of other
nations; but thefe were not by the regular Bards; for their fyftem was fo
inimical to thofe, that any of the order, who fhould compofe what was not
agreeable to the fyftem would be for ever degraded from it.

† Yr iaith Gynmraeg.
Dyçymyg a Çrebwyll.
Amcan a diben Cerdd.
Rhyw ac anfawdd cyviawn Vyvyrdawd.
Trevyn o barth Ymddwyn.
Trevyn ar gyviawn Ddyvalu.
Amlder Deunydd a Dyçymyg.

Trevyn

Rules of Compofition, with refpect to verfe, rhyme, ftanza, confonancy, or alliteration, and accent.

Truth.

Varieties of Compofition, with refpect to defign, fancy, occafion, and meaning. Of thefe there are eight kinds : panegyric, hiftorics, didactics, gratulation, defcription, elegy, fatire, and dialogue.

Rather than attempt a defcription of them, it may be thought more curious, perhaps, if their appropriate Triades are introduced, to ferve as a compendium of the whole—

1. The three radical parts of an Art : nature, benefit, and originality.
2. The three primary points of Nature and Originality : where it cannot be better, where it cannot be otherwife, and where there is no neceffity of its being otherwife.

3. The

Trevyn ar Ganiadaeth, o barth bàn, awdyl, pennill, cynghanedd, ac acan.

Gwirionedd.

Rhywiau Cerdd, herwydd fylvon, crebwyll, açaws, ac yftyr. Wyth ryw y fydd : cerdd vawl, cerdd vaneg, neù hanefgerdd, cerdd addyfg, cerdd anerç, dyvalgerdd, cerdd alargwyn, gogan, neu ddyçan a fôn, hawl ac atteb.

1. Tair cynran Celvyddyd : anian, llès, a phriodoldeb.
2. Tri çynnod Anian a Hanvod : lle ni ellir gwell, lle ni ellir amgen, a'r lle ni raid amgen.

3. The three primary points of the benefit of Science: its being patronized by the world, its virtue in improving the world, and its perfection in supporting itself.

4. The three marks of the propriety of a Science: juft caufe, juft organization, and juft conformity.

5. The three times of Science: when it is juft, when it is becoming, and when it is neceffary.

6. The three to whom Science is fuitable: he that delights in it, he that underftands it, and he that deferves it.

7. The three intentions of Poetry: increafe of good, increafe of underftanding, and increafe of happinefs.

8. The three qualifications of Poetry: endowment of genius, judgment from experience, and happinefs of mind.

9. The three foundations of Judgment: bold defign, frequent practice, and frequent miftakes.

10. The three foundations of Learning: feeing much, fuffering much, and ftudying much.

11. The

---

3. Tri cynnod llês Celvyddyd: ei hofi gan y byd, ei rhinwedd yn gwellâu'r byd, : i pherfeith-gamp yn cynnal ei hun.

4. Tri nôd priodoldeb Celvyddyd: iawn açaws, iawn ymdrevyn, ac iawn gyvunied.

5. Tri amfer Celvyddyd: pan vo iawn, pan vo hardd, a phan vo raid.

6. Tair hyweddiant Celvyddyd: ar a'i hofo, ar ei deallo, ac ar a'i dirper.

7. Tri diben Prydyddiaeth: cynnydd daioni, cynnydd deall, a çynnydd diddanwç.

8. Tair anfawdd Barddoniaeth: athrylith awen, barn wrth ddyfg, a gwynvyd meddwl.

9. Tair colovyn Barn: eon amcan, mynyç arver, a mynyç gamfynied.

10. Tair colovyn Dyfg: gweled llawer, dyoddev llawer, ac yftyried llawer.

11. Tair

11. The three foundations of Happinefs: a fuffering with contentment, a hope that it will come, and a belief that it will be.

12. The three fountains of Knowledge; invention, ftudy, and experience.

13. The three fountains of the Underftanding: boldnefs, vigour, and exertion.

14. The three foundations of Thought: perfpicuity, amplitude, and juftnefs.

15. The three ornaments of Thought: perfpicuity, correctnefs, and novelty.

16. The three canons of Perfpicuity: the word that is neceffary, the quantity that is neceffary, and the manner that is neceffary.

17. The three canons of Amplitude: appropriate thought, variety of thought, and requifite thought.

18. The three properties of juft Thinking: what is poffible to be, what ought to be, and what is commendable to be.

20. The

---

11. Tair colovyn Gwynvyd: goddȩv o voddlonrwydd, gobaith y daw, a ȼred y bydd.

12. Tair fynon Gwybodaeth: crebwyll, yftyriaeth, a dyfgeidiaeth.

13. Tair fynon Deall: eonder, nwyv, ac ymgais.

14. Tair colovyn Synwyr: eglurdeb, llawnder, a ȼyviawnder.

15. Tri harddwȼ Synwyr: eglurdeb, cywirdeb, a newydd-deb.

16. Tair colovyn Eglurdeb: y gair à vo raid, y maint à vo raid, a'r ddull à vo raid.

17. Tair colovyn Llawnder: priodawl veȡdwl, amyl veddwl, ac angen veddwl.

18. Tair cynneddyv ȼyviawn Vyvyrdawd: à ddiçoȵ vôd, à ddylai vôd, ac y fydd hardd ei vôd.

19. The three requisites of Song: thought that shews genius, fancy directed by art, and truth.

20. The three embellishments of Song: fine invention, happy subject, and a masterly harmonious composition.

21. The three excellencies of Song: simplicity of language, simplicity of subject, and simplicity of invention.

22. The three necessaries of Song: dignified intention, thought, and matter.

23. The three commendables of Song: praise without flattery, amorous pleasantry without obscenity, and satire without abuse.

24. The three diversities of Song: diversity of thinking, diversity of language, and diversity of versification.

25. The three beauties of Song: attraction, eloquence, and boldness.

26. The three sweets of Song: facility of comprehension, sprightliness of language, and sweetly-soothing thoughts.

27. The

19. Tri anhepgor Cerdd: awen-yryd, celvydd-bwyll, a gwirionedd.

20. Tri thecäad Cerdd: hardd grebwyll, hardd berthynas, a hardd gywrein-gamp ar vydryddu.

21. Tri ardderçogrwydd Cerdd: godidawg iaith, godidawg yftyr, a godidawg grebwyll.

22. Tri rhaid Cerdd: godidawg, amcan, fynwyr, a deunydd.

23. Tri harddwç Cerdd: mawl heb druth, nwyv heb anlladrwydd, a dyçan heb ferthyd.

24. Tri amrywiaeth Cerdd: amrywiaeth myvyrdawd, amrywiaeth iaith, ac amrywiaeth colovyn cerdd.

25. Tri gwyçder Cerdd: hygaredd, hyawdledd, ac eonder.

26. Tri melufder Cerdd: hawfder deall, trynwyv iaith, a mwythus-ber vyvyrdawd.

27. Tri

27. The three elegancies of Song: a highly compre-
hensive language, charming luminous thoughts, and
ingenious compofition.

28. The things which give relifh to a Song: diverfity of
language, diverfity of thinking, and diverfity of
ftructure in the metres.

29. The three agreements that ought to be in a Song: between digreffion and uniformity, between an elevated
and common language, and between truth and the
marvellous.

30. The three things that improve the Song: the ftudying
it thoroughly, the examining of it frequently, and
exerting to the utmoft.

31. The three appropriates of Song: its quantity, its purpofe, and its occafion.

32. The three proprieties of Song: correct fancy, correct
order, and correct metre.

33. The three honours of Song: the verity of the thing
treated of, the excellency of it, and the ingenuity of
the manner in which it is managed.

35. The

27. Tri pheth blqdeuawg at Gerdd: yftyrhell iaith, goleu-ber fynwyr, a
çywrain gelvyddyd.

28. Tri pheth à wnânt vlâs ar Gerdd: amryvel iaith, amryvel vyvyrdawd,
ac amryvel gainc ar vefur.

29. Tri çyttundeb à ddylai vôd ar Gerdd: rhwng amryveiliant a çyvundeb,
rhwng rhagor-iaith, a çyfredin-iaith, a rhwng gwir a rhyveddawd.

30. Tri pheth à bair Gerdd yn dda: ei llwyr vyvyriaw, ei mynyç çwiliaw,
ac ollawl ymegnïaw.

31. Tri phriodoldeb Cerdd: ei maint, ei hamcan, a'i haçaws.

32. Tri iawnder Cerdd: iawn grebwyll, iawn drevyn, ac iawn vydyr.

33. Tair urddas Cerdd: gwired y peth à fonier am dano, godidoced y peth
à fonier am dano, a çelvydded y dull à fonier am dano.

34. Tri

34. The three attractions of Song: its excellent novelty, ease of comprehension, and correct poetry.

35. The three things which ought to pervade the Song: perfect learning, perfect vigour, and perfect nature.

36. The three perspicuities of Song: perspicuous language, subject, and intention.

37. The three intentions of Song: to improve the understanding, to improve the heart, and to soothe the mind.

38. The three natural things in Song: a natural occasion, natural language, and a natural regulation of the fancy.

39. The three aptnesses of Song: apt language, apt thinking, and apt order in the composition.

40. The three perfections of Song: perfect language, perfect invention, and perfect art.

41. The three materials of Song: language, invention, and art.

42. The three indispensables of Language: purity, copiousness, and aptness.

43. The

---

34. Tri hofder Cerdd: ei godidawg newyddiant, yr hawfder o'i deall, a'i cywrain brydyddiaeth.

35. Tair trwyogaeth Cerdd: trylen, trynwyv, a thrynaws.

36. Tri gloywineb Cerdd: gloyw iaith, gloyw yftyr, a gloyw ddiben.

37. Tri diben Cerdd: gwellâu'r deall, gwellâu'r galon, a diddanu'r meddwl.

38. Tri gweddufder Cerdd: gweddus açaws, gweddus iaith, a gweddus drevyn ar ddyçymyg.

39. Try hoywder Cerdd: hoyw iaith, hoyw vyvyrdawd, a hoyw drevyn ar y ganiadaeth.

40. Tri çyvlawnder Cerdd: cyvlawn iaith, cyvlawn ddyçymyg, a çyvlawn gelvyddyd.

41. Tri deunydd Cerdd: iaith, crebwyll, a çelvyddyd.

42. Tri anhepgor Iaith: purdeb, amledd, ac hyweddiant.

43. Tair

43. The three ways that a Language may be rendered copious: by diverfifying fynonymous words, by a variety of compound epithets, and a multiformity of expreffion.

44. The three qualities wherein confift the purity of a Language: original formation, ufe, and matter.

45. The three branches of the aptitude. of a Language: what is underftood, what affords pleafure, and what is believed.

46. The three fupports of Language: order, ftrength, and fynonymy.

47. The three correct qualities of a Language: correct conftruction, correct etymology, and correct pronunciation.

48. The three ufes of a Language: to relate, to excite, and to defcribe.

49. The three things that conftitute juft Defcription: juft felection of words, juft conftruction of language, and juft comparifon.

50. The

---

43. Tair fordd yr amléir Iaith: amryvelu geiriau cyvyftyr, amryvodd gylmeiriau, ac amryddull ymadrawdd.

44. Tair cynneddyv purdeb ar Iaith: priv anfawdd, priv arver a phriv ddeunydd.

45. Tair cainc hyweddiant Iaith: à ddëellir, à hofir, ac à gredir.

46. Tri cynnorthwy Iaith: trevyn, nwyv, a cyfelyb-air.

47. Tri iawnder, y fydd ar Iaith: iawn eirioli, iawn ymddwyn, ac iawn leverydd.

48. Tair fwydd Iaith: adrawdd, cynnhyrvu, a dyvalu.

49. Tri pheth à bair iawn Ddyvalu; iawn ddewis ar air, iawn ieithyddu, ac iawn gyfelybu.

50. Tri

50. The three things appertaining to juft Selection : the beft language, the beft order, and the beft object.

51. The three dialects of the Welfh Language: the Ventefian, or Silurian, the Dimetian, and the Venedocian; and it is proper in Poetry to ufe all of them inrdifcriminately, agreeable to the opinion, and authority of the primitive Bards.

52. The three things which conftitute a Poet : genius, knowledge, and impulfe.

53. The three primary purpofes of a Bard with refpect to Intention and Duty: to do the will of God, to benefit man, and to reverence love.

54. The three primary excellencies of a Bard: art fo eafily comprehended that none can be fo generally fimple, a dignity of thinking not to be furpaffed in appropriate fimplicity, and a fuperior originality not to be excelled in natural fimplicity.

55. The three duties of a Bard: juft compofition, juft knowledge, and juft criticifm

56. The

50. Tri pheth y fydd ar iawn Ddewis: y iaith oreu, y drevyn oreu, a'r gwrthddryç goreu.

51. Tair llavarwedd y fydd ar y Gynmraeg : y Wennwyfeg, y Ddeheubartheg, a'r Wyndodeg; a çyviawn ar gerdd ymarver â phob un o'r tair ynghymmyfg, blith-dra-phlith, yn ol barn ac awdurdawd y priv veirdd.

52. Tri pheth à wnânt Brydydd: awen, gwybodaeth, a çynnhyrviad.

53. Tri phriv amcan Bardd herwydd Pwyll a Dyled: boddiaw Duw, llefâu dyn, a pharçu ferçogrwydd.

54. Tair priv orçeft Bardd : celvyddyd gyrwydded ei deall ni's gellir cynnevinaç o'r fymledd, godidawg vyvyrdawd ni's gellir addafaç, o'r fymledd, a rhagorawl briodoldeb ni's gellir gweddufaç o'r fymledd.

55. Tair dyledfwydd Bardd: iawn ganu, iawn ddyfgu, ac iawn varnu,

56. Tair

56. The three honours of a Minftrel : ftrength of imagination, profundity of learning, and purity of morals.

57. The three excellencies of a Minftrel: profound difcrimination of all things, complete illuftration, and luminous compofitioh.

58. The three excellencies of Compofition : juft verfification, juft defcription, and juft arrangement.

The Bards divided their canons of verfification, or metricities,* into nine *Gorçanau*, elements of fong, or primary principles, and fifteen *Adlawiaid*, fecondary, or compound principles, making in all twenty-four ; to which all poffible varieties, and combinations of metres, in any language, are reducible. To thefe, and the laws of confonancy, accent, and rhyme, the following Triades are applicable—

1. The three requifites of Verfification : metricity, confonancy, and rhyme.

2. The three principles of Metre : length of the verfe, form of the ftanza, and the power of the accent.

3. The

56. Tair rhagorgamp ar Gerddawr : cyvlawn ddynodiant ar bob peth, cyvlwyr vanegiant, a çyvlwys ganiadaeth.

57. Tri dyledogrwydd Cerddawr : grymufder athrylith, cyvlawnder dyfg, a glendyd ei gampau.

58. Tair rhagoriaeth Canu : iawu vydryddu, iawn ddyvalu, ac iawn ymddwyn.

* The term in the *Welfh* is *Cybydeddau*, for which, as well as fome others, I have been obliged to ufe words not common, by endeavouring to convey the exact idea of the originals.

1. Tri anhepgor Mydryddiaeth : colovyn, cynghanedd, ac awdyl.

2. Tri phriodoldeb Mefur : hyd y bân, dull y pennill, a phwys yr acan.

3. Tri

3. The three primary diſtinctions of Metre: the Cowydd, the Ynglyn, and the Awdyl.

4. The three excellencies of Metre: correctneſs, freedom, and harmonious accent.

5. The three variations of Verſe: variation of metricity, variation of conſonancy, and variation of accent.

6. The three primary principles of Conſonancy: the rhyming conſonancy, the alliterative conſonancy, and the compound conſonancy of rhyme and alliteration.

By the nine *Gorçanau*, or canons of metricity, are to be underſtood ſo many varieties of lengths, or number of ſyllables in a verſe, including from four to twelve ſyllables, being adequate to every poſſible change that can be uſed, agreeable to the laws of harmony. The names of theſe metrical elements are—

	Vèr,	Syll. 4	Short.	
	Gaeth,	5	Confined.	
	Droſgyl,	6	Rugged.	
	Levyn,	7	Smooth.	
Cyhdeydd,	Waſtad,	8	Regular.	Metricity,
	Draws,	9	Croſs.	
	Wèn,	10	Flowing.	
	Laes,	11	Heavy.	
	Hîr,	12	Long.	

3. Tri phriv rywiogaeth ar Veſur: cowydd, ynglyn, ac awdyl.

4. Tri rhagoriaeth Mydyr: cywreindeb, rhwyddineb, ac acan bêr.

5. Tri amrywiaeth Bàn: amrywiaeth cyhydedd, amrywiaeth cynghanedd, ac amrywiaeth acan.

6. Tair Cynghanedd y ſydd o briv anſawdd; cynghanedd ſain, cynghanedd groes, a cynghanedd luſg.

The

The *Adlawiaid*, fecondary, or compound principles, being fifteen in number, are all the poſſible variety of combinations of the *Gorçanau*, depending upon the different lengths or quantity, and rhyme; the firſt ariſing from a junction of unequal verſes; and the latter from changes, or variety of rhymes: The names of the *Adlawiaid* are—

Bàn cyrç,	Recurrent pauſe.
Toddaid,	Confluency.
Triban milwr,	Warrior's triplet.
Triban cyrç,	Recurrent triplet.
Cowydd,	Recitative.
Traethodyn,	Compound Recitative.
Proeſt cadwynawdyl,	Combined alternate rhyme.
Proeſt cyvnewidiawg,	Combined vowel alternity.
Clogyrnaç,	Rugoſity.
Lloſtodyn,	Cuſpidated ſtrain.
Llamgyrç,	Recurrent tranſition.
Cadwyngyrç,	Recurrent catenation.
Ynglyn,	Continuity.
Cynghawg,	Complexity;
Dyri,	Unconnected quantity.

The *Cynghanedd*, or confonancy, is generally termed alliteration, the nature of which is very imperfectly ſeen in *Engliſh* compoſitions, compared with the regular ſyſtem by which it is governed in the *Welſh*; but to give a proper analyſis of it would require too much attention, ſo it ſhall be paſſed over, and a few words beſtowed on the two remaining heads of rhyme and quantity. There is nothing peculiar in the rhyme, but that it is required to be literally

perfect

perfect in all cafes. As to the metrical feet, or quantity,
the Welsh in this respect is the same as the Latin poetry:
The feet are called *Corvanau*, of which there are seven,
under the following denomination—

Corvan crwn	‿́	long syllable.
Corvan byr	——	—— long syllable.
Corvan hir	‿́	— spondee.
Corvan cryç disgynedig		— dactyl.
Corvan cryç derçavedig		— anapest.
Corvan talgrwn		—— iambic.
Corvan rhywiawg		— trochee.

I have been thus diffuse in noticing the Bardic system of
poetry, for the sake of making known to the world
the existence of what is altogether original, and curious. It has been a thing totally unknown for ages, except to those few who were of the regular order of the
primitive Bards. It never was regularly known to the
Poets of *Wales*, who were not Bards * ; but they, and also
the musicians, had peculiar laws to themselves, far less perfect seemingly, and borrowed from slight hints, and inti-
mations, procured of this ancient system of British Bardism.

* It is a little unfortunate for the perspicuity of this sketch that the term
of *Bard* is become synonymous with *Poet*. The latter character I shall pass
over, with informing the reader, that he may meet with a variety of curious information respecting him in Mr. E. Jones's Musical and Poetical
Relics, the second edition of which is now publishing, greatly enlarged.

REMARKS

REMARKS

WELSH ORTHOGRAPHY.

THERE are thirty-eight Letters in the Language; fixteen of thofe are radicals, that exprefs the primary founds; the others may be called ferviles, ufed as the inflections, or mutations of the firft; for each of which there is a fimple appropriate character. But fince the invention of Printing, and the introduction of the Roman Letters, it has been neceffary, for want of a fufficient variety of Letters caft for the purpofe, to adopt two, and even three of thofe Letters, to exprefs one found, or character; by which the fimplicity and beauty of the proper Alphabet of the Language is loft.

No Letter has any variation of found, except the accented vowels, which are lengthened, or otherwife, according to the power of the accent; and all are pronounced, as there are no mutes. The following are the Letters that differ in power from the Englifh Letters.

A, is as *a* in *Man*.
C, is always as a *K*.
Ç, is a gutteral, as χ, or ⴖ, generally exprefled by *Ch*.
Dd, founds like *Th* in *The*.
G, always as *G* in *Go*.
I, as *ee*, in *Been*.
Ll, as an afpirated *L*.
U, as *I*, in *Sin*.
W, is a vowel like ∞, in *Soon*.
Y, is like *u* in *Burn*.

CANIADAU

LLYWARÇ HEN.

MARWNAD GERAINT AB ERBIN,

TYWYSAWG DYVNAINT. (a)

PAN aned Geraint oedd agored pyrth nev,
   Rhoddai Grift à arçed,
Pryd mirain Prydain ogoned.

Moled pawb y rhudd Eraint,
Arglwydd; molav innau Eraint,
Gelyn i Sais, car i faint.

Rhag Geraint gelyn dyhad, (b)
Gwelais i veirç cymmrudd o gad, (c)
A gwedy gawr garw bwylliad.

(a) *Ll. arall:* Marwnad Geraint ab Erbin: *Arall:* Canu o Eraint ab Erbin. Tri Llyng-efawg Ynys Prydain: Geraint ab Erbin; Gwenwynwyn ab Nav; a Març ab Meirchiawn.
(b) Glyn dibat. *Un llyfyr:* Glynn dibat. *Arall.*
(c) Gwelais y veirch kymrut o gat; neu, crumeudd.

ELEGIES AND OTHER PIECES
LLYWARÇ HEN.

ELEGY UPON GERAINT AB ERBIN,

PRINCE OF DEVON. (*a*)

WHEN GERAINT was born the gates of heaven were open,
    CHRIST then granted what was requested,
A countenance beautiful, the glory of *Britain.*

Let all celebrate the red-ftained *Geraint*
Their lord; I will alfo praife *Geraint*,
The *Saxon*'s foe, the friend of faints.

Before *Geraint*, the terrifier of the foe,
I faw the fteeds hagged with mutual toil from battle,
Where, after the fhout was given, frightful deeds began.

(*a*) *Geraint ab Erbin* was commander of a fleet of fhips fitted out by the Britons to oppofe the Saxons; and he fell fighting againft them, about the year 530. There were two other princes of the name of *Geraint*, in *Cornwall*; one of whom was alive in 589, and the other in 710. When the yellow plague was depopulating *Wales*, and among the reft, had carried off *Maelgwn Gwynedd*, *Teilaw* then bifhop of *Llandav*, and feveral attendants came into *Cornwall*, and was kindly entertained by *Geraint*. From thence *Teilaw* paffed over into *Armorica*; and after ftaying near eight years, being upon his return to *Wales*, vifited *Geraint* again, and found him upon his death-bed. *Borl. Ant. of Cornwall, p. 371.* The *Geraint* mentioned in the *Saxon Chronicle* to be at war with *Ina*, about the year 710, is the laft of the three of that name.

Rhag Geraint gelyn cythrudd, (*a*)
Gwelais i veirç tan gymmrudd, (*b*)
A gwedy gawr (*c*) garw açludd.

Yn Llongborth gwelais drydar,
Ac elorawr yn ngwyar,
A gwyr rhudd rhag rhuthr efgar.

Rhag Geraint gelyn ormes, (*d*)
Gwelais meirç can eu creës ;
A gwedy gawr garw açes.

Yn Llongborth gwelais i wythaint,
Ac elorawr mwy no maint,
A gwyr rhudd rhag rhuthr Geraint !

Yn Llongborth gwelais waedfrau,
Ac elorawr rhag arvau,
A gwyr rhudd rhag rhuthr angau.

Yn Llongborth gwelais i ottoyw (*e*)
Gwyr ni giliynt (*f*) rhag ovn gwayw,
Ac yved gwin o wydr gloyw.

Yn Llongborth gwelais i vygedorth,
A gwyr yn godde ammorth,
A gorvod gwedi gorborth.

(*a*) *Ll. arall :* Gelyn cyftudd.
(*b*) Neu gymryd, neu gymryad, neu grymrudd.
(*c*) Neu guawr, neu gwawr.
(*d*) Neu gelein ormes.
(*e*) Neu otteu.
(*f*) Neu gyllynt, neu gylyn.

Before *Geraint*, that breathed terror on the foe,
I saw steeds bearing the maimed sharers of their toil ;
And after the shout of war a fearful obscurity.

At *Llongborth* (a) I saw the noisy tumult,
And biers with the dead drenched in gore,
And ruddy men from the onset of the foe.

Before *Geraint*, the molester of the enemy,
I saw the steeds white with foam,
And after the shout of battle a fearful torrent,

At *Llongborth* I saw the rage of slaughter,
And biers with slain innumerable,
And red-stain'd men from the assault of *Geraint*.

At *Llongborth* I saw the gushing of blood,
And biers with dead from the rage of weapons,
And red-stain'd men from the assault of death.

In *Llongborth* I saw the quick-impelling spurs
Of men, who would not flinch from the dread of the spear,
And the quaffing of wine out of the bright glass. (b)

In *Llongborth* I saw a smoaking pile,
And men enduring the want of sustenance,
And defeat, after the excess of feastings.

(a) The *Haven of Ships*, some harbour on the south coast, probably Portsmouth.
(b) It seems, from a number of authorities, that the Britons were very early acquainted with
the process of making glass. The vitrified Forts in *Scotland*, are an indisputable proof; and
the Druid Beads, or Adder Stones, we must own to be vitrified by art, or we must credit the
common opinion of the country, that they are b'own by snakes, in the manner described by
Pliny. Strange as this opinion may seem, there are people in *Wales*, who still furnish the curious with Adder Stones, thus procured, as they say, at a particular time of the summer.

Yn Llongborth gwelais i arvau
Gwyr, a gwyar yn dineu,
A gwedi gawr garw adneu.

Yn Llongborth gwelais gymminad (*a*)
Gwyr yn ngryd, a gwaed ar iâd,
Rhag Geraint mawr mab ei dâd.

Yn Llongborth gwelais drabludd
Ar fain, brain ar goludd,
Ac ar grân cynran man-rudd. (*b*)

Yn Llongborth gwelais i vrithred
Gwyr ynghyd, a gwaed ar draed ;
" A vo gwyr i Eraint, bryfied !"

Yn Llongborth gwelais vrwydrin (*c*)
Gwyr ynghyd, (*d*) a gwaed hyd ddeuliu,
Rhag rhuthr mawr mab Erbin.

Yn Llongborth y llâs Geraint,
Gwr dewr (*e*) o goettir Dyvnaint,
Wyntwy yn lladd gyd a's lleddaint. (*f*)

(*a*) Neu, Cymmanat.—Nid yw y pennill hwn yn y *Ll: Coch* ; onid yw yr hwn a ganlyn, ya
fyr o fralç yr un un, yr hwn fydd hevyd yn y *Ll: Du*——
         Yn Llongborth gwelais gymmynad——
         Porthid gniv pob cynniviad.
(*b*) Neu, Ac ar grawn Cynran madrudd.
(*c*) Neu, Ryw drin.
(*d*) Neu, Gwyr rhuthr.
(*e*) Neu, Gwyr dewr.
(*f*) Neu, A chyn ry lleddid hwy lladdyffeint.

In *Llongborth* I faw the weapons
Of heroes, with gore faft dropping,
And after the fhout a fearful return to earth.

In *Llongborth* I faw the edges of blades in contact,
Men furrounded with terrour, and blood on the brow,
Before *Geraint*, the great fon of his father.

In *Llongborth* I faw hard toiling
Amidft the ftones, ravens feafting on entrails,
And on the chieftain's brow a crimfon gafh. (*a*)

At. *Llongborth* I faw a tumultuous running
Of men together, and blood about the feet :—
" Thofe that are the men of *Geraint* make hafte !"

In *Llongborth* I faw a confufed conflict,
Men ftriving together, and blood to the knees,
From the affault of the great fon of *Erbin*.

At *Llongborth* was *Geraint* flain,
A ftrenuous warrior from the woodland of *Dyvnaint*, (*b*)
Slaughtering his foes as he fell.

(*a*) Alluding probably to *Geraint* : the meaning of *Cynran* is *firft participator* ; which feems to be an epithet for the eldeft fon, or reprefentative of the family ; alluding to the law of Gavelkind, by which the younger child was to make the divifion ; and the eldeft had the choice, or firft fhare.

(*b*) *Dyvnaint* implies a country abounding with deep vales ; and is the ancient name of *Devonfhire*; and from which the modern Englifh name of Devon is undoubtedly derived.

Yn Llongborth llâs i Arthur
Gwyr dewr, cymmynynt a dur; (a)
Ammherawdyr, llywiawdyr llavur.

Oedd re redaint dan vorddwyd Geraint,
Garhirion, grawn hydd,
Rhuthr goddaith (b) ar ddifaith vynydd.

Oedd re redaint dan vorddwyd Geraint,
Garhirion, grawn odew, (c)
Rhuddion, rhuthr eryron glew.

Oedd re redaint dan vorddwyd Geraint,
Garhirion, grawn wehyn, (d)
Rhuddion, rhuthr eryron gwyn.

Oedd re redaint dan vorddwyd Geraint,
Garhirion, grawn voloç,
Rhuddion, rhuthr eryron coç.

Oedd re redaint dan vorddwyd Geraint,
Garhirion, grawn eu bwyd, (e)
Rhuddion, rhuthr eryron llwyd.

Oedd re redaint dan vorddwyd Geraint,
Garhirion, grawn addas,
Rhuddion, rhuthr eryron glas.

(a) Neu, Cymmynt o dur.
(b) Neu, Twrv goddaith.
(c) Neu, Grav a odeu; neu, Grawn o dew.
(d) Neu, Yehyn.
(e) Neu, Grawn eubwyd.

At *Llongborth* were flain to *Arthur*
Valiant men, who hewed down with fteel;
He was the emperor, and conductor of the toil of war.

Under the thigh of *Geraint* were fwift racers,
With long legs, that fed on the grain of the deer,
Their courfe was like the confuming fire on the wild hills. (*a*)

Under the thigh of *Geraint* were fleet runners,
With long hams, fattened with corn;
They were red ones; their affault was like the bold eagles.

Under *Geraint*'s thigh were fleet runners,
With long legs. they fcattered about the grain;
They were ruddy; their affault was like the white eagles.

Under *Geraint*'s thigh were fleet runners,
With long legs, high-mettled, fed with grain;
They were ruddy; bold their affault, like the red eagles.

Under *Geraint*'s thigh were fleet racers,
Long their legs; their food was corn;
Red were they; fierce their courfe, like the brown eagles.

Swift racers were under the thigh of *Geraint*;
Their legs were long; they well deferved the grain;
Red were they; bold their courfe as the grey eagles.

(*a*) Goddaith, is a term applied to the burning of furze, or heath, on the mountains; which
is done at feafonable times of the year.

Oedd re redaint dan vorddwyd Geraint, .
Garhirion, grawn vagu,
Rhuddion, rhuthr eryron du.

Oedd re redaint dan vorddwyd Geraint,
Garhirion, grawn gwenith, (a)
Rhuddion, rhuthr eryron brith.

Oedd re redaint dan vorddwyd Geraint,
Garhirion, grawn anchwant, ·
Blawr, blaen eu rhawn yn ariant. (b)

(a) Neu, Grawn wenith.
(b) Neu, Blayr blaen eiriawn yn ariant.

Swift racers were under the thigh of *Geraint* ;
Whofe legs were long ; they were reared up with corn,
They were red ones ; their affault was as the black eagles.

Swift racers were under the thigh of *Geraint* ;
Whofe legs were long ; wheat their corn ;
They red ones were ; their affault was as the fpotted eagles.

Swift racers were under the thigh of *Geraint* ;
Whofe legs were long ; they were fatiated with grain ;
They were grey, with tails tipt with filver.

Y GORWYNION.

GORWYN blaen òn, hir-wŷnion vyddant,
    Pan dyvant yn mlaen naint:
Bron gwla hiraeth ei haint.

Gorwyn blaen naint dewaint hir;
Ceinmygir pob cywraint:
Dyly bun pwyth hun i haint. (a)

Gorwyn blaen helyg; eilyg pyſg yn llyn;
 Goçwiban gwynt uwç blaen gwryſg mân
Treç anian nag addyſg.

Gorwyn blaen eithin; a çyvrin a doeth,
Ac annoeth dyſgethrin;
Namyn Duw nid oes dewin.

Gorwyn blaen mcillion; digalon llwvr; (b)
Lluddedig eiddigion: (c)
Gnawd ar eiddil ovalon.

Gorwyn blaen cawn; gwythlawn eiddig,
 Ys odid a'i digawn: (d)
Gweithred call yw caru yn iawn. (e)

(a) *Ll. Du.* Dyly bun puyth hun y heint.
(b) Neu, Diellon llyfur; neu, digallon llyfur.
(c) Neu, Lluddedic eigyawn; neu, lludedic eidyawn; neu, lludedic edigyon.
(d) Neu, ys odid ae digaun.
(e) Neu, Gueithred call yn caru yn iaun.

THE GORWYNION. (a)

THE tops of the afh gliften, that are white and ftately,
   When growing on the top of the dingle:
The breaft rackt with pain, longing is its complaint.

Brightly glitters the top of the cliff at the long midnight hour;
Every ingenious perfon will be honoured:
'Tis the duty of the fair, to afford fleep to him that is in pain.

Brightly gliften the willow tops; the fifh are merry in the lakes,
Bluftering is the wind over the tops of the fmall branches:
Nature over learning doth prevail.

Brightly gliften the tops of furze; have confidence with the wife,
But from the unwife tear thyfelf afar;
Befides God, there is none that fees futurity.

Brightly gliften the clover tops; the timid has no heart;
Wearied out are the jealous ones:
Cares attend the weak.

Brightly gliften the tops of reed-grafs; furious is the jealous,
If any fhould perchance offend him:
'Tis the maxim of the prudent to love with fincerity.

(a) There is a difficulty in finding an Englifh word that can give the exact idea of this title: it means things that have a very bright whi·enefs, or glare—*corufcanti.*

The laft line of thefe verfes generally contains fome moral maxim, unconnected with the preceding, except in the metre; it is a plan to affift the memory practifed by the *Beirdd,* in conveying their inftruction by oral means, without being liable to be corrupted.

Ġorwyn blaen mynyddedd rhag anhunedd gaeav,
Llawn crùl cawn ; trwm yw trawfedd :
Rhag newyn nid oes wyledd.

Gorwyn blaen mynyddedd hydyr oervel gaeav ;
Crin cawn ; crwybyr ar vedd ;
Çwevris gwall yn alltudedd. ·

Gorwyn blaen derw, çwerw brig òn,
Rhag hwyaid gwefgeraid tòn :
Pybyr twyll ; pell oval i'm calon.

Gorwyn blaen derw, çwerw brig òn ;
Çweg evwr ; (a) çwerthiniad tòn :
Ni çêl grudd gyftudd calon.

Gorwyn blaen egroes ; nid moes caledi
Cadwed bawb ei eirioes : (b)
Gwaethav anav yw anvoes.

Gorwyn blaen banadyl ; cynnadyl i ferçawg ;
Gorvelyn cangau bacwyawg ;
Bâs rhyd ; gnawd hyvryd yn hunawg.

Gorwyn blaen avall ; amgall pob dedwydd ;
Hirddydd merydd mall ;
Crwybyr ar wawr carçarawr dall. (c)

(a) Neu, Chuec Evyr Chuerthinat tonn.
(b) Neu, Katuet bawh y eiryoes.
(c) Neu, Cruybyr aruaur carcharaur dall.

Brightly glare the tops of mountains from the bluftering of winter,
Full are the ftalks of reeds; heavy is oppreffion :
Againft famine, bafhfulnefs will vanifh.

Brightly glare the tops of mountains affail'd by winter cold ;
Brittle are the reeds; the mead is incrufted over ;
Playful is the heedlefs in banifhment.

Bright are the tops of the oaks, bitter are the afh branches ;
Before the ducks the dividing waves are feen :
Confident is deceit ; care is deeply rooted in my heart.

Brightly gliften the tops of the oaks, bitter are the afh branches ;
Sweet is the fheltering hedge ; the wave is a noify grinner ;
The cheek cannot conceal the trouble of the heart. (a)

Bright is the top of the eglantine ; hardfhip difpenfes with forms ; (b)
Let every one keep his fire-fide :
The greateft blemifh is ill manners.

Brightly glitters the top of the broom ; may the lover have a home ;
Very yellow feem the cluftered branches ;
Shallow is the ford ; fleep vifits the contented mind.

Brightly glitters the top of the apple-tree ; the profperous is circumfpect ·
In the long day the ftagnant pool is warm ;
Thick is the veil on the light of the blind prifoner.

(a) This ftanza feems to be but a different reading of the preceding one.
(b) Neceffity has no law,

Gorwyn blaen coll ger Digoll bre; (a)
Diaele vydd pob foll; (b)
Gweithred cadarn cadw arvoll.

Gorwyn blaen corfydd, gnawd merydd yn drwm;
A ieuanc dyfgedydd;
Ni thyr, (c) namyn fôl y fydd.

Gorwyn blaen eleftyr, bid veneftyr pob drud;
Gair teulu yn yfgwn;
Gnawd gan anghywir air twn.

Gorwyn blaen grug gnawd feuthug ar lwvyr; (d)
Hydyr vydd dwvyr ar dàl glàn:
Gnawd gan gywir air cyvan.

Gorwyn blaen brwyn; cymmwyn biw;
Rhedegawg vy neigyr heddiw,
'Amgeledd a dyn nid ydiw.

Gorwyn blaen rhedyn melyn cadavarth
Mor vydd buarth deillion; (e)
Rhedegawg manawg meibion. (f)

Gorwyn blaen cyriawal; gnawd goval ar ñen;
A gwenyn yn ynial;
Namyn Duw nid oes dial.

(a) Neu, Geyr digyll bre.
(b) Neu, Difell vyd pob foll.
(c) Neu, Na thyr.
(d) Neu, Gnaut feuthu ar lyfur.
(e) Neu, Morfyd duarth deillon.
(f) Neu, Manau meibon.

Very glittering are the hazel tops by the hill of Dig
Every prudent one will be free from harm;
'Tis the act of the mighty to keep a treaty.

Glittering are the tops of the reeds; the fat are drowsy
And the young imbibe instruction;
None but the foolish will break the faith.

Glittering is the top of the lilly; let every bold one be a drinker;
The word of a tribe is superior;
'Tis usual for the unjust to break his word.

Bright are the tops of heath; miscarriage attends the timid;
Boldly laves the water on its banks:
'Tis the maxim of the just to keep his word.

The tops of the rushes glitter; the kine are gentle;
Running are my tears this day,
Social comfort from man there is not.

Glittering are the tops of fern, yellow is the wild marygold;
The sea is a fence for blind ones;
Swift and active are the young men.

Glittering are the tops of the service tree; care attends the old;
And bees frequent the wilds;
Vengeance only to God belongs.

(*s*) There is an extensive mountain in the neighbourhood of Montgomery called *Cova Digull*; which may be the same as the one here mentioned.

C

Gorwyn blaen dâr didor drychin ;
Gwenyn yn uçel, geuvel crin ;
Gnawd gan rewydd ryçwerthin.

Gorwyn blaen celli, gogyhyd yſwydd, (*a*)
A dail deri dygayddyd ; (*b*)
A wyl à gâr gwyn ei vyd !

Gorwyn blaen derw ; oer-verw dwvyr ;
Cyrçyd bwy blaen bedwerw ;
Gwnelid aeth ſaeth y ſyberw.

Gorwyn blaen celyn caled, ac ereill aur agored ;
Pan gyſgo pawb ar gylçed,
Ni çwſg Duw pan rydd gwared.

Gorwyn blaen helyg hydyr elwig,
Gorwydd hirddydd derlyëdig ;
A garo eu gilydd ni's dig.

Gorwyn blaen brwyn, brigawg wydd ; (*c*)
Pan dýner dan obenydd,
Meddwl ſerçawg ſyberw vydd.

Gorwyn blaen yſbyddad ; hydyr wyliad gorwydd,
Gnawd ſerçawg erlyniad ;
Gwnelid da diwyd gènad.

Gorwyn blaen berwr ; byddinawr gorwydd ;
Ceingyvreu coed i lawr ;
Çweryd bryd wrth a garawr.

(*a*) Neu, gogyhyt yſuyd.
(*b*) Neu, A deil deri dygaydyt.
(*c*) Neu, Brigawg vyd.

Brightly glitters the top of the oak; inceffant is the tempeft;
The bees are high in their flight, brittle is the charr'd brufhwood;
The wanton is apt to laugh too frequently.

The hazel grove brightly glitters, even and uniform feem the brakes;
And with leaves the oaks envelope themfelves;
Happy is he who fees the one he loves!

Glittering feems the top of the oak; coolly purls the ftream;
I wifh to obtain the top of the birchen grove;
Abruptly goes the arrow of the haughty to give pain.

Brightly glitters the top of the hard holly, that opens its golden leaves;
When all are afleep on the furrounding walls,
God flumbers not when he means to give deliverance.

Glittering are the tops of the willows, brittle and tender;
In the long day of fummer the war-horfe flags,
Thofe that have mutual friendfhip will not offend.

Glittering are the tops of rufhes, the trees are full of branches;
When drawn under the pillow,
The wanton mind will be haughty. (a)

Bright is the top of the hawthorn; confident is the fight of the fteed;
It behoves the dependant to be grateful;
May it be good what the fpeedy meffenger brings.

Glittering are the tops of creffes; warlike is the fteed;
Trees are fair ornaments of the ground;
Joyful is the foul with the one it loves.

(a) There is an obfcurity in this ftanza; as it is not clear whether the middle line is connected with the firft, or laft. If with the firft, the true reading is in the notes of various
readings.

Gorwyn blaen perth; hywerth gorwydd;
Ys da pwyll gyda nerth;
Gwnelid anghelvydd annerth.

Gorwyn blaen perthi, ceingyvreu adar,
Hir ddydd dawn goleu;
Trugar daphar Duw goreu.

Gorwyn blaen erwain, ac elain yn llwyn;
Gwyçyr gwynt gwydd ni gywain; (a)
Eiriawl ni gorawl, ni gyngain.

Gorwyn blaen yſgaw, hydr anaw unig;
Gnawd taer i dreiſiaw; (b)
Gwall a ddwg daphar o law. (c)

(a) Neu, Guychyr guynt guydd nigyein.
(b) Neu, Gnaut y dreiſiyau.
(c) Neu, Gual a duc daffar o lau.

Brightly glares the top of the bufh, valuable is the fteed;
Reafon joined with ftrength is effectual;
Let the unfkilful be void of ftrength.

Glittering are the tops of the brakes, birds are their fair jewels;
The long day is the gift of the radiant light,
Mercy was formed by God, the moft beneficent.

Glittering are the elmweed tops, fweet the mufic of the grove;
Boifterous amongft the trees the wind doth whiftle;
Interceding with the obdurate will not avail.

Glittering are the tops of elder-trees; bold is the folitary fongfter;
Accuftomed is the violent to opprefs;
By want of care the food in hand may be loft. (a)

(a) Want of regular connection is obfervable in this poem; but perhaps much of that arifes from our being ignorant of myftical allufions that might have been anciently intended by the various fcenes that are mentioned. All that can now be done is to give the literaforcel of the words.

MARWNAD URIEN REGED.

DYM cyvarwyddiad ynhwç dywal, *(a)*
Baran yn nghyvlwç ; *(b)*
Gwell yd ladd nog yd ydolwç.

Dym cyfarwyddiad ynhwç ; dywal
Dywedyd yn nrws Lleç,
" Dunawd vab Pabo ni theç."

Dym cyfarwyddiad ynhwç dywal, çwerw, *(c)*
Blwng çwerthin mor ryvel dorvloeddiad,
Urien Reged greidiawl gravel.

Eryr gâl ŷn hwç glew hael, *(d)*
Ryvel goddig buddig vael,
Urien greidiawl gavael. *(e)*

(a) *Ll. Du.* Dym kywarwydyat unhuch dywal.
Ll. Coç. Dim cyfarwyddiad yn Hwch dywal,
(b) Barau ynghyfolwch ; neu, Baran ygkyoluch.
(c) *Ll. Du.* Dym kywarwydat unhuch dywal.
Chwerthin mor ryvel dorvloedyat
Urien Reged greidyaul gravel.
Ll. Coç. Dim cyfarwyddiad yn Hwch ddywal, chwêrw
Blwng chwerthin mor rhyfel
Darfloeddiad Urien Reged graiddiol.
(d, Ll. Coç. Graiddiol eryr gâl yn Hwch gleu haul rhyfel .
Goddig buddig fael
Urien greiddiol gafael.
(e) *Ll. Du.* Urien grudyawl gavael.

ELEGY ON URIEN REGED. (*a*)

LET me be guided onward, thou afhen fpear of death, (*b*) fierce
Thy look in the mutual conflict ;
'Tis better that thou fhould kill, than parley on terms.

Let me be guided onward, thou afhen thrufter ; fiercely
Was it faid in the pafs of *Lleç*
" *Dunawd* the fon of *Pabo* will never fly !"··

Let me be guided onward, thou fierce afhen fpear ; bitter
And fullen as the maddening fea was the hoarfe fhouting of the war,
Where the fiery foul of Urien raged.

Like the eagle, (*c*) a foe with an afhen fpear, bold and generous,
The torment of the war, fure of conqueft,
Was *Urien* with the fiery grafp.

(*a*) See fome account of him in the Life of *Llywarç*:—He was one of the greateft en-
couragers of the Bards of his age ; efpecially of *Taliefin* ; and of *Trifwardd,* his domeftic bard,
none of whofe works have reached our time. *Taliefin* enumerates ten great battles fought by
Urien, againft the *Saxons* ; and he was flain treacheroufly about the year 567.

(*b*) In the original *Ynbwç,* or the *Afben Thrufter* ; and which is alfo a proper name of men ;
and it has been taken by ſ me to be fo in this poem ; but by taking into confideration all the
paffages wherein the word occurs, it feems moft natural to take it in the fenfe as if the Bard was
addreffing his fpear, and bent on revenging the death of his friend.

(*c*) *Eryr Gâl,* in the original : *Gâl* fignifies a *Gaul,* and alfo an enemy ; thus it feems that
the *Belgic Gauls* were the earlieft, and greateft molefters of the *Cynmry* ; hence a *Gaul* and an
enemy were confidered as fynonym ius.

Gavael Eryr Gâl ỳn hwç (a)
Berçen enawr,
Cell llyr, cain ebyr gwyr glawr.

Pen a borthav o vy nhu, (b)
Bu cyrçyniad rhwng deu-lu, (c)
Mab Cynvarç balç bieuvu !

Pen· a borthav ar vy nhu : Pen Urien,
Llary, llyw ei lu ; (d)
Ac ar ei vron wen fran ddu !

Pen a borthav mywn vy nghrys : pen Urien,
Llary llywiai lys ; (e)
Ac ar ei vron wen vran ai hŷs !

Pen a borthav i'm neddair,(f)
Eryr eçwydd, oedd ni gair ; (g)
Teyrn-vron treuliad gynniwair. (h)

. (a) Ll. Du. Eryr gal unbuch berchen enaur
            Kell llyr ebyr guyl glaur.
(b) Ll. Du. Pen a borthav a untu ; neu, a bu tu;
    Ll. Coç. Pen a borthav a ynty.
(c) Ll. Du. By kyrch ynat rug deutu;
(d) Ll. Du. Pen a borthav ar vyntu
            Pen Urien llary llyu eilu.
(e) Ll. Coç. Llary llyw eu llys.
(f) Ll. Coç. Fedeir.
(g) Ll. Du. Yryr echwydd aedd vugeil ; neu, yrrechwyd, &c.
    Ll. Coç. Yr erechwydd aedd nu geil.
(h) Ll. Coç. Genweir.

The *Eagle* of *Gâl* holds the pusher of the spear's
Soul in possession,
In the cell of the water of the smooth inlets with green surface. (*a*)

I bear by my side a head,
That has been an assaulter between two hosts—
The son of *Cynvarg*, magnanimous he has been ! (*b*)

I bear by my side a head : the head of *Urien*,
The mild leader of his army.—
And on his white bosom the sable raven is perch'd !

I bear in my shirt a head : the head of *Urien*,
That governed a court with mildness :—
And on his white bosom the sable raven doth glut.

A head I bear in my hand,
He that was a soaring eagle, whose like will not be had ;
His princely breast is assailed by the devourer (*c*)

(*a*) This stanza begins with *Eryr Gâl*, like the preceding ; but it is here rendered in a contrary sense ; which is right is very doubtful. This last stanza is very obscure altogether ; and seemingly incomplete in the middle line.

(*b*) The preceding part of the Elegy breathes revenge, but here it changes to lament the fate of *Urien*. It seems that *Llywarg* secured the head of his friend ; if he actually did so, what was the intention ? Does it not allude to some custom peculiar to the Britons ?

(*c*) This Elegy has suffered by transcribing, as may be seen by the various readings ; but whether the reading adopted is the best, must be left to the Welsh critics, without a translation, lest the English reader should be tired with trifles.

Pen a borthav tu morddwyd,
Oedd yſgwyd ar ei wlad, oedd olwyn yn nghâd,
Oedd cledyr cywlad (*a*) rhwydd. (*b*)

Pen a borthav ar vy nghledd,
Gwell ei vyw, nog yt ei vedd;
Oedd dinas i henwredd. (*c*)

Pen a borthav o Godir Pènawg, (*d*)
Pellyniawg ei luŷdd: (*e*)
Urien geiriawg glodrydd;

Pen a borthav ar vy yſgwydd;
Ni'm arvollai waradwydd—(*f*)
Gwae vy llaw; lladd vy arglwydd !

Pen a borthav ar vy mraiç,
Neus gorug o dir Brynaiç; (*g*)
Gwedy gwawr gelorawr veirç.

Pen a borthav yn angad vy llaw,
Llary udd llywiai wlad ; (*b*)
Pen poſt Prydain ryallad.

(*a*) *Ll. Du.* Oedd cledyv cad cywlad; neu, Oed cledyr cad cywlad.
(*b*) *Ll. Coſ.* Oedd yſgwyd ar ei wlad,
          Oedd owyn ynghad cywlad rwydd.
(*c*) *Ll. Du.* Gwell y vyu noc yt y ved
          Oedd dinas y henured.
(*d*) Neu, Godir pennauc ; neu, Gorddir pennog.
(*e*) *Ll. Du.* Penllynyawc y luyd.
(*f*) *Ll. Coſ.* Ny marfyllai wâr at wydJ.
(*g*) *Ll. Coſ.* Nys goruc o dir Bryneich.
(*b*) *Ll. Du.* Llaryud llywyei wlat.
     Ll. Coſ. Llarywydd llyw ei wlad.

I bear by the fide of my thigh a head,
That was the fhield of his country, and a wheel in battle;
That was the prompt defender of his neighbourhood.

I bear a head on my fword;
Better his being alive, than to thee his mead;
He was a caftle to old age.

I bear a head from the bordering land of *Pénawg*, (*a*)
Widely extended was his warfare :—
Urien, the eloquent, whofe fame went far!

A head I bear on my fhoulder,
That would not bring on me difgrace—
Woe to my hand, (*b*) that my lord is flain!

A head on my arm I bear,
He that overcame the land of *Brynaif*, (*c*)
But after the fierce onfet comes the fteeds with biers.

A head I bear in the grafp of my hand,
Of a chief who mildly governed a country;
The head, and moft powerful pillar of *Britain*.

(*a*) *Urien* was flain befieging *Deoderic* in the ifle of *Medcaut*; fome fmall ifland on the coaft, fouth of the *Forth*; and *Penawg* might be the headland, to which it was contiguous.

(*b*) A common exclamation amongft the Britons.

(*c*) The ancient principality of *Bernicia* comprehended a tract of hilly country, as the name implies, beginning north about the *Picts Wall*, and extending fouthward into *Yorkſhire*. It was a part of the territory of a people in the time of the *Romans* called *Brigantes*, that is, *Bri-gantwys*, or the people of the uplands.

Pen a borthav o du pawl,
Pen Urien, udd dragonawl;
A çyd dêl dydd brawd, ni'm tawr !

Pen a borthav a'm porthes;
Neud adwen nad arvylles, (a)
Gwae vy llaw, lle 'm digones !

Pen a borthav o dy Rhiw, (b)
Ac ei enau ewynvriw gwaed—(c)
Gwae Reged o heddiw !

Ni thyrvis vy mraiç; rhygarddwys vy ais ; (d)
Vy nghalon neu'r dòres ? (e)
Pen a borthav a'm porthes !

Y gelain veinwen a oloir heddiw, (f)
A dan bridd a main—
Gwae vy llaw, lladd tâd Owain !

Y gelain veinwen a oloir heddiw,
Ynmhlith pridd a derw—
Gwae vy llaw, lladd vy nghevynderw !

(a) *Ll. Du.* Neut atuen nat ar vylles.
   Ll. Coç. Neud adwen nad yrfylles.
(b) *Ll. Du.* O dy Riu.
   Ll. Coç. O ddu Riw.
(c) *Ll. Du.* Ac y eneuriw gwaet.
   Ll. Coç. Ac y eneu ewynrhiw gwaid.
(d) *Ll. Du.* Ny thyr vis vymbreich rygarduys vy eis.
   Ll. Coç. Ny thyrrwys fy mreich rygarddwys fy ais.
(e) Neu, Neut dorres ; neu, Neur dorreis.
(f) A oleuir heddyw.   *R. Thomas.*

I bear a head on a pole,
The head of *Urien*, the magnificent chief:
And fhould the day of judgment come, it concerns me not!

I bear a head that fupported me;
Is there any known but he welcomed?—
Woe to my hand, gone is he that gave me content!

I bear a head from the *Rhiw*, (*a*)
With his lips foaming with blood—
Woe to *Reged* (*b*) from this day!

My arm has not flagg'd; but my bofom is greatly troubled;
Ah, my heart! is it not broken?—
A head I bear that was my fupport!

The delicate white corpfe will be interr'd this day,
Under earth and ftones.—
Woe to my hand, that the father of *Owain* is flain!

The delicate white corpfe will be covered over this day,
Amongft earth and oak—
Woe my hand, that my coufin is flain!

(*a*) The declivity, or afcent: many places are fo called; and here it feems to be the name of a place.

(*b*) The patrimony of *Urien*: one of the four parts into which *Cumbria* was then divided; and it feems to have been the north eaft divifion.

Y gelain veinwen a oloir heno,
A dan vain ai dewid (*a*)
Gwae vy llaw, llam rym tyngid ! (*b*)

Y gelain veinwen a oloir heno
Ynmhlith pridd a thywarç :—
Gwae vy llaw, lladd mab Cynvarç !

Y gelain veinwen a oloir heddiw
Dan weryd ac arwydd :—
Gwae vy llaw, lladd vy arglwydd !

Y gelain veinwen a oloir heddiw
A dan bridd a thywawd :
Gwae vy llaw, llam rym daerawd !

Y gelain veinwen a oloir heddiw,
A dan bridd a main glâs :—
Gwae vy llaw, llam rym gallas ! (*c*)

Y gelain veinwen a oloir heddiw,
A dan bridd a dynad :—
Gwae vy llaw, llam rym gallad !

Anoeth byd brawd bu yn cynnull ; (*d*)
Am gyrn buelyn am drull, (*e*)
Rhebydd viled Reged dull. (*f*)

(*a*) Neu, Aedcuit ; neu, a dewyd.
(*b*) Neu, Llad rym tyghit ; neu, Llamrym tynged.
(*c*) *Ll. Du.* Llam ryn gallas.
(*d*) *Ll. Du.* Annoeth byd braut buyn kynnull.
    Ll. Coç. Annoeth bydd brawd yn cynnydd.
(*e*) *Ll. Coç.* Amgyrn buelyn am drull.
(*f*) Rebyd vilet (neu, wyled) Reget dull.

The delicate white corpfe will be covered this night ;
Under ftones will he be left—
Woe my hand, what a ftep has fate decreed me !

The delicate white corpfe will be interr'd this night,
Amidft earth and green fods ;—
Woe my hand, that the fon of *Cynvarɕ* fhould be flain !

The delicate white corpfe will be interr'd this day,
Under the green-fward with a tumulus ;—
Woe my hand, that my lord is flain !

The fair white corpfe will be interr'd this day
Under earth and fand—
Woe my hand, the ftep that is decreed to me !

The fair white corpfe will be interr'd this day,
Under earth and blue ftones :—
Woe my hand, the ftep that befel me !

The fair white corpfe will be covered this day
Under earth and nettles :—
Woe my hand, that fuch a ftep could have happened to me !

A mafter-feat of the world (*a*) the brother has been in purfuit of; (*b*)
For the horns of the buffalo, for a feftive goblet,
He was the depredator with the hounds in the covert of *Reged!*

(*a*) Or perhaps, more literally, *the bidden*, or *myfterious thing of the world* ; any great exploit
a warrior was to accomplifh to eftablifh his chara&er. In the age of chivalry the *Anoethau* came
to fignify the impoffibilities that were enjoined to be performed by the knights of rom 'nce.

(*b*) *The brother has been in purfuit of.*—Meaning *Urien* ; as he was the brother of *Eurddyl*,
whom the bard addreffes here.

Anoeth byd brawd bu yn cynnwys, (*a*)
Am gyrn buelyn amwys, (*b*)
Rhebydd viled Regedwys. (*c*)

Handid Eurddyl avlawen henoeth, (*d*)
A lluofydd amgen :
Yn Aber Lleu lladd Urien !

Ys trift Eurddyl o'r drallawd heno,
Ac o'r llam a'm daerawd (*e*)
Yn Aber Lleu lladd ei brawd !

Dyw Gwener gwelais i ddiwyd mawr, (*f*)
Ar vyddinawr bedydd ; (*g*)
Haid heb vodrydav hy bydd. (*h*)

Neu'm rhoddes i Run ryvelvawr (*i*)
Cant haid, a çant yfgwydawr ?
Ac un haid oedd well pell mawr. (*k*)

(*a*) *Ll. Coſ.* Anoeth bydd (neu, byd) brawd bu yn cynnwys.
(*b*) *Ll. Coſ.* Amgyrn buelyn a mwys.
(*c*) *Ll. Coſ.* Rhebydd filed Rhegethwys.
   Ll. Du. Rhebyd vilet regeduis (neu, rededwys.)
(*d*) *Ll. Du.* Handit euyrdyl (neu, evyrddyl) avlauen.
(*e*) *Ll. Coſ.* Yn Aber Lley lladd *Uries.*
(*f*) Ac or llam amdaerawt.
(*g*) *Ll. Du.* Gweleis y divyd mawr ; neu, difydd ; neu ddinydd mawr.
   Ll. Coſ. Gweleis i ddiwyd mawr.
(*h*) Neu, bedit, neu bedydd, neu hubydd. *Ll. Du.*
(*i*) *Ll. Du.* Heid heb vodrydav.
   Ll. Coſ. Heid heb fodrydau hy byd.
(*k*) Neu ryvedliawr ; neu, rhyfeddfawr ; neu rhyfeddliawr
(*l*) *Ll. Coſ.* Ac un oedd well pell mawr.

A mafter-feat of the world the brother has eagerly fought;
For the equivocal horn of the buffalo, (*a*)
He was the chacer with the hound with the men of *Reged!*

Eurddyl (*b*) will be joylefs this night,
Since the leader of armies is as if he was not:—
In *Aber Lleu Urien* has been flain!

Eurddyl will be forrowful from the tribulation of this night,
And from the fate that is to me befallen:
That her brother fhould be flain at *Aber Lleu!*

On Friday I faw great anxiety
Amongft the baptifed embattled hofts;
Like a fwarm without a hive, bold in defpair.

Were there not given to me by *Rhun*, (*c*) greatly fond of war,
A hundred fwarms, and a hundred fhields?
But one fwarm was better far than all.

(*a*) *Equivocal horn of the buffalo*—Alluding to the two ufes made of the horn: To found the alarm of war; and to drink the mead at feafts.

(*b*) Sifter to *Urien*, married to *Elifer Gofgordd-vawr*, or *Elifer* with the great Clan; a prince of a diftrict in the neighbourhood of *Edinburgh*.

(*c*) This *Rhun* cannot be the bafe fon of *Maelgwn*; as *Maelgwn* was alive at this period, though he furvived *Urien* but a fhort time; he died in 568. *Urien* dying before *Maelgwn*, the government could not be claimed by *Elidyr Mwynvawr* in right of his wife *Eurgain*, the daughter of *Maelgwn*, till fome time after; and it was that claim which occafioned the expedition of *Rhun ab Maelgwn* into the north. This fhews that the *Rhun* mentioned in the Elegy, muft be another: the fame, probably, as *Rhun Rhyveddvawr*, in *Gutyn Owain's* Pedigrees; where he is made the fon of *Einiawn ab Magreig Glôf, ab Cenau ab Coel Godebawg*; and father to *Perweir*, wife to *Rhun* the fon of *Maelgwn*.

D

Neu'm rhoddes i Run rwyv iolydd cantrev, (*a*)
A çant eidionydd ; (*b*)
Ac un rodd oedd well nog ydd, (*c*)

Yn myw Rhun, rheawdyr dihedd, (*d*)
Dyrain enwir enbydedd ; (*e*)
Heiyrn ar veirç enwiredd.

Mor yw, gogwn, vy anav ; (*f*)
Arglyw pob un yn mhob hâv :
Ni wyr neb nebawd arhav. (*g*)

Pwyllai Duñawd, (*h*) varçawg gwain,
Er eçwydd (*i*) gwneuthur celain,
Yn erbyn cryſaid Owain. (*k*)

Pwyllai Dunawd, (*l*) ydd preſen,
Er eçwydd (*m*) gwneuthur cadwen,
Yn erbyn cyvryſedd Paſgen.

(*a*) *Ll. Coç.* Rhwyfydydd cantref.
(*b*) *Ll. Du.* A chant eudyonyd.
(*c*) *Ll. Du.* Ac un (rod) oedd uell nogyd.
(*d*) Neu rheawdyr dyhedd ; neu, creaudyr dyhed.
(*e*) *Ll. Du.* Dyrein enwir eu byded (neu, enbydded.)
     Ll. Coç. Direin enwir eu bydedd.
(*f*) *Ll. Du.* Mor vi gogun vy anaf.
     Ll. Coç. Mor yw gogwn fy arnaf (neu, arwaf)
(*g*) Neu, arnaf.
(*h*) Neu, Pwyllic Dunawd ; neu, Pyllei Dunawd.
(*i*) Neu, Erechwydd.
(*k*) Neu, cryſoedd Owein ; neu, cyfryſedd Owain.
(*l*) Neu, Pwyllic Dunawd.
(*m*) Neu, Erechwydd.

Were there not given to me by. *Rhun*, the celebrated chief, a *Cantrev*,
And a hundred lowing kine?
But one gift was better far than thofe.

In the life-time of *Rhun*, the peacelefs wanderer,
The unjuft will wallow in dangers:
May there be fetters of iron on the fteeds of rapine.

The extreme I know of my trouble;
It is what all will hear, in every feafon of warfare:
No one hath known a greater fcene of violence.

Dunawd, (*a*) the knight of the warring field, would fiercely rage,
With a mind determined to make a dead corpfe,
Againft the quick onfet of Owain. (*b*)

Dunawd, the hafty chief, would fiercely rage,
With mind elated for the battle,
Againft the confliⅽt of *Pafgen*. (*c*)

(*a*) Called in the Triades one of the three pillars of battle of the ifle of Britain; the other two were *Cynvelyn Drwfgyl*, and *Urien* the fon of *Cynvarς*.

" Tri phoft Câd ynys Prydain ; Dunawd vab Pabo, Cynvelyn

" Drwfgyl, ac Urien vab *Cynvarς*. Trioedd.

Pabo, the father of *Dunawd*, obtained the title of *Poft Prydain*, or Pillar of *Britain*, from his great valour in fighting againft the *Scots* and *Picts*: He was the fon of *Mor ab Cenau ab Coel Godebawg*, grandfather of *Conftantine* the great. *Pabo* built a church in *Anglefey*, called after him *Llanbabo*; where his tomb was opened in the reign of *Charles* II. *See the Infcription in Rowl. Mon. Antiq. Ed. 2. p. 151.*

(*b*) Eldeft fon of *Urien*.

(*c*) Third fon of *Urien*.

D 2

Pwyllai Wallawg, marçawg trin,
Er eçwydd (*a*) gwneuthur dyvin,
Yn erbyn cyvryfedd Elphin.

Pwyllai Vran, vab y Mellyrn, (*b*)
Vu'n d'iol i lofgi vy ffyrn ; (*c*)
Blaidd a vygai wrth ebyrn. (*d*)

Pwyllai Vorgant, ev a'i wyr,
Vu'n d'iol i lofgi vy nhymmyr; (*e*)
Llug a gravai wrth glegyr. (*f*)

Pwyllais i, pan lâs Elgno ;
Frowyllai lavyn a rciddio Pyll, (*g*)
A phebyll o'i vro.

Eilwaith gwelais, gwedy gweithien, (*h*)
Aur yfgwyd ar yfgwydd Urien : (*i*)
Bu ail yno Elgno hen.

Ar ereçwydd ethyw gwallt. (*k*)
O vraw marçawg yfguall ; (*l*)
A vydd wrth Urien arall ! (*m*)

(*a*) Neu, Erechwydd.
(*b*) *Ll. Du.* Melfyrn; neu, mellyrn.
(*c*) *Ll. Du.* Vyn Dihâl llofgi uy ffyrn.
(*d*) *Ll. Du.* Bleid ullgei (neu, fu gai; neu, milgi) wrth Ebyrn.
(*e*) *Ll. Du.* Cyn dihol llofgi uyn tymyr.
(*f*) *Ll. Du.* Llye a gravei wrth Glegyr.
(*g*) *Ll. Du.* Ffrouyllei lavyn o reidyo Pyll.
    Ll. Coç. Ffrowylle lafyn ar eiddo Pyll.
(*h*) *Ll. Du.* Gwelcis i gwedy gweithieu.
(*i*) *Ll. Du.* Uryein.
(*k*) *Ll. Du.* Ar erethuyd (crechuyd) ethyw gwallt (guall.)
(*l*) Neu, Yfgueill; neu, ys gweill.
(*m*) *Ll. Coç.* A fydd fyth Urien arall.

Gwallawg, the knight of tumult, would violently rave,
With a mind determined to try the sharpest edge,
Against the conflict of *Elphin*. (*a*)

Bran, the son of *Mellyrn*, would violently rave,
That collected an army to burn my ovens;
He was a wolf smothered by his own load.

Morgant, (*b*) and his men, would fiercely rage,
Who collected a host to burn my lands;
He was like a mouse scratching against a rock.

My fury also raged, when *Elgno* fell;
Terribly rapid moved the blade when lifted up by *Pyll*, (*c*)
Whilst a tent stood in his country.

A second time I saw, after that conflict,
A golden shield on the shoulder of *Urien*;
There again befel the fate of old *Elgno*.

The hair bristled up anend,
With the fear of the blood-spilling knight:
Will there ever be another to match with *Urien*!

(*a*) Fifth son of *Urien.*
(*b*) This probably is the *Morgant*, by whose instigation *Urien* was murdered.
(*c*) The second son of *Llywarç.*

Ys moel vy arglwydd er evras gwrth, (a)
Ni's câr cedwyr ei gâs ; (b)
Lliaws gwledig rhydreulias

Angerdd Urien îs, agro gènyv ; (c)
Cyrçyniad yn mhob bro,
Yn wyfg Llovan Llawddifro. (d)

Tawel awel, ti hirglyw ! (e)
Odid a vo moledyw,
Nam Urien, cen nid yw !

Llawer ci geilig, a hebawg wyrenig,
A lithiwyd ar y llawr,
Cyn bu Erlleon llawedrawr. (f)

Yr aelwyd hon a'i goglud gawr, (g)
Mwy gorddyvnafai ar ei llawr
Mêdd, a meddwon eiriawr ! (h)

Yr aelwyd hon neu's cudd dynad !
Tra vu vyw ei gwarçeidwad,
Mwy gorddyvnafai eirçiad !

(a) Ll. Coç. Ys moel yn fy arglwydd yr (ys) euras gwrth.
(b) Ll. Du. Nys car cadwyr y gas.
(c) Neu, Ys a gro (agro) gennyv.
(d) Ll. Du. Yn uifc lovan law diffro.
(e) Ll. Du. Tauel auel ty hirglyu.
(f) Ll. Du. Cyn by Erlleon llauedraur.
     Ll. Coç. Cyn y bu Erlleon Llyweddriawr,
(g) Ll. Coç. Ae goglyd gawr ; neu, ai goglud gawr.
(h) Ll. Coç. Eiriawl.

Tho' decapidated be my lord, yet from his manly youth, till now
The warriors loved not his refentment;
Many fovereigns has he confumed.

The fiery breath of *Urien* is ftill'd, I am affail'd by grief;
There is commotion in every region
In fearch of *Llovan*, with the detefted hand. (*a*)

Silent breathing gale, long wilt thou be heard !
There is fcarcely another deferving praife,
Since *Urien* is no more !

Many a dog that fcented well the prey, and aerial hawk,
Have been trained on this floor
Before *Erlleon* became polluted.

This hearth, deferted by the fhout of war,
More congenial on its floor would have been
The mead, and loquacious drunken warriors !

This hearth, ah, will it not be covered with nettles ?
Whilft its defender lived,
More congenial to it was the foot of the needy petitioner.

(*a*) This act by *Llovan Llawddifro* is recorded in the Triades, one of the three villainous mur-
ders of *Britain*; the other was committed by *Eiddyn* the fon of *Eirygan*, who flew *Aneurin*,
monarch of the bards; and the third by *Llawgad Trwm Bargawd Eiddyn*, on *Avaon*, the fon of
Taliefin.

Yr aelwyd hon neu's cudd glefin l
Yn myw Owain ac Elphin;
Breuafai ei phair breiddin.

Yr aelwyd hon neu's cudd callawdyr llwyd,
Mwy gorddyvnafai am ei bwyd
Cleddyval dywal diarfwyd l

Yr aelwyd hon neu's cudd caen vieri, (b)
Coed cynneuawg oedd iddi : (c)
Gorddyvnafai Reged roddi l

Yr aclwyd hon neu's cudd drain, (d)
Mwy gorddyvnafai ei çyngrain
Cymmwynas cyweithas Owain l   ·

Yr aelwyd hon neu's cudd myr, (f)
Mwy gorddyvnafai babir gloyw,
A çyveddau çywir l

Yr aelwyd hon neu's cudd tavawl ; (g)
Mwy y gorddyvnafai ar ei llawr,
Mêdd, a meddwon eiriawl l l

Yr aelwyd hon neu's cladd hwç;
Mwy gorddyvnafai elwç gwyr,
Ac am gyrn cyveddwç l (b)

(a) *Ll. Du.* Berwaffei ei phair breiddin.
(b) *Ll. Du.* Neus cud cein vieri coed.
(c) *Ll. Du.* Cynnevaut oed idi.
(d) *Ll. Coç.* Yr aelwyd hon fai ddrein.
(e) *Ll. Coç.* Cymmwynas, cymdeithas Owein.
(f) Neu, Neus cyd my..
(b) *Ll. Coç.* Neus cyd tafawl.
(i) *Ll. Coç.* Ac amgyrn cyfeddwch.

This hearth, will it not be covered with the green fod!
In the lifetime of *Owain* and *Elphin*,
Its ample pot boil'd the prey taken from the foe.

This hearth, will it not be covered with mufty toad-ftools,
Around the viands it prepared, more cheering was
The clattering fword of the fierce dauntlefs warrior!

This hearth, will it not be overgrown with fpreading brambles!
Till now logs of burning wood lay on it,
Accuftomed to prepare the gifts of *Reged!* (a)

This hearth, will it not be covered with thorns!
More congenial on it would have been the mixed group
Of *Owain*'s focial friends, united in harmony.

This hearth, will it not be covered over by the ants!
More adapted to it would have been the bright torches,
And harmlefs feftivities!

This hearth, will it not be covered with dock leaves!
More congenial on its floor would have been
The mead, and the talking of intoxicated warriors.

This hearth, will it not be turned up by the fwine!
More congenial to it would have been the clamour of men,
And the circling horns of the banquet.

(a) The original of this paffage is rather equivocal; as it might be rendered, the gifts beftowed by *Urien*; however it is intended, in the tranflation to fignify the contrary; or the gifts,
and contributions of the country of *Reged* to their prince.

Yr aelwyd hon neu's cladd cywen ;
Ni's eiddiganai angen, (*a*)
Yn myw Owain, ac Urien !

Yr yſtwfwl hwn, a'r hwn draw,
Mwy gorddyvnaſai amdanaw
Elwç llu, a llwybyr anaw ! (*b*)

(*a*) *Ll. Coſ.* Ni eiddiganel angen.
(*b*) *Ll. Coſ, a'r Ll. Du.* A Lluybyr arnaw.

This hearth, will it not be fcratched up by fowls!
It never experienced a fcarcity,
While *Owain*, and *Urien* lived!

This buttrefs here, and that one there,
More congenial around them would have been
An army's clamour, and the path of melody!

TRIBANAU.

CALANGAUAV caled grawn,
Dail ar gyçwyn, llynwyn llawn:—
Y bore cyn noi vyned,
Gwae a ymddiried i eſtrawn!

Calangauav cain gyvrin,
Cyvred awel a drychin:
Gwaith celwydd yw celu rhin.

Calangauav cul hyddod,
Melyn blaen bedw, gweddw havod:
Gwae a haedd mevyl er byçod!

Calangauav crwm blaen gwryſg:
Gnâwd o ben diried dervyſg;
Lle ni bo dawn ni bydd dyſg.

Calangauav garw hin,
Annhebyg i gyntevin:
Namwyn Dụw nid oes dewin.

Calangauav caled cras,
Purddu bran, buan o vras:
Am gwymp hen çwerddid gwên gwâs.

Calangauav llwm goddaith,
Aradyr yn rhyç, ŷç yn ngwaith:
O'r cant odid cydymmaith.

T R I P L E T S.

ON All Saints' Day hard is the grain,
  The leaves are dropping, the puddle is full:—
At fetting off in the morning,
Woe to him that will truft to a ftranger!

On All Saints' Day, a time of pleafant goffipping,
The gale and the ftorm keep equal pace:
It is the labour of falfehood to keep a fecret.

On All Saints' Day the ftags are lean,
Yellow are the tops of birch, deferted is the fummer dwelling:
Woe to him who for a trifle deferves a curfe!

On All Saints' Day the tops of the branches are bent:
In the mouth of the mifchievous difturbance is congenial;
Where there is no natural gift there will be no learning.

On All Saints' Day bluftering is the weather,
Very unlike the beginning of the paft fair feafon:
Befides God there is none who knows the future.

On All Saints' Day 'tis hard and dry,
Doubly black is the crow, quick is the arrow from the bow:
For the ftumbling of the old the looks of the youth wear a fmile.

On All Saints' Day bare is the place where the heath is burnt,
The plough is in the furrow, the ox at work:
Amongft a hundred 'tis a chance to meet a friend.

CANU MÁENWÝN.

MAENWYN trá vum i'th oed,
Ni fethrid vy llen i â throed,
Nid erddid vy nhir i heb waed.

Maenwyn tra vum i'th erbyn,
A'm ieuenctid i'm dylyn,
Ni thòrai gofail vy nhervyn. (*a*)

Maenwyn tra vum i'th erlid,
Yn dylyn vy ieuenctid,
Ni çarai gofail vy ngwythlid. (*b*)

Maenwyn tra vum i evras,
O ddylyn dywal galanas, (*c*)
Gwnawn weithred gwr cyd byddwn gwas. (*d*)

Maenwyn, meidyr di yn gall; (*e*)
Angen ceffail ar wall ; (*f*)
Ceified Vaelgwn vaer arall.

(*a*) *Ll. Coç.* Ni thorrei gaffeil fyn terfyn.
(*b*) *Ll. Coç.* Ni charei geffeil fy ngwythlid.
    Ll. Du. Ni charei goffail uy ngwrthlit.
(*c*) *Ll. Du.* Oedvli dywal galanas.
(*d*) *Ll. Coç.* Tra byddwn gwas.
(*e*) Neu, Meddir, medr, meidr, medhyr di yn gall.
(*f*) *Ll. Du.* Anghen cyffweid (kyffyeil) ar wall.
    Ll. Coç. Angen cyffeil ar wall.

TO MAENWYN. (a)

MAENWYN, when I was of thy age,
My garment should not be trodden under foot,
My land should not have been ploughed without blood.

Maenwyn, when I was in thy condition,
With youth attendant on me,
The outlaw would not have broken my boundary.

Maenwyn, whilst I was as thou art,
Following the course of my youth,
The enemy loved not the fury of my resentment.

Maenwyn, whilst I was in the bloom of youth,
Addicted to fierce slaughter,
I performed the part of a man, though but a boy.

Maenwyn, take thy aim discreetly;
Or through necessity, instead of a heedless guardian,
Let Maelgwn provide another mayor. (b)

(a) An exhortation to Maenwyn, a young warrior, who it seems had been commanded to capitulate, and deliver up his arms. Llywarç endeavours to encourage him to resist the offer, and shew his fidelity to Maelgwn.
(b) The original is Maer; of the same import as the English bailiff; the head officer of a town, district, or farm.

Vy'm dewis i gyvran, (*a*) a'i gaen arnaw,
Yn llym, megis draen ;
Nid over gniv i'm hogi maen.

Anreg rym gallad o Ddyfryn Mewyrniawn, (*b*)
Yn nghudd yn nghelwrn :
Haearn llym llaes o ddwrn.

Boed bendigaid yr anghyfbell wraç,
A ddywed o ddrws ei çell : (*d*)
Maenwyn nag addaw dy gyllell.

(*a*) *Ll. Du.* Vyn deuis i gyvran.
     Ll. Coç. Vym dewis gyvran.
(*b*) *Ll. Coç.* Anrheg rym gall o Ddyffryn Meirniawn.
     Ll. Du. Anrhegyn ryn gallad o Ddyffryn.
(*c*) *Ll. Du.* A dynaut o drus y chell.

My choice is to have a portion, with its sheath on it,
And sharp-pointed as a thorn;
It is not labour lost for me to whet a stone. (*a*)

A present was bestowed on me, from the vale of *Mewyrnion*,
Concealed in a case;
It was a keen iron far projecting from the hand. (*b*)

Blessed be the solitary old hag,
That said from the door of her hut—
"*Maenwyn*, do not deliver up thy whittle."

(*a*) This seems intended as a pun upon the name of the youth. *Maenwyn* implies—*having
the nature, or hardness of a stone*; and still the Poet thought that the *stone* that he was speaking of
wanted a little more hardening.

(*b*) A sword is here described; but the name designedly omitted.

ENGLYNION DUAD.

BID coç crib ceiliawg, bid anianawl
Ei lev, o wely buddugawl:
Llawenydd dyn Duw ai mawl.

Bid lawen meiçiad (*a*) wrth uçenaid gwynt;
Bid tawel yn delaid; (*b*)
Bid gnawd avlwydd ar ddiriaid.

Bid gyhuddawg ceifiad, bid gniviad gwyd, (*c*)
A bid gynnwys dillad:
A garo bardd bid hardd roddiad.

Bid lew unben, a bid awy vryd, (*d*)
A bid vlaidd ar vlaidd ar adwy; (*e*)
Ni çeidw wyneb ar na roddwy. (*f*)

Bid vuan redaint yn ardal mynydd;
Bid yn ngheudawd oval;
Bid anniwair anwadal.

Bid amlwg marçawg, bid ogelawg lleidyr,
Twyllid gwraig oludawg:
Cyvaillt blaidd bugail diawg.

(*a*) Neu, Meichieu.
(*b*) Neu, Bit tauel yndileit.
(*c*) Neu, Bit gnifgat guyd; neu, Gnifyat guyd, (gwydd.)
(*d*) *Ll. Coç.* Bit avuy unben a bit leu.
(*e*) Neu, A bit lleiniad yr ardwy.
(*f*) Neu, Ni cheidw ei wyneb ri reddwy.

SATIRICAL TRIPLETS. (a)

L ET the cock's comb be red, naturally loud be
His voice, from his triumphant bed:
Man's rejoicing God will commend.

Let the fwine-herd be merry at the fighing of the wind; (b)
Let the filent appear graceful;
Let the mifchievous be accuftomed to misfortune.

Let the bailiff impeach, let evil be a tormentor;
May garments be full and ample:
He that loves a bard let him be a generous giver.

Let a prince be brave, with a mind enlarged,
And let him be a wolf againft a wolf on the breach;
He will not fhew his face that will not give.

Fleet let the racers be on the mountain fide;
Let care be in the bofom;
Unchafte let the inconftant be.

The knight, confpicuous let him be, and the thief be fneaking,
The woman that is rich may be deceived;
The friend of the wolf is the lazy fhepherd.

(a) Thefe are moftly proverbial fayings, here connected together by the metres of the ftanzaa.
(b) Becaufe then the fwine would have acorns without his being at any trouble.

Bid gwir baglawl, bid ryngyngawd gelwydd; (*a*)
Bid vab lleen yn çwannawg: (*b*)
Bid anniwair daueiriawg.

Bid gwrm biw, a bid llwyd blaidd;
Efgud gorwydd i ar haidd;
Gwefgyd gwawn-grawn yn ei wraidd. (*c*)

Bid grwm byddar, bid trwm cau;
Efgud gorwydd yn nghadau;
Gwefgyd gwawn-grawn yn adneu.

Bid aha! byddar, bid anwadal ehud;
Diriaid bid ymgeingar; (*d*)
Dedwydd, ar a'i gwŷl a'i câr.

Bid dwvyn llyn, bid llym gwaywawr;
Bid gran clav glew wrth awr: (*e*)
Bid doeth dedwydd, Duw a'i mawr. (*f*)

Bid llym eithin, bid dyfgethrin drud;
A bid eddain alltud;
Bid çwannawg ynvyd i çwerthin. (*g*)

(*a*) Neu, Bid gwir baglawl, bid rygyngawd gorwydd.
(*b*) Neu, Bid val llen yn chwannawg.
   Bed amlwg marçawg, bid redegawg gorwydd.
(*c*) Neu, Guefcyt guangraun yn y ureid.
(*d*) *Ll. Coſ.* Bid ynvyt ymladgar.
(*e*) *Ll. Coſ.* Bit gran clef gleu wrth aur.
  Ll. arall. Bid gwanandeu glau wrth awr.
(*f*) Neu, Bid doeth dedwydd, Duw ai nawdd.
(*g*) *Ll. Coſ.* Bit evein alldut, bit dyfgethrin drut,
   Bit çuannauc ynvyt y çuerthin.

Let truth hobble on crutches, let lies fly swiftly;
Let the clerical man be covetous; (a)
The unchaste, let him be prevaricating.

Let the cow be brown, and the wolf be grey,
Swift the steed fed with barley,
Let the tender grain be press'd at the roots.

Let the snare be bent, let bonds be heavy;
The horse nimble in battles;
The tender grain be press'd when deposited in the ground. (b)

Let the deaf be dubious, the rash be fickle;
The mischievous, let him be wrangling;
The prudent need but be seen to be beloved.

Let the pool be deep, the spears be sharp;
Let the eye of the sick be bold at the shout of war;
Let the wife be happy, God commends him.

Let the furze be prickly, let the fierce hurl ruin;
And let the exile wander;
Let the fool be fond of laughter.

(a) More literally—Let the son of learning be covetous.
(b) The concluding line of this, and the preceding stanza, seem very obscure.

Bid wlyb rhyç; bid vynyç maç;
Bid gŵyn clav, bid lawen iaç;
Bid çwyrn colwyn, bid wenwyn gwraç. (*a*)

Bid diaſbad aeleu, bid ae byddin;
Bid beſgitor dyre;
Bid drud glew, a bid rew bre.

Bid wen gwylan, bid van tòn;
Bid hyvagyl gwyar ar òn;
Bid lwyd rew; bid lew calon.

Bid las lluarth; bid diwarth eiriad;
Bid reiniad yn nghyvarth;
Bid wraig ddrwg â mynyç warth.

Bid gogor gan iar, bid trydar gan lew; (*b*)
Bid ynvyd ymladdgar; (*c*)
Bid tòn calon gan alar.

Bid hofder llawer a'i heirç;
Bid wyn twr, bid orun feirç;
Bid lwth çwannawg; (*d*) bid ryngawg cleirç.

Bid anhygar diriaid, bid fêr pob ewaint;
Bid henaint i dylodedd;
Bid addvwyn yn ancwyn medd.

(*a*) *Ll. arall.* Bid çwyrniad colwyn, bid wenwyn gwraç,
　　　　　　　Bid cwynfan claf, bid lawen iaç.
(*b*) *Ll. Coç.* Bit gravangauc iar bit trydar leu.
(*c*) *Ll. arall.* Bid oval ar ei car.
(*d*) *Ll. Coç.* Bit lyth chuannauc.

Let the furrow be wet; let bail be frequent;
The fick be complaining, the one in health be merry;
Let the lap-dog fnarl, the old woman let her be peevifh.

Let the hurt cry out, an army be it moving;
Let the well-fed be wanton;
Let the ftrong be bold; and let the hill be flippery.

Let the gull be white, let the wave be loud;
Let the gore be aptly clotted on the afhen fpear;
Let the ice be grey; the heart be bold.

Let the camp be green; let the talkative be reproachlefs;
Let there be pufhing of fpears in the conflict;
The wicked woman let her be with frequent reproaches.

With the hen let there be cackling, let the lion roar;
Let the foolifh be quarrelfome;
Let the heart affailed with grief be broken.

Let beauty be defired by many;
Let the tower be white, let harnefs clatter;
Let the glutton hanker; let the clergy be interceding.

Let the mifchievous be unlovely, youths be they ftrong;
Let old age attend poverty;
In the banquet let the mead be delicious.

Bid çwyrniad colwyn, bid wenwyn neidyr;
Bid noviaw rhyd wrth beleidyr;
Nid gwell yr otwr no'r lleidyr.

Bid gwyrdd gweilgi, bid gorawen tòn;
Bid cwyn pob galarus;
Bid avlawen hen heinus.

. A fnarler let the lap-dog be, and the adder poifonous ;
In paffing a ford with fpears, let there be fwimming ;
The adulterer is not better than the thief.

Let the fea be green, the wave be it with clamour flowing ;
Every one oppreffed with grief let him complain ;
Penfive be the old afflicted with pain.

I'R GÔG, YN ABER CUAWG.

GOREISTE ar vryn, aerwyn vy mryd, (a)
A hevyd ni'm cyçwyn :
Byr vy nhaith, difaith vy nhyddyn !

Llem awel, llwm beŋyd er byw, (b)
Pan orwiſg coed telyw hav ; (c)
Terydd glav wyv heddyw ! (d)

Nid wyv enhued, miled ni çadwav ; (e)
Ni allav ddarymred !—
Tra vo da gan Gôg, caned !

Côg lavar a gân gan ddydd,
Cyvreu ciçiawg yn nolydd Cuawg : (f)
" Gwell còrawg na çybydd."

Yn Aber Cuawg yd ganant Gogau,
Ar gangau blodeuawg ;
Gwae glav, a'u clyw yn voddawg !

Yn Aber Cuawg Côgau a gonant ;
Ys advant gan vy mrŷd ; (g)
A'u cygleu na's clwyv hevyd ! (h)

(a) Neu, Goreiſle (goreiſti) ar vryn, aervryn vym bryt.
(b) Neu, Llem auel llum benedyr hyu.
(c) Neu, Par oruiſe coed telyu haf.
(d) Neu, Ceryd glaf uyf hedyu.
(e) Neu, Neud wyf anhyed milet ny chaduaf.
(f) Ll. Du. Cyfra eichiawg yn molydd tuawg.
(g) Neu, Ys adwant (atvant) gan fy mryd.
(h) Neu, Na's clyw hefyd.

TO THE CUCKOO,

IN THE

VALE OF CUAWG, (a)

SITTING to reſt on a hill, cruelly inclined is my mind,
And yet it doth not impel me onward;
Short is my journey, and my dwelling wretched!

Sharply blows the gale, it is bare puniſhment to live,
When the trees array themſelves in their ſummer finery;
Violent is my pain this day!

I am no follower of the chace, I keep no hound;
I cannot move myſelf about!——
As long as it ſeemeth good to the cuckoo, let her ſing!

The loud-voiced cuckoo ſings with the dawn,
Her melodious notes in the dales of *Cuawg*:
" Better the liberal than the miſer." (b)

By the waters of *Cuawg* the cuckoos ſing,
On the bloſſom-covered branches;
Woe to the ſick, that hears their contented notes!

By the waters of *Cuawg* cuckoos are ſinging;
To my mind grating is the ſound;
Oh, may others that hear not ſicken like me!

(a) Some have aſcribed this poem to a *Mabclev ab Llywarç*; who is ſaid to have flouriſhed towards the end of the fourteenth century. But the *Llyvyr Du o Gaervyrddin*, one of the MSS. wherewith it is collated is full as old as that period; and yet in that we ſee it had then ſuffered much by time. *Mabclev* might be an epithet aſſumed by *Llywarç*; and it implies—*Sick for a ſon*.

(b) It ſeems that this proverb is to be conſidered as the ſong of the cuckoo.

Neu's endewais i Gôg, (a) ar eiddiorwg bren,
Neu'r laeſwys vy nghylçwy ;
Edlid a gerais, a gerais neud mwy ! (b)

Yn y van odduwç llon dâr,
Ydd endewais i lais adar: (c)
Côg vàn, côv gan bawb à gâr !

Cethlydd cathyl-voddawg, hiraethawg ei llev,
Taith oddev, tuth hebawg,
Cog vreuer (d) yn Aber Cuawg!

Gorddyar adar gwlydd naint, (e)
Llewyçyd lloer, oer dewaint,
Çrau vy mryd rhag govyd hainð !

Gwyn gwarthav naint, dewaint hir—
Ceinmygir pob cywraint :
Dylȳwn pwyth hun i henaint ! (f)

Gorddyar adar, gwlyb gro,
Dail cwyddid, divryd divro ;
Ni wadav, wyv clâv heno !

Gorddyar adar gwlyb traeth,
Eglur nwyvre, ehelaeth tòn ;
Gwyw calon rhag hiraeth !

(a) Neu, Neus edeueis i Gog.
(b) Neu, Edlit a gereis neut muy.
(c) Neu, Yr endeueis (edeueis) y leis adar.
(d) Neu, Cog vrever.
(e) Neu, Gulyt veint ; neu, gwld neint.
(f) Neu, Dyluyn (dylynn) puyth hun i heint.

Have I not liftened to the cuckoo, on the tree encircled with ivy?
And did it not caufe me to hang down my fhield?
But hateful is what I loved! if I loved, hence fhall it ceafe!

On a hill that overlooked the merry oak,
I have liftened to the fong of birds—
The loud cuckoo, that is in every lover's thoughts!

Sweet fongftrefs with her fong of content, her voice creates longing;
She is fated to wander;—like the hawk fcuds
The loud cuckoo by the waters of *Cuawg!*

The birds are clamorous, humid are the hollow glens;
Let the moon refleft her light! cold is the midnight hour;
Outrageous is my mind from the torment of diforder.

Illuminated is the top of the cliff, in the tedious midnight—
Every ingenious merit is honourably rewarded: (a)
I deferve a little indulgence of fleep to old age!

The birds are clamorous, the beach is wet;
Let the leaves fall, the exile is unconcerned;
I will not conceal it, I am fick this night!

The birds are clamorous, the ftrand is wet,
Clear is the welkin, high fwells the wave:
The heart is palfied with longing!

(a) This is a common proverb; and is introduced here without conneftion; probably with a view
to fhew difarrangement of thoughts, arifing from a delirium.

Gorddyar adar gwlyb traeth.
Eglur tòn, taith ehelaeth: (*a*)
A grëad yn mabolaeth,
Carwn, pei cafwn etwaeth ! (*b*)

Gorddyar adar ar edrywedd, (*c*)
Bàn llev cwn yn nifaith ;
Gorddyar adar eilwaith.

Cyntevin cain pob amhad ! (*d*)
Pan vryfiant cedwyr i gâd,
Mi nid av, anav ni'm gad !

Cyntevin, cain ar yftre,
Pan vrŷs cedwyr i gadle ; (*e*)
Mi nid av, anav a'm de ! (*f*)

Llwyd gwarthav mynydd, brau blaen ôri,
O ebyr dyhepgyr tòn
Pevyr, pell çwerthin o'm calon !

Affymi heddyw pen y mis,
Yn y weftva ydd edewis :
Crau vy mryd, (*g*) cryd a'm dewis !

(*a*) Neu, Tuth ehelaeth.
(*b*) Mae y braiç hwn yn gyntav o'r pennill caniynawl,
     Yn y Llyvyr Du.
(*c*) Neu, Gordyar adar orredryuaed.
     Neu, Gorddyar adar ar edrywiardd ban.
(*d*) Neu, cein pub amat.
(*e*) Neu, Pan vryt ketuyr y gadle.
(*f*) Neu, Nidaaf anaf am edy.
     Neu, Ni nad af anaf amdde.
(*g*) *Ll. Du.* Crei vymb, t.

The birds are clamorous, the ftrand is wet ;
Bright is the wave, taking its ample range :
That was formed for my youth,
I could love, if again on me beftowed ! (a)

Clamorous are the birds on the fcent of the prey,
Loud is the cry of the dogs in the defert ;
Again clamorous are the birds.

When the harbinger of fummer comes every varied feed is gay,
When the warriors haften to the conflict,
I do not go, infirmity prevents me !

When the fummer comes, glorious, on the impatient fteeds
Seem the warriors, when haftening to the field of battle ;
I fhall not go, infirmity keeps me back !

Grey is the mountain's brow, the tops of the afh are brittle ;
The difembogueing waters impel the fair wave onward ;
Far is laughter from my poor heart !

Ah ! what a lot is mine this day, but a month is paft
Since the focial feaft I left ;
Diftracted is my mind—a fever preys upon me !

(a) This paffage is dark in the original ; but it feems to imply that, if he could be again
changed to youth, it would be a pleafure, notwithftanding all the misfortunes and viciffitudes he
had experienced in the world.

Amlwg golwg gwyliadur,
Gwnelyd fyberwyd fegur:
Crau vy mryd, (a) clevyd a'm cûr!

Alav, yn ail mail am vedd,
Nid eiddun dedwydd dyhedd; (b)
Amaerwy adnabod amynedd.

Alav, yn ail mail am lâd,
Llithredawr llyry, llon cawad,
A dwvyn ryd; berwyd bryd brâd!

Berwyd brâd anvad ober: (c)
Byddant dolur pan burer,
Gwerthu byçod er llawer.

Berwitor brâd yr anwir; (d)
Pan varno Dovydd, dydd hir,
Tywyll vydd gau, golau gwir.

Perygyl yn burthiad cyrçyniad cewig;
Llawen gwyr odduwç llâd;
Crin calav, alav yn eiliad. (e)

(a) Ll. Du. Crei vymbryt.
(b) Ll. Du. Nyt eidun detuyd dyhed.
(c). Neu, Berwyd brad anfad o ber.
(d) Ll. Du. a'r Ll. Coç. Preator preemir pan varno dovyd dyd hir
              Tyuyll vyd geu goleu guir.
(e) Ll. Du. Perygyl yn dirthivat (dirthinat) kyrchynyat Kewic.
    Ll. Coç. Cerygyl yn dirthiwad Cyrchyfiad Cewig.
(f) Ll. Du. Llauen guyr o dy uet llat
              Crin calav alav yn deilyat.

TO THE CUCKOO, IN THE VALE OF CUAWG.

Quick is the fight of the centinel;
Let the idle perform acts of complacency;
Diftracted is my mind, I am confumed by ficknefs!

Riches, like a bowl encircling mead, (*a*)
The contented man of peace will not covet:
Perfeverance is the key to knowledge.

Riches, like a bowl that encircles the cheering beverage,
Glides away, like the fnake, the refrefhing fhower,
Or deceives like the deep ford: it ftirs the mind to treachery!

Treachery ferments every evil deed,
That will be torture, when the time of purifying comes;
It is felling a little for much.

Let the wicked be fomenting treachery; (*b*)
But on that great day, when the Renovator fhall judge,
Falfhood will be darker ftill, and truth illuminated.

Danger chaces thofe who are on their career with chains for captives,
Joyous are men over the beverage;
Frail is the reed, of riches a meet emblem.

(*a*) The fenfe of this and the following ftanza, as it is rendered here, depends upon the way
the tranflator has punctuated the originals; but they might be pointed to mean very differently,
their conftruction being equivocal.
(*b*) The original of this line is very obfcure from the blunders of tranfcribers; and the fame may
be faid of the firft line of the next ftanza.

F

Cygleu dòn drom ei tholo, vàn, (*a*)
Yrhwng graian a gro : (*b*)
Crau vy mryd rhag lledvryd heno !

Ofglawg blaen derw, çwerw çẃaith òn, (*c*)
Çweg evwr çwerthiñiad tòn ;
Ni çel grudd gyftudd calon !

Ymwng uçenaid a ddywaid arnav, (*d*)
Yn ol vy ngorddyvnaid,
Ni âd Duw dda i ddiriaid ! (*e*)

Da i ddiriaid ni ater, (*f*)
Namyn triftyd a phryder : (*g*)
Ni adwna Duw ar à wnêl.

Oedd macwy mabclav, oedd goelin (*b*)
Gyvran yn llys brenin ;
Poed gwyl Duw wrth y dewin ! (*i*)

O'r a wneler, deryw ; (*k*)
Yftyried ar a'i derlly, (*l*)
Câs dyn yman yw câs Duw vry.

(*a*) *Ll. Coç.* Cigleu don drom ith olo fau
(*b*) *Ll. Coç.* Rhwng gran a gro.
(*c*) *Ll. Coç.* Ofglod blaen derw chwerw chwerw chweith ona.
(*d*) Neu, A dyvet arnav ; neu, A dyfeiad heno.
(*e*) Neu, Da y diryet ; neu, y da i diried.
(*f*) *Ll. Du.* Da y diryet nyatter.
     Ll. Coç. Dau ddiricid ny atter.
(*g*) *Ll. Coç.* Namyn triftyd a phrudder.
(*b*) *Ll. Coç.* Oedd macwy Mabclav oedd goein gyfran.
     Ll. Du. Oed gein gyfion ; neu, oed goewin gyfion.
(*i*) *Ll. Du.* Poed guyl Dyu urth edein.
(*k*) *Ll. Du.* Or a uneler yn derut.
(*l*) *Ll. Du.* Yftyryeit yr aç derlly.

Hear the heavy-falling wave, how loud,
Amidft the gravel and the ftony beach!
My mind burns with delirious rage this night!

Branching is the top of the oak, bitter the tafte of the afh,
Sweet the fheltering hedge, the wave is bluftering:
The cheek will not conceal the trouble of the heart! (a)

The heaving figh tells of me,
After all my craving defires,
That God will not fuffer the mifchievous to enjoy wealth.

To the mifchievous wealth will not be given,
But forrow and anxiety:
Whatever God hath done, he will not reverfe. (b)

The fon of ficknefs (c) has been a brifk youth, he had the lot
Of fharing in a king's court;
May he fee God when he is going hence!

Of what is doing, it is now concluded,
Let him that reads it confider,
That what is detefted here by man is detefted by God above.

(a) This proverb is prettily given in *Englynion y Clywaid*, by a bard of the tenth century:

A glyweifti a gânt Avaön,
Vab Taliefin, gerdd gyvion:
Ni çêl grudd cyftudd calon.

Didft thou hear how Avaön fang,
The fon of *Taliefin*, whofe mufe was juft:
The countenance cannot conceal the forrow of the heart.

(b) *Davydd ab Gwilym*, a bard who flourifhed in the latter part of the fourteenth century, (an edition of whofe works were lately printed in *London*,) hath paraphrafed this, in his elegant poem to *Dwynwen*—

Nid adwna, da ei dangnev,
Duw a wnaeth, nid ai o nêv.

(c) *The fon of ficknefs.* There is a doubt, whether this is an epithet for the bard, or a proper name; it has been taken for the latter. The original, if written a compound word is *Mabglav*; or, *fick for a fon*; if uncompounded; as *Mab clav*, it implies the fick fon, fick man; or, the man of ficknefs. According to fome manufcripts, *Llywarg* had a fon called *Mab Clav*; but perhaps it is making the epithet a proper name by miftake.

YNGLYNION.

GNAWD gwynt o'r deheu; gnawd adneu yn llari;
Gnawd gwr gwan godeneu:
Gnawd i ddyn ovyn çwedlau;

Gnawd gwynt o'r Dwyrain; gnawd dyn bronrain balç;
Gnawd mwyalç ynmhlith drain;
Gnawd rhag traha tra llevain;
Gnawd yn ngwig gael cig o vrain.

Gnawd gwynt o'r Gogledd; gnawd rhianedd çweg,
Gnawd gwr teg yn Ngwynedd;
Gnawd i deyrn arlwy gwledd;
Gnawd gwedy llŷn lledvrydedd.

Gnawd gwynt o'r Môr; gnawd dygyvor llanw;
Gnawd i vanw vagu hôr;
Gnawd i voç turiaw cylor.

Gnawd gwynt o'r Mynydd; gnawd merydd yn mro;
Gnawd gael tô yn ngweunydd;
Gnawd dail, a gwyail, a gwydd.

Gnawd nyth Eryr yn mlaen dâr,
Ac yn nghyvyrdy gwyr llaçar;
Golwg vynud ar a gâr.

Gnawd dydd a thanllwyth yn nghynllaith gauav,
Cynreinion cynrwyddiaith;
Gnawd aelwyd ddifydd yn ddifaith.

PROVERBIAL VERSES. (a)

WIND comes from the fouth; the church-yard is a receiver of
The weakling will be flender: [pledges ;
A man is ufed to enquire after news.

Winds from the eaft ; proud is the man that fwells out his breaft ;
The thrufh is accuftomed to be among the thorns ;
Againft oppreffion there will be an outcry ;
The crows are ufed to find a carrion in the corner of the park.

Wind comes from the north ; young damfels are lovely,
In *Gwynedd* a comely man may be feen ;
A prince is accuftomed to provide a feaft ;
After drink derangement of the fenfes is ufual.

Wind comes from the fea ; the high tide will overflow ;
The fow is ufed to breed vermine,
The fwine are ufed to turn the ground for their nuts.

Wind comes from the mountain, the vale abounds with ftagnant pools,
In the marfhes it is ufual to find thatch ;
There will be leaves, tender fhoots, and trees.

In the top of the oak there will be an eagle's neft ;
And in the alehoufe intemperate loquacious men ;
The eye will glance upon the one it loves.

When winter begins to pour its moifture, a roufing fire is ufual,
With the eloquent men of fpears ;
The hearth of the faithlefs will be made a defert.

(a) Some MSS. attribute thefe to *Llywarç*; fuppofing that he did arrange the proverbs into ftanzas, for the more eafy retaining in memory, it is for that only any merit is due to him; as the maxims were feparately known time immemorial.

MARWNAD CYNDDYLAN AB CYNDRWYN.

SEVWC allan vorwynion, a fyllwç werydre Gynddylan;
Llys Pengwern neud tandde?
Gwàe ieuainc à eiddynt brodre! (a)

Un pren â gwyddvid arno, (b)
O dianc ys odid: (c)
A vỳno Duw dervid !(d)

Cynddylan calon iaën gauav,
A wânt Twrç trwy ei ben, (e)
Ti a roddaift cwrwv Tren. (f)

Cynddylan calon goddaith wanwyn,
O gyvlwyn am gyviaith, (g)
Yn amwyn Tren, trev ddifaith.

Cynddylan bevyr-boft cywlad, (b)
Cadwynawg cyndyniawg câd, (i)
Amyfgai Tren, (k) trev ei dâd.

(a) Ll. Du. Gwae ieuanc a eiddyn brodyrdde (neu, brodyrde.)
(b) Neu, Unpren a govit arnau.
(c) Neu, O diemic yr odit.
(d) Neu, Ac a fynno Duw derffid.
(e) Neu, A unant turch truy y benn.
(f) Neu, Cu (tw) a rodeift curuf (twrwf) Trena,
(g) Neu, O gyfly yn amgyfieith.
(b) Neu, bwyiboft kyulat.
(i) Neu, Cildynnauc eat.
(k) Neu, A myfcei (myfce) tren; neu, A muefei Tren.

ELEGY ON CYNDDYLAN AB CYNDRWYN.

STAND out ye virgins, and behold the habitation of *Cynddylan* ;
The royal palace of *Pengwern* (*a*) is it not in flames ?
Woe to the young ones that long to enter into focial ties !

One tree, around which the twining woodbine clafps,
Shall perchance efcape ;
But what God wills let that be done !

Cynddylan, thy hearfis like the ice of winter,
Thou wert pierced by *Twrç* through the head:
Thou haft given the ale of *Tren !* (*b*)

Cynddylan, thy heart was like fire confuming heath in fpring ;
In embracing the fociety of thy countrymen,
And in defending *Tren*, now a town laid wafte !

Cynddylan, the glorious pillar of his country,
The obftinate toiler in the conflict that wore the chain, (*c*)
The defender of *Tren*, the patrimony of his fire.

(*a*) Or the *head of the meadow* ; now Shrewfbury. The fcene of this whole poem lies in the neighbourhood.

(*b*) *Tren*, the name of a town, and alfo a river: it might be *Trent* in *Staffordshire*; but more likely *Tern*, in *Shropshire*. This *Tren* was the property of *Cyndrwyn*, the father of *Cynddylan*.

(*c*) *Cadwynawg* and *Eurdorçawg* are fynonymous; that is, wearing a chain, or, wearing a golden torquois; which was the badge of honour of an ancient Britifh warrior.

Cynddylan vyvyr-bwyll o vri, (a)
Cadwynawg, cyndyniawg llu,
A myfgai (b) Tren hyd tra vu !

Cynddylan calon milgi,
Pan ddifgynai yn nghymhelri câd,
Celanedd a laddai.

Cynddylan calon hebawg,
Buddai'r enwir cynddeiriawg, (c)
Cenau Cyndrwyn cyndyniawg.

Cynddylan calon gwyth-hwç; (d)
Pan ddifgynai yn mhriv-lwç câd, (e)
Celanedd yn ddeu-drwç.

Cynddylan gulhwç gynniviad llew
Blaidd ddylyn ddifgyniad; (f)
Nid adver Twrç trev ei dâd.

Cynddylan, hyd tra attad
Ydd adai ei galon mor wylad,
Gantaw, mal y twrwv i gâd. (h)

(a) *Ll. Du.* Cynddylan vyvyrbwyll (bevyrbwyll) off ri (ry.)
(b) Neu, A mufcei; neu, a mycfei.
(c) Neu, Buddair, (neu, Bu talr) enwir cynddeiriawg.
(d) Neu, Cyndylan callon guythhuch.
(e) Neu, Priffwch cad.
(f) Neu, llei (blai) dilyn dis gynnyat.
(g) Neu, Mal y guruf y gat.

Cynddylan, eminent for fagacity of thought,
Wearing the chain of honour, (*a*) foremoft in the hoft,
The protector of *Tren*, whilft he lived.

Cynddylan, with the heart of a greyhound,
When he defcended into the mutual conflict of battle,
A carnage he would make.

Cynddylan, with a heart like a hawk,
In the caufe of truth obftinately-outrageous he would be :
The cub of *Cyndrwyn*, the ftubborn one.

Cynddylan, with the heart of a wild boar ;
When he defcended into the commencing tumult of battle,
There was carnage heaped on carnage.

Cynddylan, the hungry boar, a depredator as a lion bold,
Or like the wolf tracing the fallen carcafe ;
Twrf will not reftore the patrimony of his fire.

Cynddylan, whilft towards thee he
Beftowed his heart, how warm the affection
He had ; but like the ftorm in the battle.

(*a*) *Aneurin*, in his *Gododin*, celebrates feveral heroes, who were in the battle of *Cattraeth*, that
wore the golden chain:

> Gwyr a gryfiafant, buant gydnaid,
> Hoedylvyrion meddwon uç medd hidlaid ;
> Gofgordd Vynyddawg eurawg yn rhaid,
> Gwerth eu gwledd o vedd vu eu henaid !

Heroes armed with fpeed and leapt together onward,
Short were their lives, drunk with fweet mead diftill'd ;
The men of *Mynyddawg*, who in the conflict wore the golden badge,
The price of their caroufal over mead were their fouls.

Cynddylan Powys borfor wyç yt,
Cell efbyd bywyd ior ; (a)
Cenau Cyndrwyn cwynitor !

Cynddylan wyn vab Cyndrwyn,
Ni mâd wifg baryv am ei drwyn, (b)
Gwr ni bu gwell no morwyn. (c)

Cynddylan, cymmwyad wyt, (d)
Ar meithyd na veddyliwyd, (e)
Am drebull tull dy yfgwyd. (f)

Cynddylan, cae di y rhiw,
Er yddaw Lloegyrwys heddiw : (g)
Amgeledd am un nid gwiw ! (h)

Cynddylan, cae di y nen, (i)
Yn i ddaw (k) Lloegyrwys drwy Dren :
Ni elwir coed o un-pren. (l)

Gan vy nghalon i mor dru,
Cyffylltu yftyllod du,
Gwyn-gnawd Cynddylan cynran canllu ! (m)

(a) Neu, Cell a byt bywyt jor.
(b) Neu, Fy mad-wifc baraf am ei drwyn.
(c) Neu, Gwr ny les gwell no morwyn.
(d) Neu, Cymoyt (cynwuyt) wyt.
(e) Neu, Ar meithyd na vedylyuyt (bydylwyt.)
(f) Neu, Am drebwll twll dy yfgwyt.
(g) Neu, Yr ydau (yng ddaw) Lloegrwys heddiw.
(h) Neu, Nid ýw gwiw ; neu, nid iw ; neu, nydiu.
(i) Neu, Cae di dy nenn.
(k) Neu, Yng ddaw ; neu, yn y dau.
(l) L'. Du. Ny elvir coel o unpren.
(m) Neu, Cyngran canllu.

Cynddylan, the fplendid purple of *Powys* to thee belonged,
The retreat of ftrangers was the life of my lord—
The warlike fon of *Cyndrwyn* for thee my moaning !

Cynddylan, thou comely fon of *Cyndrwyn*,
It is not proper that a beard fhould be worn round the nofe,
By a man who has been no better than a maid.

Cynddylan, thou wert a fierce antagonift,
Thou wouldeft perform feats till then unthought of,
Around the fcope of the fhelter of thy fhield.

Cynddylan, guard thou the cliff, (a)
Againft any *Lloegyrians* (b) that may come this day ;
Concern for one fhould not avail !

Cynddylan, guard thou the height,
Until the *Lloegyrians* come through *Tren :*
One tree cannot be called a wood.

My heart how it throbs with mifery,
That the black boards fhould be joined, to inclofe
The fair flefh of *Cynddylan*, the foremoft in a hundred hofts !

(a) The *Rbiw*, or *Cliff*, may be the name of a place ; though the contrary fenfe feems moft
probable to be right here, when the next ftanza is taken into confideration, where it is expreffed
in another word.

(b) *Lloegyrians*, the people of *Lloegyr*. The fouth part of *England*, bounded by the *Severn*
and the *Humber*, exclufive of *Cornwall*, was the ancient *Lloegyr* ; but there is reafon to conclude
that the name was once confined to a ftill leffer extent of country ; or fo much of the fouthern
coaft as the *Belgic Gauls* poffeffed ; who did not coalefce in the *Cymry*, and there was a confiderable difference in their dialects. But *Lloegyr* now implies *England* in general.

Yſtavell Cynddylan ys tywyll heno,
Heb dân, heb wely—
Wylav dro, tawav wedy!

Yſlavell Cynddylan ys tywyll heno,
Heb dân, heb ganwyll—
Namyn Duw, pwy a'm dyry pwyll!

Yſtavell Cynddylan ys tywyll heno,
Heb dân, heb oleuad—
Elid amdaw am danad!

Yſtavell Cynddylan ys tywyll ei nen,
Gwedy gwên gyweithydd—
Gwae ni wna da a'i dywydd! (*a*)

Yſtavell Cynddylan neud aethwyd heb wedd, (*b*)
Mae yn medd dy yſgwyd; (*c*)
Hyd tra vu, ni bu doll glwyd!

Yſtavell Cynddylan ys digariad heno
Gwedy 'r neb pieuvad— (*d*)
Wi! o angau, byr a'm gad! (*e*)

Yſtavell Cynddylan nid eſmwyth heno, (*f*)
Ar ben Careg Hydwyth, (*g*)
Heb nêr, heb niver, heb ammwyth!

(*a*) Neu, Ae dyvyd; neu, Ae dywydd,
(*b*) Neu, Aethuyt heb ued.
(*c*) Neu, Mae ym bed dy yſcuyt (aſcwyt.)
(*d*) Neu, Guedy'r neb pieu vat.
(*e*) Neu, Owi a angeu byr im gad; neu, Wi a agheu byr am gat.
(*f*) Neu, Neud eiſinwydd heno.
(*g*) Neu, Carreg hydwydd (hytuyth.)

The hall of *Cynddylan* is gloomy this night,
Without fire, without bed—
I muſt wheep awhile, and then be ſilent !

The hall of *Cynddylan* is gloomy this night,
Without fire, without candle—
Except God doth, who will endue me with patience !

The hall of *Cynddylan* is gloomy this night,
Without fire, without being lighted—
Be thou encircled with ſpreading ſilence !

The hall of *Cynddylan*, gloomy ſeems its roof,
Since the ſweet ſmile of humanity is no more—
Woe to him that ſaw it, if he negleȼts to do good !

The hall of *Cynddylan*, art thou not bereft of thy appearance,
Thy ſhield is in the grave ;
Whilſt he lived, there was no broken roof !

The hall of *Cynddylan* is without love this night,
Since he that owned it is no more—
Ah, Death ! it will be but a ſhort time he will leave me !

The hall of *Cynddylan* is not eaſy this night,
On the top of the rock of *Hydwyth*,
Without its lord, without company, without the circling feaſts ! (a)

(a) *Aneurin* acquaints us, in the *Gododin*, what ſort of company frequented theſe feaſts—
  Crau cynhynt cynnullynt reiawr,
  Yn gynvan, mal taran twryv aeſawr—
  Cydyvent vedd gloyw wrth liw babir ;
  Cyd vai da ei vlas ei gâs bu hir !
To the firſt onſet for blood the warriors would repair,
With fronts uplifted, harſh thunder the tumult of their ſhields—
On ſparkling mead they mutually carouſed by the light of torches ;
Though its taſte was ſweet, long was the woe it brought !

Yſtavell Cynddylan ys tywyll heno, (*a*)
Heb dân, heb gerddau—
Dygyſtudd deurudd dagrau!

Yſtavell Cynddylan ys tywyll heno;
Heb dân, heb deulu—
Hidyl mau ŷd gynu! (*b*)

Yſtavell Cynddylan a'm gwân ei gweled, (*c*)
Heb doëd, heb dân— (*d*)
Marw vy nglyw, byw my hunan! (*e*)

Yſtavell Cynddylan ys peithiawg heno; (*f*)
Gwedy cedwyr-voddawg:
Elvan, Cynddylan, Caeawg. (*g*)

Yſtavell Cynddylan ys oefgrai heno;
Gwedy y parç a'm buai;
Heb wyr, heb wragedd a'i cadwai!

Yſtavell Cynddylan ys arav heno,
Gwedy colli ei hynav—
Y mawr drugarawg Dduw, pa wnav! (*h*)

Yſtavell Cynddylan ys tywyll ei nen,
Gwedy diva o Loegyrwys, (*i*)
Cynddylan, ac Elvan Powys!

(*a*) Neu, Stavell Gynddylan yſtywyll heno.
(*b*) Neu, Hidyl ineu ytgynnu.
(*c*) *Ll. Coç.* Yſtavell Cynddylan amgen ei gweled.
(*d*) *Ll. Coç.* Heb doeth heb dan; *Ll. Du.* Heb doet heb dan.
(*e*) *Ll. Du.* Maru vyglyu byu mu hunan.
(*f*) *Ll. Coç.* Ys peithwae heno; neu, Ys peithwg heno.
(*g*) Neu, Cueawc.
(*h*) *Ll. Coç.* Y mawr-drigawe Dduw pa wnaf.
(*i*) Neu, Gwedy dyva o Loegyruys.

The hall of *Cynddylan* is gloomy this night,
Without fire, without fongs—
Tears afflict the cheeks !

The hall of *Cynddylan* is gloomy this night,
Without fire, without family—
My overflowing tears gufh out !

The hall of *Cynddylan* pierces me to fee it,
Without a covering, without fire—
My general is dead, and I alive myfelf!

The hall of *Cynddylan* is openly expofed this night, (*a*)
After being the contented refort of warriors :
Elvan, Cynddylan, and *Caeòg !*

The hall of *Cynddylan* is the feat of chill grief this night,
After the refpect I experienced ;
Without the men, without the women, who refided there !

The hall of *Cynddylan* is filent this night,
After lofing its mafter—
The great merciful God, what fhall I do !

The hall of *Cynddylan,* gloomy feems its roof,
Since the *Lloegyrians* have deftroyed
Cynddylan and *Elvan* of *Powys !*

(*a*) The word rendered EXPOSED, is PEITHIAWG, from PAITH, a being bare, naked, or in full view; fo *dyffryn paith* is a plain valley, without houfes, inclofures, or any thing to interrupt the fight. All words that are common to the *Latin* and the language of the *Cymmry,* that have fyllables terminating with CT in the former, have always TH to correfpond in the latter; hence it feems that PICT and PAITH are the fame. So *Paith* is the root of the name of the *Picts,* in *Britain;* and *Peithwy,* from *Paith,* alfo of the people of *Poictou* in *France.*

Yſtavell Cynddylan ys tywyll henô
O blant Cyndrwyn:
Cynon, a Gwion, a gwyn.

Yſtavell Cynddylan a'm erwan, pob awr,
Gwedy mawr amgynnyrddan, (a)
A welais ar dy bentan!

Eryr Eli, ban ei lev,
Llewſai gwyr llyn, (b)
Crau calon Cynddylan wyn! (c)

Eryr Eli, gorelwi heno,
Yn ngwaed gwyr gwynnovi:
Ev yn nghoed, trwm hoed i mi! (d)

Eryr Eli a glywav henô,
Creulyd yw, ni's beiddiav—
Ev yn nghoed, trwm hoed arnav!

Eryr Eli gorthrymed heno,
Dyfrynt Meiſir, mygedawg
Dir Broçvael; hir rhygodded!

Eryr Eli eçcidw myr,
Ni thraidd pyſgod yn ebyr;
Gelwid gweled o waed gwyr. (e)

(a) Ll. Du. Yſdavell Gyndylan amorwan pob awr
    Gwedy mawr anghyvran (anghyvyrdan.)
(b) Ll. Coç. Lleiſieu gwyr llyn.   Ll. Du. Guyr llyni.
(c) Ll. Du. Creu callon Kyndylan roynn.
(d) Neu, Oet y mi; neu, Arnaf ñ.
    Ll. Du. Eryr Eli gorelwi heno eu gwaed gwyr gwynnoſi
        Eſi goſt trwm hoet arnaf ymi.
(e) Ll. Du. Geluit guelet (gwelit) o waet gwyr.

The hall of *Cynddylan* is gloomy this night,
Bereaved of the fons of *Cyndrwyn*,
Cynon, and *Gwion*, and *Gwyn*.

The hall of *Cynddylan*, thou piercest me through every hour,
After all the great re-echoing clamour
That I have feen around thy hearth!

The eagle of *Eli*, (a) loud his cry,
After drinking frefh beverage,
The throbbing fluid of the heart of fair *Cynddylan!*

Eagle of *Eli*, thou doft loudly fcream to night,
In the blood of men thou doft eagerly wallow—
He is in the wood : (b) heavy is my longing!

The eagle of *Eli* I hear this night,
He is bloody, I will not dare him—
He is in the wood : heavy is my load of grief!

The eagle of *Eli*, let him opprefs this night
The valley of *Meifir*, (c) the celebrated
Land of *Brofvael*; (d) long has it been afflicted!

The eagle of *Eli* narrowly watches the feas,
The fifh dare not penetrate the inlets;
He calls that he fees the blood of men.

(a) Probably fome neighbouring crag frequented by eagles; though it might have been the name of a man.

(b) It is not clear whether the allufion is to the eagle being in the wood, or that *Cynddylan* was inclofed in a fhrine; but moft likely the latter is meant.

(c) Perhaps the extenfive fpace in which *Shrewfbury* is fituated.

(d) *Brofvael*, or *Brofwel Yfgitbrawg* prince of *Powys*, who commanded the *Britons* in the battle of *Bangor*.

G

Eryr Eli, gorymdda coed,
Cyvore ciniawva; (a)
A'i llawç llwyddid ei draha ! (b)

Eryr Pengwern, pen-garn llwyd,
Aruçel ei adlais, (c)
Eiddig am gîg à gerais ! (d)

Eryr Pengwern, pen·garn llwyd,
Aruçel ei ieuan,
Eiddig am gîg Cynddylan !

Eryr Pengwern, pen-garn llwyd,
Aruçel ei adav,
Eiddig am gîg a garav ! (e)

Eryr Pengwern pell galwawd heno, (f)
Ar waed gwyr gwylawd:
Rhy gelwir Tren trev ddifawd.

Eryr Pengwern pell gelwid heno,
Ar waed gwyr gwelid:
Rhy gelwir Tren trev letbrid.

Eglwyfau Baffa ynt faeth heno,
Y diwedd ymgynnwys, (g)
Cledyr câd, calon Argoedwys.

(a) Ll. Cof. Cyvore ciniawa.
(b) Neu, Ae llauç lluydit y draha.
(c) Neu, Aruchel y atlas (neu, addes.)
(d) Ll. Cof. Eiddig am gîg a gares.
(e) Neu, gîg Cynddylan.
(f) Neu, Pell galwant heno.
(g) Neu, Y diued ymgynnuys.

The eagle of *Eli* wanders among the woods,
Early with the dawn he takes his repaft;
May he that allures him profper in his wiles!

The eagle of *Pengwern*, with the brown beak;
Very loud is his fcream,
Jealous for the flefh of him I loved!

The eagle of *Pengwern*, with the brown beak;
Very loud is his clamour,
Jealous for the flefh of *Cynddylan!*

The eagle of *Pengwern*, with the brown beak;
Very loud is his howling,
Jealous for the flefh of him I love! (*a*)

The eagle of *Pengwern*, calling far about this night,
On the blood of men keeps watching:
Hence *Tren* fhall be called a town unfortunate.

The eagle of *Pengwern* calls far about this night,
On the blood of men he is feen:
Hence *Tren* fhall be called the flaming town.

The churches of *Baffa* (*b*) are enriched this night,
Containing the departed remains
Of the pillar of battle, the heart of the men of *Argoed.*

(*a*) This ftanza feems to be only a different reading of the preceding one, crept into the text
by miftake.

(*b*) There is no certainty of the fituation of the town called *Egluyfau Baffa*; but we may
fuppofe it was near the fcene of action. According to *Nennius*, one of *Arthur's* battles was
fought near a place of this name.

G 2

Eglwyſau Baſſa ynt faeth heno; (*a*)
Vy nhavawd a'u gwnaeth:
Rhudd ynt hwy, rhwy vy hiraeth! (*b*)

Eglwyſau Baſſa ynt wng heno, (*c*)
I etivedd Cyndrwyn:
Mablan Cynddylan wyn !

Eglwyſau Baſſa ynt dirion heno,
Ys gwaedlyd eu meillion: (*d*)
Rhudd ynt hwy, rhwy vy nghalon ! (*e*)

Eglwyſau Baſſa collaſant eu braint,
Gwedy y diva o Loegyrwys
Cynddylan, ac Elvan Powys. (*f*)

Eglwyſau Baſſa ynt ddiva heno,
Eu cedwyr ni phara ; (*g*)
Gŵyr a ŵyr, a mi yma.

Eglwyſau Baſſa ynt barwar heno, (*h*)
A minnau wyv dyar :
Rhudd hwy, rhwy vy ngalar ! (*i*)

(*a*) *Ll. Dn.* Ynt tirion heno.
(*b*) *Ll. Du.* Rud ynthwy a hwy fy hiraeth.
(*c*) Neu, Ynt yng heno y etived Cyndrwyn.
(*d*) Neu, Y gwaeth eu meillyon.
   Ll. Du. Ys gwaedly (gwaedlef) ei meillion.
(*e*) *Ll. Du.* Rhudd yn hwy rhwy fy nghalon.
   Neu, Rud ynt vy rwy vygcallon.
(*f*) Neu, Kyndyl ac Elvarn Powys.
(*g*) Neu, Y chetwyr ny phara.
(*h*) Neu, Ynt barvar heno.
(*i*) Neu, Rud vy rwy vyggalur.

The churches of *Baſſa* are enriched to night;
My tongue occaſioned it;
Red are they, my longing is extreme!

The churches of *Baſſa* afford ſpace to night,
To the progeny of *Cyndrwyn*—
The grave-houſe of fair *Cynddylan!*

The churches of *Baſſa* are gay this night,
Bloody are their trefoils;
Red are they, my heart is broken!

The churches of *Baſſa* have loſt their privilege,
Since the *Lloegyrians* (a) have deſtroyed
Cynddylan, and *Elvan* of *Powys.*

The churches of *Baſſa* are fated to periſh this night,
Their warriors will not remain;
He knows, that knoweth all, and I alſo know.

The churches of *Baſſa* are ſilent this night,
And I am clamorous—
Red are they, my ſorrow is extreme!

(a) *Lloegyrians*, ſtriƈtly ſo called, were the *Belgic* colony, before-mentioned; but at this
period we may ſuppoſe they were intermixed with other people; and that *Lloegyr*, in this paſſage
implies ſuch portion of the iſland, as was inhabited by the people ſo mixed, under the denomination of *Romanized Britons.* There is not one inſtance where the *Saxons* or *Engliſh* are called
Lloegyrians, though *England* is called *Lloegyr* to this day; but *Sacſon* is the only name given to
the *Engliſh.*

Y drev wen yn mron y coed,
Ys ev yw ei hevras eirioed,
Ar wyneb ei gwellt y gwaed. (*a*)

Y drev wen yn y tymmyr,
Ei hevras, ei glas vyvyr,
Ei gwaed a dan draed ei gwyr. (*b*)

Y drev wen yn y dyfrynt,
Llawen y byddair wrth gyvamug câd, (*c*)
Ei gwerin neu'r derynt ! (*d*)

Y drev wen rhwng Tren a Throdwydd,
Oedd gnoclaç yſgwyd tòn
Yn dyvod o gâd, nog yt ŷç yn eçwydd. (*e*)

Y drev wen rhwng Tren a Thraval,
Oedd gnoclaç y gwaed (*f*)
Ar wyneb gwellt, nog eredig braenar.

Gwyn ei vyd, Freuer, (*g*) mor yw haint
Heno, gwedy colli cevnaint ; (*h*)
O anfawd vy nhavawd yd leſaint !

(*a*) Neu, Ar uyneb y guellt y guaet.
(*b*) Neu, Y drev uen ynyt (yn yd) hymyr
      Y hevras y glas vyvyr
      Y guaet a dan draet y guyr.
(*c*) Neu, Llauen y bydeir wrth gyvamud kat.
(*d*) Neu, Y gueryn neur derynt.
(*e*) Neu, Noc yt ych y cchuyd.
(*f*) Neu, Oed gnodach y gavat; neu, Gnoch y guaet (guaet yn ar.)
(*h*) Neu, Guyn y vyt Freuer; neu, Guyn y vyt Treiry.
(*i*) Neu, Ceuncint.

The white town in the fkirt of the wood,
Of its youth from time immemorial has been
On the furface of the grafs their blood.

The white town in the cultivated plain,
Its youth, its blue fons of contemplation, (*a*)
And its blood, are under the feet of men.

The white town in the valley,
Joyful were its inmates when called to mutual aid in battle,
But its citizens are they not gone !

The white town between *Tren* and *Trodwydd*, (*b*)
More ufual in it was to fee the broken fhield,
Coming from battle, than the returning ox at eve.

The white town between *Tren* and *Traval*,
More ufed was it to have the blood
On the grafs, than to plough the fallow land.

Alas, *Freuer !* how great the anguifh
This night, after the lofing of kindred ;
By the misfortune of my tongue they were flain !

(*a*) The original has *blue contemplation* ; or as it may be exprefled, *grey-clad contemplation*. It may be fuppofed that the Bards are meant ; as the general drefs of the order was unicolour of fky-blue.

(*b*) The three rivers *Tren*, *Trodwydd*, and *Traval*, here mentioned, might enable one acquainted with the topography of Shropfhire to point out, perhaps, the fpot where the town of *Tren* ftood.

G 4

Gwyn ei vyd, Freuer, mor yw van heno,
Gwedy angau Elvan.
Ac eryr Cyndrwyn, Cynddylan!

Nid angau Freuer a'm de heno;
Am ddanmorth brodyrdde,
Dihunav, wylav vore! (a)

Nid angau Freuer a'm gwna haint;
O ddeçreu nos hyd ddewaint,
Dihunav, wylav bylgaint!

Nid angau Freuer (b) a'm tremyn heno,
A'm gwna gryd iau melyn,
A çoçau dagrau dros erçwyn!

Nid angau Freuer a ernywav heno, (c)
Namyn my hun mi wan-glav; (d)
Vy mrodyr, a'm tymmyr a gwynav!

Freuer wen, brodyr a'th vaeth,
Ni hanoeddynt o'r difaeth,
Gwyr ni vegynt vygyliaeth! (e)

Freuer wen, brodyr a'th vu,
Pan glywynt gywrenin llu
Ni eçwyddai fydd ganthu! (f)

(a) Neu, Du hunav uylav vore.
(b) Neu, Ny agheu ffreuer.
(c) Neu, Ny agheu ffreuer a ernuaf heno.
(d) Neu, Ny wanglaf.
(e) Neu, Wyr ny fegynt uygylyaeth.
(f) Neu, Ny echuydei fydd ganthu.
    Ll. Du. Ni echyfyddai fydd ganthu.

Alas, *Freuer !* how loud the moaning this night,
After the death of *Elvan,*
And the eagle of *Cyndrwyn, Cynddylan !*

It is not the death of *Freuer* that afflicts me this night;
It is the ill-fated end of focial comfort,
That breaks my fleep, and I early weep !

It is not the death of *Freuer* that fills me with pain ;
From the beginning of night till midnight,
I keep awake, and weep through the morning !

It is not the death of *Freuer,* that makes me watch to night,
That gives me the yellow jaundiced fever,
That makes the red tears flow over the bed-fide !

It is not the death of *Freuer* that torments me this night,
Nor myfelf that am feebly-fick,
But it is my brothers (*a*) and my kindred that I mourn !

Fair *Freuer,* they were brothers who cherifhed thee,
That were not defcended from a bafe origin,
They were men who did not cherifh timidity.

Fair *Freuer,* to thee there were brothers,
Who when they heard the clafhing fpears of an army,
Would not fuffer the abode of reft to ftand over them.

(*a*) It does not appear that the term *brothers,* ufed here, can mean any more than the friends, with whom the Bard had formed an intimacy; though, perhaps, he might have married *Freuer,* a daughter of *Cyndrwyn,* who feems to have been dead before the fall of her brothers in the battle of *Tren.*

Mi, a Freuer, a Medlan,
Cyd vo câd yn mhob man,
Ni'n tawr ni laddawr ein rhan. (a)

Y mynydd, cyd ad vo uwç,
Nid eiddigav, av i ddwyn vy muwç,
Er yfgawn gan rai vy rhuwç. (b)

Amhaval ar Avaerwy,
Ydd aä Tren yn y Trydonwy,
Ac ydd aä Twrç yn Marçawy. (c)

Amhaval ar Elwydden, (d)
Ydd aä Trydonwy yn Nhren,
Ac ydd aä Geirw yn Alwen. (e)

•

Cyn bu vy nghylçed groenen gavyr, (f)
Galed; çwannawg i gelen,
Rhym gorug yn veddw vedd Tren. (g)

Gwedy vy mrodyr o dymmyr Havren,
J am ddwylan Ddwyryw:
Gwae vi Dduw, vy mod yn vyw!

(a) Neu, Nyn taur ny ladaur an ran.
(b) Neu, Y mynyd kyt at vo uch
          Nyt eidigafaf y duyn vym buch
          Yr ysgaun gan rei vy ruch.
(c) Neu, Amhaval ar avaeruy
          Yd y Tren yn y Trydonuy
          Ac yd aa Turch ym marchauy.
(d) Neu, Am haul ar Eluyden (Elfydden.)
(e) Ll. Du. Geirw am Alwen.
(f) Neu, Cyn bu vyghylchet croenen (groen) gawyr.
(g) Neu, Rum goruc y wedu ved Tren.
          Ll. Du. Rym gorug yn feddw fedd brynn.

Me, and *Freuer*, and *Medlan*,
Whilft there is a battle in every place,
We are not contented, if there are not flain our fhares.

The mountain, if it fhould be ftill higher,
I will not become peevifh, but will go to take my cow,
Though light fome may deem my fhaggy cloak. (*a*)

In parallel windings with *Avaerwy*,
Doth *Tren* glide into the rough *Trydonwy*, (*b*)
And alfo the ftream of *Twrç* into *Marçawy*.

In parallel windings with *Elwyddcu*,
Doth *Trydonwy* unite with *Tren*,
So alfo flows the *Geirw* into *Alwen*. (*c*)

Before my covering was made of the hide of the goat
Of the hardy fpecies ; intent after carnage,
I have been made drunk with the mead of *Tren*.

After my brothers of the bordering dales of *Havren*, (*d*) .
I wander the banks of the *Dwyryw*—(*e*)
Woe to me, my God, that I am living !

(*a*) It would be difficult to pretend to explain this ftanza.

(*b*) Uncertain what river; but *Dyvyrdonwy* is an epithet given fometimes to the *Dee*, expreffive of its foamy waves ; and *Trydonwy* gives the fame idea ; and perhaps with the fame propriety applied to the *Severn*. If the *Severn* is not meant by that appellation, the river now called *Tern* çannot be the *Tren* mentioned here.

(*c*) The *Alwen*, or the *very foamy* water, falls into the *Dee* a little above *Corwen*.

(*d*) The *Severn*; of which *Havren* is the root, with *Yi* prefixt.

(*e*) The *Dee*.

Gwedy meirç hywedd, a çoçwedd ddillad,
A phluawr melyn,
Main vy nghoes, nid oes ym dremyn !

Gwartheg Edeyrniawn ni buant gerddenin,
A çan neb nid aethant yn myw *(a)*
Gorwyniawn, gwr o Uwçnant. *(b)*

Gwartheg Edeyrniawn ni buant gerddenin,
A çhan neb ni çerddynt,
Yn myw Gorwyniawn, gwr edvynt ! *(c)*

Edwyn warth gwarthegydd,
Gwerth gwyl a negydd; *(d)*
Ar a ddyvo dragwarth a'i deubydd.

Mi a wyddwn à oedd da,
Gwaed am eu gilydd gwrda.

Rhag gwraig Gwrthmwl byddai gwân,
Heddyw byddai ban ei dyfgyr
Hi, gyn na diva ei gwyr. *(e)*

Tywarçen Ercal ar âr dywal
Wyr, o edwedd Morial;
A gwedy Rhys mae rhyfonial. *(f)*

(a) Neu, A chant (cherdd) neb nyd aethant ym buw (byw.)
(b) Neu, Gwyr a uchuunt (q. uchnant.)
(c) Neu, Ym huyf Goruynnyaun gwr Eduyn.
(d) Neu, Gwerth gwyla negydd.
(e) Neu, Rhei gureu gyrthmul bydei guan hediw
      Bydai ban y difgyr hi gyva (*Ll. Du.* gyn na) diva y guyr.
(f) Neu, Tyuarchen ercal ar er (ar) dyual wyr.
      O etwed Moryal a guedy Rys maer y fonal.

After the fleek tractable fteeds, and garments of ruddy hue,
And the waving yellow plumes,
Slender is my leg, my piercing look is gone !

The kine of *Edcyrnion* (*a*) never were aftray,
And nobody took them away for booty, in the life-time of
Gorwynion, the hero of *Uçnant*. (*b*)

The kine of *Edcyrnion* never went aftray,
And nobody took them for booty,
In the life-time of *Gorwynion*, a man now gone from us !

The reproach is known to the herdfman,
The price is fhame and refufal ;
On fuch as come into that difgrace it will befal.

I knew of what was good,
Blood for blood amongft heroes. (*c*)

For the wife of *Gwrtbmwl* (*d*) there was piercing with fpears ;
On this day loud would have been the fcreams
Of her, as on the deftruction of her men.

The fod of *Ercal* is on the afhes of fierce
Men, of the progeny of *Morial* ; (*e*)
And after *Rhys* there is great murmuring of woe.

(*a*) A diftrict near *Bala* in *Meirien.*
(*b*) A diftrict in the upper part of *Montgomeryfbire.*
(*c*) This ftanza feems incomplete.
(*d*) *Gwrtbmwl Wledig,* a prince of the northern *Britons;* who, like *Llywarç*, was driven out
of his dominions by the *Saxons.*
(*e*) A warrior of this name is often mentioned by *Aneurin ;* and *Meugant* gives an account of the
expedition of *Morial* to *Caer Lwydgeed,* or *Lincoln;* from whence he brought a booty of 1,500
bullocks.

Heledd hwyedig ym gelwir,
O Dduw ! padyw yth roddir (*a*)
Meirç vy mro, ac eu tir !

Heledd hwyedig a'm cyveirç,
O Dduw ! padyw yth roddir gwrwm feirç;
Cynddylan ar bedwar-deg-meirç.

Neu'r fyllais olygon ar dirion dir
O orfedd Orwynion—
Hir hwyl haul, hwy vy nghovion !

Neu'r fyllais o Ddinlle Vrecon
Freuer werydre ;
Hiraeth am dammorth brodyrdde ! (*b*)

Llâs vy mrodyr ar unwaith,
Cynan, Cynddylan, Cynwraith, (*c*)
Yn amwyn Tren, trev ddifaith.

Ni fangai wehelyth ar nyth Cynddylan,
Ni theçai droedvedd fyth,
Ni vagas ei vam vab llyth.

Brodyr ambwyad ni vall,
A dyvynt val gwyail coll : (*f*)
O un i un edynt oll.

(*a*) Neu, O Duw padiv yth rodir.
(*b*) Yma canlyn y darn pennill hwn.
        Marçawg o Gaer Adnau
        Nid oedd hwyr a gwynion
        Gwr o Sanneir.
(*c*) Neu, Cynvreith.
(*f*) Neu, A dyuynt val guyall coll.

Heledd (*a*) henceforth fhall I be called,
O my God! why is it that to thee is given
The fteeds of my country, and their land?

Heledd henceforth fhall I be greeted,
O my God! why is it that to thee is given the murky harnefs
Of *Cynddylan* on forty horfes?

Have not my eyes gazed on a pleafant land,
From the confpicuous feat of *Gorwynion*? (*b*)
Long is the courfe of the fun, longer my remembrances!

Have not I gazed from the high-placed city of *Wrecon* (*c*)
On the verdant vale of *Freuer*,
With grief for the deftruction of my focial friends!

Slain were my brethren all at once,
Cynan, *Cynddylan*, and *Cynvraith*,
In defending *Tren*, a town laid wafte!

No tribe dared to intrude on the abode of *Cynddylan*,
He would never retreat the length of a foot;
His mother nurfed no weakling fon.

Brethren I have had, who were free from evil,
Who grew up like hazel faplings:—
One by one they are all departed!

(*a*) *Heledd* implies a brine, or falt pit; and it is alfo the name of feveral places; and there were women of this name; one of the daughters of *Cyndrwyn* was fo called.

(*b*) The feat, or *Gorfedd*, of *Gorwynion*, the court of juftice of *Gorwynion*. The *Britons* held their courts on an eminence in the open air; and anciently within a circle of ftones.

(*c*) The *Uriconium* of the *Romans*, now *Wroxeter* in *Shropfhire*. Here was lately found an infcription on the tomb of an officer of the *Legio vicef. victrix*. The *Caer Wrygion* in the catalogues of *Bifhop Ufher* and *Dr. T. Williams*, feems to have been the fame; and it is probable that the *Caer Gorgorn* in the *Triads*, and the *Caer Guirigion* of *Nennius* were alfo the fame.

Brodyr ambwyad a ddug Duw rhagov ;
Vy anfawd ai gorug ;
Ni obrynynt faw èr fug ! (a)

Teneu awel, tew ledcynt,
Peraidd y rhyçau, ni pharad a'u goteu ; (b)
Ar a vu nad ydynt ! (c)

As clywo a Duw a dyn,
As clywo ieuanc a hyn ;
Mevyl barvau maddeu hedyn, (d)

Yn myw ehedyn ehediai, (e)
Dillad yn araws gwaed vai,
Ar glas verau nav nwyvai.

Rhyveddav dinclair nad yw, (f)
Yn ol eilydd celwydd clyw,
Yn ngwall Twrç tòri cnau cnyw.

Ni vu niwl ai mwg, (g)
Ai cedwyr yn cyvamwg ;
Yn ngweirglawdd aer yſſydd ddrwg.

(a) Neu, Ny o brynynt ffaw er ffug.
(b) Neu, Ny pharat ac goreu.
(c) Neu, Ara vu nat ydynt.
(d) Neu, Madeu hed yn.
(e) Neu, Ym byw ehedyn ehedyei.
(f) Neu, Dincleir nadiv.
(g) Neu, Ny vu nuil ae mwc.

Brethren I have had whom God hath taken from me;
My misfortune was the caufe—
They would not purchafe fame through deceit!

Tbin is the gale, thickly fly tales of mifery;
Sweet are thofe ridges, but thofe that made them do not remain;
Thofe who have been, woe to me that now they are not!

When God feparates from man,
When the young feparates from the old,
Difgrace of beards (a) forgive to the flyer.

Whilft he lives the winged animal will fly;
Garments in waiting for the bloody field,
And the blue blades, had the vigorous chief.

I wonder that he is not the loweft rambling minftrel,
After being a mufician of palpable lies—
When in want *Twrf* cracks the earth-nuts.

What has not been mift will go in fmoke;
Warriors will repair to give mutual defence;
In a meadow a flaughter is bad.

(a) **Mevyl baryv,** or difgrace of the beard, was a heinous crime, but of what nature has not been exprefsly defined: It feems to imply cuckoldom. There were three crimes, for which the *Welfh Laws* impowered a hufband to beftow a limited perfonal caftigation on his wife; and one was—*An mvow mevyl ar ei varyv*; or, *for wifhing difgrace on his beard.*

H

Endewais o weirglawdd aer yſgwyd; (a)
Digyvyng dinas i gedyrn— (b)
Goreu gwr Garanmael.

Caranmael cymmwy arnad,
Alwen dy yſtle o gâd:
Gnawd mân ar rán cynniviad.

Cynniv oedd ognaw llaw hael, (c)
Mab Cynddylan, clod avael ;
L yweddwr Cyndrwynin, Caranmael !

Caranmael oedd dihaidd,
Ac oedd deholedig trev tâd,
A geiſwys Caranmael yn ynad. (d)

Caranmael cymmwyedd ognaw, (e)
Mab Cynddylan clod arllaw,
Nid ynad cymmynad o honaw. (f)

Pan wiſgai Garanmael gadbais Cynddylan
A pheryrddiaw ei ònen, (g)
Ni çafai Franc tanc o'i ben. (h)

(a) Neu, Edeueis y veirglaud aer yſguyt.
    Ll. Du. Edeweis i weirgledd æ yſgwyd.
(b) Neu, Digyvynd dinas y Gedyrn.
(c) Neu, Kynnivoed o gnaf llav hael.
(d) Neu, Oed diheid aç oed diholedic
       Trev tat a geiſſyuys
       Karanmael yn gat.
(e) Neu, Cymwed ognaw.
(f) Neu, Nyt ynat kyt mynat ohonau.
(g) Neu, A phyryrdyau y onneu.
(h) Neu, Tranc œ ben.

I liftened from the meadow to the clattering of fhields;
A city is no reftraint to the mighty ones—
The beft of men was *Caranmael.*

Caranmael, when thou art on all fides preft,
Alwen is thy place of reft from battle—
It is ufual for a toiling warrior to have a mark on his brow.

Torment was the grafp of the generous hand
Of the fon of *Cynddylan,* that keeps faft hold of fame—
The laft man of the line of *Cyndrwyn* is *Caranmael!*

Caranmael was without claim;
And the patrimony was fequeftered,
That *Caranmael* attempted to enjoy by being a judge.

Caranmael with the afflicting grafp,
The fon of *Cynddylan,* on fame's upper hand,
His ftroke was not that of a judge. (*a*)

When *Caranmael* put on the corflet of *Cynddylan,*
And lifted up and fhook his afhen fpear,
From his mouth the *Frank (b)* would not get the word of peace.

(*a*) It feems he was a better warrior than a judge.
(*b*) How is this paffage to be cleared up, where he calls the enemy a *Frank?* Did the *Franks* emigrate with the *Saxons,* in fuch numbers, as to caufe the introduction of their name into this ifland, as a feparate body of people?

Amſer y bum i vras vwyd,
Ni ddyrçavwn vy morddwyd
Er gwr à gwynai clav gornwyd. (a)

Brodyr ambwyad innau,
Ni's cwynai glevyd cornwydau :
Un Elvan, Cynddylan dau.

Ni mâd wiſg briger nyw dirper awr,
O wr yn nirvawr gyvryſedd ;
Nid oedd levawr vy mroder. (b)

Onid rhag angau a'i aelau mawr,
A gloes glâs verau,
Ni byddav levawr innau. (c)

Maes Maoddyn neu's cudd rhew,
O ddiva da ei oddew : (d)
Ar vedd Eirinwedd eiry tew !

Tom Elwyddan neu's gwlyç gwlaw ; (e) .
Mae Maoddyn y danaw !
Dyn vai Gynon i'w gwynaw. (f)

Pedwar pwn broder a'm bu,
Ac i bob un penteulu ;
Ni wyr Tren berçen iddi. (g)

(a) Neu, Yr gur a guyneu klav gomuyt.
(b) Neu, Ny mat uiſc briger nyu dirper aur.
    Our yn dirvaur gyuryſſed
    Nyt oed leuaur vymbroder.
(c) Neu, Ny bydaf leuawr inneu.
(d) Neu, O diva da y oleu.
(e) Neu, Tom Eluithan neus gulych glau.
(f) Neu, Dyn yei Gynon y guynau.
(g) Neu, Ny uyr Tren berchen y du.

The time when I fared on rich viands,
I lifted not my thigh in contempt
Againſt a man complaining with the pang of ſickneſs.

Brothers alfo have I had,
That would not complain if a peſtilence even had raged ;
One was *Elvan, Cynddylan* was another.

The hair is difgracefully worn, if to cry out
Should a man be given in the utmoſt heat of conflict ;
My brothers they were no ſnivellers.

But for death and its fearful afflictions,
And the pang of the blue blades,
I will not be a ſniveller neither.

The field of *Maoddyn, (a)* is it not with froſt overſpread,
Since the herds of its cultivator are deſtroyed—
On the grave of *Eirinwedd*, ſee the ſnow lies thick !

The barrow of *Elwyddan*, is it not drench'd with rain ?
There is *Maoddyn* under it !——
A man that *Cynon (b)* hath to mourn.

Four brothers of a fruitful ſtock to me have been,
And each was allotted to be the head of a family—
But *Tren* knows to itſelf no owner.

(a) The portion, moſt likely, of *Maoddyn*, the brother of *Cynddylan*; as it ſeems the ſhare
of each was called after its owner. So *Dyfryn Meifyr*, and *dyfryn Freuer*, were the ſhares of the
two daughters of *Cyndrwyn.*
(b) Probably *Cynon Garwyn*, the ſon of *Bryſwael Yfgithrawg*, prince of *Powys.*

Pedwar pwn broder a'm buant
Ac i bob gorwyv nwyviant:
Ni wyr Tren, perçen cyngant!

Pedwar pwn terwyn (a) o addwyn vrodyr
A'm buant o Gyndrwyn: '
Nid oes i Dren berçen mwyn !

Gofgo yngod addoed arnad, (b)
Nid wyv bylgaint gÿvod ;
Neu'm gwânt yfgwr o gwr dyvod ? (c)

Gofgo di yngod, a theç ;
Nid wyd ymadrawdd dibeç : (d)
Nid gwiw clain yth grain y greç.

Amfer i buant addvwyn,
I cerid merçed Cyndrwyn,
Heledd, Gwladus, a Gwenddwyn.

Çwiorydd a'm bu diddan ; (e)
Mi a'u collais oll açlan,
Freuer, Medwyl, a Medlan !

Çwiorydd a'm bu hevyd,
Mi a'u collais oll i gyd,
Gwledyr, Meifyr, a Çeinvryd !

(a) Neu, Peduar pun tervyn.
(b) Neu, Gofgo yngod adot arnat.
(c) Neu, Neum gunant yfgur o gurr dyvot.
(d) Ll. Du. Nid ymadrawdd diboch.
(e) Neu, Chwiorydd am bydiddan.

Four brothers of a fruitful stock to me there were,
And each of these princely heirs possessed vigour—
But *Tren* knows no congenial owner!

Four, of a fruitful stock, courageous and comely brothers
There were to me, the sons of *Cyndrwyn*,—
There is not to *Tren* the possession of any comfort!

Fly thee hence, the time of fate is upon thee;
I do not rise with the dawn;
Shall I not be transfixed by a shaft from the coming rows?

Fly thee hence and hide thyself;
Thou art not of a sinless conversation—
It will not avail thee to lye along, thy creeping will make a crash! (a)

At the time they were fair and pleasing,
Beloved were the daughters of *Cyndrwyn*,
Heledd, Gwladus, and *Gwenddwyn*.

Sisters I had who made me happy;
I have lost them all together,—
Freuer, Medwyl, and *Medlan!*

Sisters to me there were besides,
I have lost them one and all,—
Gwledyr, Meifyr, and *Ceinvryd!*

(a) This stanza concludes the Elegy in the *Llyvyr Coç*, or the *Red Book of Hergeft*; but other MSS. have the following additional stanzas.

Llâs Cynddylan, llâs Cynwraith,
Yn amwyn Tren, trev ddifaith—
Gwae vi vawr araws eu llaith !

Gwelais ar lawr Maes Togwy,
Byddinawr, a gawr gymmwy—
Cynddylan oedd cynnorthwy.

Celain a fyç o du tân ; (a)
Pan glywyv godwryv godaran,
Llu Llemenig, mab Mahawen.

Arbènig lleithig llurig
Yn nghyhoedd aer gwyth gwaith-vuddig, (b)
Flam daphar, llaçar Llemenig.

(a) Neu, Celein a fych o dy tan.
(b) Neu, Ynghyhoedd airggwyth gwaith fuddig.

Cynddylan has been flain, *Cynvraith* has been flain,
In defending *Tren*, a town laid wafte—
Great is my woe, that I furvive their death !

I have feen on the ground of the field of *Togwy*
An embattled hoft, with the fhout of mutual onfet—
Cynddylan was the auxiliary fupport.

A carcafe fhall parch by the fide of the fire,
When I hear the murmer of the thundering din
Of the hoft of *Llemenig*, (a) the fon of *Mabawen*.

A fovereign of a throne, in arms
In the confpicuous rage of flaughter, conquering
See the fpreader of the flame, the violent *Llemenig*.

(a) Llemenig was, like *Llywarg*, one of the three free guefts, difcontented in the court of *Arthur*.

TRIBANAU.

CRIN calav a lliv yn nant ;
Cyvnewid Sais a'i ariant,
Digu enaid mam geu-blant.

Y ddeilen à drevyd gwynt,
Gwae hi a'i thynged (a)
Hên hi—eleni y ganed ! (b)

Cyd boed vyçan ys célvydd
Ydd adail adar yn ngorwydd ;
Cyvoed vydd dà â dedwydd.

Oer-wlyb mynydd oer-las iâ ;
Ymddiried i Dduw ni'th dwylla ;
Nid edry hir-bwyll hir-bla.

Baglawg byddin, bagwy òn ;
Hwyaid yn llyn, graenwyn tòn ;
Treç na çant cyftudd calon (c)

Hir nôs gorddyar morva ;
Gnawd tervyfg yn nghymmanva ;
Ni çyvyd diriaid â da.

    .

(a) Neu, Gwae hi ae thyghet.
(b) Neu, Hen hi elein y ganet.
(c) Neu, Trech na chant cyftyt calon

PROVERBIAL TRIPLETS.(*a*)

BRITTLE is the reed, there is flood in the ravine;
Like the commerce of a *Saxon* with his money,
Void of love is the foul of a ftep-mother.

The leaf that is hurried by the wind,
Alas! how perifhable its fate—
It is old—this year only was it born!

Though it be fmall, yet ingenious
Is the dwelling of the bird in the fkirt of the wood—
Of equal age will the good and the happy be.

Chill and wet is the mountain, cold and grey is the ice;
Truft to God, and he will not deceive thee:
Perfevering patience will not leave thee long afflicted.

Intangling is the fnare, cluftered is the afh;
The ducks in the pond, white breaks the wave—
More powerful than a hundred is the affliction of the heart.

The long night clamorous is the fea-fhore;
A tumult is common in a congregation—
The naughty cannot bear with the good.

(*a*) It has been faid before of fimilar verfes, that the different fentiments in each ftanza have no connection with one another, except what may arife from chance; they are claffed merely to agree with the metre.

Hir nôs, gorddyar mynydd,
Goçwiban gwynt uwç blaen gwŷdd;
Ni thwyll drycanian dedwydd.

Marçwyail dryſi a mwyar arni, (a)
A mwyalç ar ei nyth,   ·
A çelwyddawg ni theu vyth. .

Gwlaw allan gwlyçyd rhedyn,
Gwyn gro mor, goron ewyn; (b)
Tecav canwyll pwyll i ddyn.

Gwlaw allan yngan glydwr,
Melyn eithin, crin evwr—
Duw Reen, py beraiſt lyvwr !

Gwlaw allan gwlyçyd vy ngwallt,
Cwynvànus gwan, diphwys allt,
Gwelwgan gweilgi, heli hallt.

Gwlaw allan gwlyçyd cigiawn,
Goçwiban gwynt, uç blaen cawn;
Gwedy pob camp heb y dawn.

(a) Neu, Marchuyeil dryſſi a muydr (mwgan) erni.
(b) Neu, Guyn gro mor goron cuyn.

The long night clamorous is the mountain;
Bluftering is the wind over the tops of trees—
Ill-nature will not deceive the contented mind.

The luxuriant growing thorn will have berries on it;
And the thrufh on her neft,
And the liar will never be filent.

Rain without, the fern are drenched,
White the gravel of the fea, floating is the fpray—
Reafon is the faireft light for man,

Rain without, loquacious is the fhelter,
Yellow is the furze, rotten is the hedge—
Thou creating God, why didft thou give exiftence to a coward!

Rain without, my hair is drenched,
Full of complaint is the feeble, fteep is the cliff;
Darkly-white is the torrent, the fea is falt.

Rain without, let it drench the ocean,
Bluftering is the wind over the reeds—
After every feat ftill without a genius.

MARWNAD CADWALLAWN, VAB CADVAN,

BRENIN PRYDAIN.

CADWALLAWN cyn noi ddyvod,
A'i gorug a'n digonod ; (*a*) pedair priv-gad ar ddeg
Am briv-deg Prydain, a thri-ugain cyvarvod.

Llueſt Cadwallawn ar Gaint,
Lloegyr ardres ormes arnaint, (*b*)
Llaw ddillwng ellwng oed vraint. (*c*)

Llueſt Cadwallawn ar Yddon, (*d*)
Avar anwar ei alon, (*e*)
Llew llwyddawg ar Saeſon. (*f*)

Llueſt Cadwallawn glodrydd,
Yn ngwarthav Digoll Vynydd,
Seith-mis, a ſeith-gad beunydd.

(*a*) Neu, Ae goruc an divragot.
(*b*) Neu, Lloegyr ar dres ormes ednaint.
    Neu, Lloegr ardres armes arneint.
(*c*) Neu, Oed yreint; neu, Oed ureint; neu, Oed braint.
(*d*) Neu, Arydon; neu, Ar ydon; neu, Ar y don; neu, Ar yd don.
(*e*) Neu, Yn alon.
(*f*) Neu, Lleu lluydauc ar Saeſon.
    Neu, Llew llwyddawg o'r Saeſon.

ELEGY ON CADWALLON, THE SON OF CADVAN,

KING OF BRITAIN. (a)

CADWALLON, fince he is come,
He that formed him did amply fatisfy us; he fought fourteen
Great battles for the moft fair *Britain*, and fixty fkirmifhes.

The army of *Cadwallon* encamped on *Caint*,
Of *Lloegyr* he was the enthraller, he was their oppreffor,
His hand was open, and honour flowed.

The army of *Cadwallon* encamped on *Yddon*,
The fierce affliction of his foes,
A lion profperous over the *Saxons*.

The army of *Cadwallon*, the illuftrious,
Encamped on the top of the mount of *Digoll*,
For feven months, and feven fkirmifhes daily.

(a) *Cadwallon* became king of *North Wales* in 613, and nominally of *Britain* in 635, and reigned till about 646. One of the moft memorable events that happened to him in the early part of his life, was his defeat by *Edwyn* king of the *Saxons* of *Deira*; who was brought up with him. In confequence of this he was obliged to fly to *Ireland*; where he remained feven years, according to the following *Triad*.

Tri diwair Deulu Ynys Prydain; Teulu Cadwallawn mab Cadvan, a vuont faith mlynedd yn Ywerddon gyd ag ev; ac yn hyny o yfbaid, ni ovynafant ddim iawn iddo rhag gorvod arnaddynt ei adaw: A Theulu Gavran mab Aeddan, pan vu y divancoll, a aethant i'r mor dros eu harglwydd: A'r trydydd Teulu Gwenddolau mab Ceidiaw, yn Arderydd, a gynnaliafant y vrwydyr bymthegnos a mis wedy lladd eu harglwydd. Sev oedd rivedi Teuluoedd pob un o'r gwyr hyny un canwr ar ugaint.

Llueſt Cadwallawn ar Havren,
Ac o'r tu draw i 'Ddygen,
A breiaid yn llofgi Meigen. (*a*)

Llueſt Cadwallawn ar Wy,
Maranedd wedi mordwy,
A ddylynad câd cylçwy. (*b*)

Llueſt Cadwallawn ar Fynnawn Vedwyr,
Rhag milwyr magai dawn ;
Dangoſai Gynon yno haeru iawn. (*c*)

Llueſt Cadwallawn ar Dâv,
Ys lluoſawg y gwelav
Cyvrenin vraiſg nâv. (*d*)

Llueſt Cadwallawn ar Dawy, (*e*)
Lleiddiad adav yn adwy, (*f*)
Clodrydd ceiſydydd cyſtwy.

Llueſt Cadwallawn tra çaer
Caew, byddin a çynnwrv taer (*g*)
Can câd, a thòri can caer.

(*a*) Neu, Afrield yn llofgi Meigen.
(*b*) Neu, A delinat kat kylçhuy.
(*c*) Neu, Haery dawn ; neu, Haearn daun.
(*d*) Neu, Cywrennin vre is nav.
(*e*) Neu, Ar Dafwy ; neu, Ar Dauy.
(*f*) Neu, Lleiddiad addaf yn adwy.
(*g*) Neu, (Caeu) Byddin a chynnwr caer (taer.)

The army of *Cadwallon* encamped on *Havren*,
And on the farther fide of *Dygen*, (a)
And the devourers were burning *Meigen*.

The army of *Cadwallon* encamped on the *Wy*, (b)
The common men, after paffing the water,
Following to the battle of fhields.

The army of *Cadwallon* encamped by the well of *Bedwyr* ; (c)
With foldiers virtue is cherifhed ;
There *Cynon* fhewed how to affert the right.

The army of *Cadwallon* encamped on the *Tav*, (d)
Very numerous may I fee
The fharers in the fame of the potent chief.

The army of *Cadwallon* encamped on *Tawy* ; (e)
He had the hand of flaughter in the breach ;
Spreading was his fame, eagerly he fought the conflict.

The army of *Cadwallon* encamped towards the city
Of *Caew*, (f) a hoft that was ftubborn in the tumult,
Of a hundred battles, and the falling of a hundred caftles.

(a) Probably this is *Dygen Vreiddin*, near *Welfh Pool*.

(b) The river *Wye*.

(c) In the upper part of *Gwaun Llwg*, *Monmouthfhire*.

(d) The river that gives name to *Caerdiff*.   Nearly oppofite *Llandaff*, on the other fide of the *Tav*, there are the ruins of a *Britifh* camp in a place called *Gwaun y Trodau*.   The tradition ? the neighbourhood is, that the *Saxons* fuffered a great defeat there.

(e) The river on which the town of *Swanfea* ftands.

(f) There is a place called *Caeo* in *Caermarthenfhire*.

Llueſt Cadwallawn ar Gowyn ; (a)
Llaw lluddedig ar awyn; (b)
Gwyr Lloegyr lluoſawg eu cwyn.

Llueſt Cadwallawn heno,
Trathir yn nhymmyr Penvro; (c)
Am nawdd vawr anhawdd i fo.

Llueſt Gadwallawn ar Deivi,
Cymmyſgai waed â heli ; (d)
Angerdd Gwynedd gwynygai. (e)

Llueſt Cadwallawn ar Dyfyrdd Avon, (f)
Gwnaeth eryron yn llawn; (g)
Gwedy trin dywyneu dawn. (h)

Llueſt Gadwallawn vy mrawd,
Yn ngwerthevin Bro Dunawd,
Ei vâr anwar yn foſawd. (i)

Llueſt Cadwallawn ar Veinin, (k)
Llew lluoſawg ei werin,
Twrwv mawr traças i orddin. (l)

(a) Neu, Ar gowyn (gyuyn.)
(b) Neu, Llau lludedic ar auyr (arawyn.)
(c) Neu, Trathit yn tymyn (tymyr) Penvro.
(d) Neu, Cymmyſgi uaet a heli.
(e) Neu, Angerdd Gwynedd Gwy ny gei (guynigei.)
(f) Neu, Ar Dyfyrdd (dyfyrd) Avon.
(g) Neu, Gwnaeth erſion yn llawn.
(h) Neu, Guedi trin dyuinːu (dyfineu) daun.
(i) Neu, Y var anuar yn ffoſſaut.
(k) Neu, Ar Fcirin (veirin.)
(l) Neu, Twrwf mawr tra chas Forddin.
    Neu, Turuf maur trochas y ordin.

The army of *Cadwallon* encamped on the *Cowyn*; (*a*)
There the hand was weary on the rein;
The men of *Lloegyr* abounded with complaints of woe.

The encampment of *Cadwallon* is this night
In the extremity of the watery region of *Penvro*, (*b*)
For refuge to retreat where the difficulty was great.

The encampment of *Cadwallon* on the *Teivi*, (*c*)
The blood mixed with the briny wave;
There the fury of *Gwynedd* (*d*) violently raged.

The army of *Cadwallon* encamped on the *Dyfyrdd River*, (*e*)
He made the eagles full;
After the conflict virtue was difgraced.

The encampment of *Cadwallon*, my brother,
In the upper part of the country of *Dunod*, (*f*)
His wrath was violent in wielding the blade.

The army of *Cadwallon* encamped on *Meinin*, (*g*)
The lion with the numerous hoft,
Great the tumult bringing affliction on the borders.

(*a*) A river dividing the counties of *Pembroke* and *Caermarthen.*
(*b*) The prefent *Pembrokefhire*; that is, the *Land's End.*
(*c*) The *Teivi* falls into the fea at the town of *Cardigan.*
(*d*) *North Wales*, exclufive of *Powys.*
(*e*) Probably a miftake for the *Dyvi River*, between the counties of *Cardigion* and *Meirionydd.*
(*f*) *Bro Dunawd*, or *Cantrev Dunodig*, a diftrict comprehending the fea-coaft of *Meirion*, and part of *Caernarvonfhire.*
(*g*) Perhaps where the abbey of *Maenen* ftood, near *Llanrwft.*

O gyſſul eſtrawn, ac anghyviawn venaiç,
Dillydd dwvyr o fynnawn:
Trig trym-ddydd am Gadwallawn ! (*a*)

Gwiſgwys coed cain dudded hâv;
Dybryſid gwyth wrth dynged— (*b*)
Cyvarwyddom ni am Elved. (*c*)

(*a*) Neu, Tri (tryc) thrymddydd am Gadwallawn.
(*b*) Neu, Dy bryſſit guych wrth dyghet.
   Neu, Dybrys o fyſid gwyth wrth dynged.
(*c*) Neu, Cyfarfyddom ni a Melfed.

From the plotting of ftrangers, and unjuft monks,
As the water flows from the fountain—
Sorrowful will be our lingering day for *Cadwallon!* (a)

The trees have put on the gay covering of fummer;
Let the wrath of flaughter haften quickly, led by fate,
Let us be guided onward to the plain of *Elved!*

(a) When *Cadwallon* returned from *Ireland*, to retrieve his honour, he directed his forces a fecond time againft *Edwyn*, whom he flew at a place called *Meigen*. In this battle the men of *Powys* greatly fignalized themfelves; and in return *Cadwallon* granted them fourteen peculiar privileges, which are enumerated by the celebrated *Cynddelw*, in a poem written in 1160, which concludes thus:

> Gwyr Powys pobyl difgywen,
> Câd orllawes orllawen:
> Pedair cynneddyv, cadw cadyr urdden,
> Ar ddeg erddygant o Veigen.

The *Powyfians*, a renowned people,
May exult of their prowefs in the conflict:
Four famed privileges, honourably confirmed,
And ten befides they acquired from *Meigen*.

CANU LLYWARÇ HÊN,

I'W HENAINT A'I VEIBION.

CYN bum cain vaglawg, bum cyfes eiriawg, (a)
Ceinvygir ni eres—
Gwyr Argoed eirioed a'ın porthes !

Cyn bum cain vaglawg bum hy,
A'm cynnwyfid yn nghyvyrdy
Powys, paradwys Cynmry.

Cyn bum cain vaglawg bum eirian,
Oedd cynwayw vy mhar, (b)
Oedd cynnwyv cevyn-grwm ; wyv trwm, wyv truan !

Baglan bren, neud cynhauav, (c)
Rhudd rhedyn, melyn calav ?—
Neu'r digerais a garav !

Baglan bren, neud gauav hŷn,
Yd vydd llavar gwyr ar lŷn (d)
Neud diannerç vy erçwyn ! (e)

Baglan bren, neud gwanwyn
Rhydd côgau, goleu ewyn ? (f)
Wyv digariad gan vorwyn !

(a) Neu, Bun (bwn) cyffes eiryauc.
(b) Neu, Oed kymueu vym par.
(c) Neu, Neut kyn trayaf.
(d) Neu, Ytuyd (ydwyt) llavar guyr ar lyn.
(e) Neu, Neut diannerch vy euryn.
(f) Neu, Rud cogeu goleu euyn.

ELEGY OF LLYWARÇ HEN,

ON OLD AGE, AND THE LOSS OF HIS SONS.

BEFORE I appeared with crutches, I was eloquent in my complaint,
It will be extolled, what is not wonderful—
The men of *Argoed* (a) have ever fupported me !

Before I appeared with crutches I was bold,
I was admitted into the congrefs houfe
Of *Powys*, the paradife of the *Cynmry*. (b)

Before I appeared on crutches I have been comely,
The foremoft of the fpears was my lance,
My round back was firft in vigour—I am heavy ; I am wretched !

My wooden crook, is it not the time of harveft,
When the fern is brown, the reeds are yellow ?—
Have I not once difliked what now I love !

My wooden crook, is not this winter,
When men are noify over the beverage ?
Is not my bedfide void of greeting vifits !

My wooden crook, is it not the fpring,
When the cuckoos are at liberty, when the foam is l right ?
I am deftitute of a maiden's love !

(a) *Argoed* implies *on, or above the wood.* It has been before obferved that this feems to have
been the name of the patrimony of *Llywarç*, bordering on the foreft of *Celyddon.* It is more probable to fuppofe that the Bard alludes to that country, than that *Argoed* fhould be confidered here
as an epithet for *Powys*; as the name does not apply to the defcription of the latter,

(b) The *Welfh.*

Baglan bren, neud cyntevin,
Neud rhudd rhyç, neud cryç egin·?
Edlid ym edryç yth ylvin! (*a*)

Baglan bren, gangen voddawg
Cynnelyç hên hiraethawg: (*b*)
Llywarç leverydd nodawg! (*c*)

Baglan bren, gangen galed,
A'm cynnwyſi: Duw difred! (*d*)
Elwir pren cywir cynnired.

Baglan bren, bydd yſtywell,
A'm cynnelyç a vo gwell:
Neud wyv Llywarç lawer pell? (*e*)

(*a*) *Ll. Coç.* Etryt ym edrych yth linin.
　　　Neu, Edryd i'm edrych ith ylfin.
　　　Ll. Du. Edlid yn edryd ith ylfin.
(*b*) Neu, Cynhellych hen hiraethauc.
(*c*) Neu, Lleveryd vodauc.
(*d*) Neu, Am cynhellych Duw diffred.
(*e*) *Ll. Coç.* Neut uyt Lyuarch lawer gwell.
　　　Neu, Neut uyd hyttrach lawer pell.
　　　Ll. Du. Neud wyt Llywarch llawer pell.

My wooden crook, is it not the beginning of fummer, (a)
Are not the furrows brown, doth not the young corn begin to ruffle.—
My paffions rife when I look at thy beak !

My wooden crook, be thou a contented branch
To fupport a mourning old man—
Llywarç accuftomed much to talk !

My wooden crook, thou hardy branch,
Bear with me—God grant !
Thou fhalt be called a wood whofe wanderings are juft.

My wooden crook, be thou fteady,
So that thou mayeft fupport me the better—
Am not I *Llywarç*, much more compact ?

(a) *Cyntevin*, or the firft appearance of fummer, is *May-Day*; and in that fenfe it is ufed in the Welfh Laws. At that time the vegetation expanding luxuriantly the profpect of the harveft feafon, there ufed to be in old times many ceremonies of rejoicing on the occafion; but the principal one was the bonefire. The firft day of *November* was confidered as the conclufion of the fummer; and this was celebrated in the fame manner with bonefires, accompanied with ceremonies fuitable to the event; and fome parts of *Wales* ftill retain thefe cuftoms. *Ireland* retains fimilar ones; and the fire that is made at thefe feafons, is called *Beal Taine* in the *Irifh* language; and fome antiquaries of that country, in eftablifhing the eras of the different colonies that planted the ifland, have been happy enough to adduce as an argument for their *Phœnician* origin this term of *Beal Taine*.

Baal was the great deity of the *Phœnicians*; and he was one, by all accounts, that exceedingly delighted in feeing his votaries confign themfelves with fortitude to fiery ordeals peculiar to his own tafte. Now according to the authorities of the before mentioned antiquaries, there are various cuftoms in their country that preferve the memory of *Baal*; and even his very name joined to *Taine*, or fire, his own element, in the term *Beal Taine*; or, (according to their authority) the *Fire of Baal*.

If the above elucidation of *Beal Taine* had not been fo clear, the *Welfh* words *Bâl Dân*, and *Tân Bâl*, would probably have been of fome weight: The meaning of *Tân*, like the *Irifh Taine*, is *fire*, and *Bâl* is fimply a projecting, fpringing out, or expanding; and when applied to vegetation, it means a budding or fhooting out leaves and bloffoms, the fame as *Balant*, of which it is the root; and it is alfo the root of *Bala*; and of *Blwydd*, *Blwyddyn*, and *Blynedd*, a year, or the circle of vegetation. So the fignification of *Bâl Dân*, or *Tân Bâl*, would be, *the rejoicing fire for the vegetation*, or *for the crop of the year*.

Yn cymmwedd y mae henaint â mi,
O'm gwallt i'm daint,
A'r cloyn à gerynt yr ieuaint. (a)

Dyrgweny gwynt, (b) gwyn gne godre gwŷdd,
Dewr hydd, diwlydd bre; (c)
Eiddil hên, hwyr yd re. (d)

Y ddeilen hon neu's cynnired gwynt?
Gwae hi o'i thynged—
Hi hên—eleni y ganed!

A gerais er yn wâs ys fy gâs gènyv,
Merç estrawn, a març glàs:
Neud nad mi eu cyvaddas! (e)

Vy mhedwar priv-gâs erymoed, (f)
Ymgyvarvyddynt yn unoed, (g)
Pâs, a henaint, haint, a hoed.

(a) *Ll. Arall.* Y mae henaint yn cymued a mi
        Om guallt ym danned
        Ar cloyn a gerynt y gwragedd.
  Ll. Du. Ar cloyn a gerynt yr ieuainc.
  Ll. Côf. Ar cloyn a gar yr ieuaint (ieueinc)
(b) Neu, Dyr guenn (dyr gweny) guynt.
(c) Neu, Deurhyd diulyd bre (Dewr hyd ddiwlydd bre)
(d) Neu, Huyr ydyre (hwys y dyre)
(e) *Ll. Du.* Y sy (yfydd) gennyf yn gâs
        A gercis er yn was.
  Neu, Deubeth a gereis er yn was
        Merch i estron a march glas
        A heddyw nid ynt gyfaddas.
(f) *Ll. Du.* Fy (ym) pedwar prifgas erioed.
(g) Neu, Yn gyvarvydynt yn unoet.
  Neu, Pan gyfarfyddynt unoed.

Surely old age is fporting with me,
From my hair to my teeth,
And that glancing look, once fo loved by fair young ones !

The wind grinningly blufters out, white is the fkirt of the wood,
Lively is the ftag, there is no moifture on the hill ;
Feeble is the aged, flowly doth he move.

This leaf, is it not blown about by the wind?
Woe to it of its fate !
It is old—in this year only was it born !

What I loved when I was a youth are hateful to me now ;
The ftranger's daughter, and the grey fteed :
Am not I for them unmeet?

The four moft hateful things to me through life,
They have met together with one accord,
The cough, old age, ficknefs, and grief.

Wyv hên, wyv unig, wyv anelwig oer,
Gwedy gwely ceinvyg ;
Wyv truan, wyv tridyblyg !

Wyv tridyblyg hên, wyv anwadal drud,
Wyv ehud, wyv anwar :
Y fawl a'm caroedd ni'm câr !

Ni'm câr rhianedd, ni'm cynnired neb,
Ni allav ddarymred—
Wi ! o angau, na'm dygred !

Ni'm dygred na hun, na hoen ;
Gwedy y lleas Llawr a Gwên, (a)
Wyv anwar abar, wyv hên !

Truan o dynged a dyngwyd (b)
I Lywarç, ar y nos y ganed ; (c)
Hir gniv heb efgor lludded !

Na wifg wedy cwyn ; na vid vrwyn dy vryd ;
Llem awel, a çwerw gwanwyn—(d)
Na'm cyhudd vy mam (e)—mab yt wyv !

(a) Neu, Guedy lleas (gwedy y llas) Llawr a Gwen.
(b) Neu, Truan o dyngwy a ddygeydd.
      Ll. Du. Truan o dynged a ddygwydd i Llywarch.
(c) Neu, I Llywarch er y nos y ganed.
(d) Neu, Llem awel a cherw gwenebyn.
(e) Neu, Amgybyd (am gyhydd) fy mam.

I am old, I am alone, I am decrepid and cold,
After the fumptuous bed of honour;
I am wretched, I am triply bent !

I am triply bent and old, I am fickly bold,
I am rafh, I am outrageous:
Thofe that loved me once, now love me not !

Young virgins love me not, I am reforted to by none,
I cannot move myfelf along—
Ah! death, why will he not befriend me !

I am befriended by neither fleep, nor gladnefs;
Since the flaughter of *Llawr* and *Gwén*, (a)
I am outrageous and loathfome, I am old !

Wretched the fate that was fated
For *Llywarç*, on the night he was born :
Long pains, without being delivered of his load of trouble ! (b)

Array not thyfelf after thy wailing ; let not thy mind be vexed :
Sharp is the gale, and bleak is the fpring !—
Accufe me not, my mother—I am thy fon !

(a) Two fons of *Llywarç*.

(b) There is a ftanza in the latter part of this Elegy that varies but a very little from this ;
and perhaps one was brought in by miftake, at fome period or other, from memory.

Neud adwen ar vy ngwên, (a)
Yn hanvod cun açen, (b)
Tri gwyddorig elwig awen ? (c)

Llym vy mhâr, llaçar yn ngryd ; (d)
Armaav i wyliaw rhyd: (e)
Cynnydd anghwyv Duw gennyd! (f)

O diengyd a'th wylwyv, (g)
O'th ryleddir a'th gwynwyv :
Na çoll wyneb gwyr argnwyv. (h)

Ni çollav dy wyneb, trin wofe ber, (i)
Pan wifg glew yr yftre ; (k)
Porthav gniv, cyn mudav lle. (l)

Rhedegawg tòn ar hyd traeth ;
Eçadav tòrid arvaeth câd acdo, (m)
Gnawd fo ar fraeth.

(a) Neu, Neut atuen ar uy auen.
(b) Neu, Ynghanfiod cun a chen.
(c) Neu, Tri gwydd orig elwig awen (wen)
    Ll. Du. Trigwyddorig elwid wen (awen)
(d) Neu, Llachar y gryd.
(e) Neu, Armaf (armaif) i uylaw (wylyaw) ryt
(f) *Ll. Cof.* Rhydd cynnydd anghyf Duw gennyd.
    Neu, Kynnydd cyn nid anghwyf Duw gennyt
    Neu, Ynnyt anghyf; neu, cyn ni ddiangwyf.
    Neu, Cyn nid anghwyf; neu, Cynni ddiangwyf.
    Ll. Du. Cynnydd anghyf Duu genhyd.
(g) Neu, O diegyd ath ueluyf.
(h) Neu, Gwyr argnif; neu, gwyr ar gnif.
(i) *Ll. Du.* Ni chollafdy trin wofeb er (wr)
(k) Neu, Penwifg glew yr yftre.
(l) Neu, Porthaf gnif kyn mudef (mydif) lle (le)
(m) Neu, Echadef torrit arvaeth (kat ac ado) cad (acddo.)

Do I not recognize by my finile,
My defcent, fway and kindred;
Three themes of the harmonious mufe?

Sharp is my fpear, furious in the onfet; (a)
I will prepare to watch on the ford:
Support againft falling may God grant me!

If thou fhouldeft run away I fhall be to weep for thee;
If thou fhouldeft be flain I fhall mourn thee:
Lofe not the countenance of the men of conflict.

I will not lofe thy countenance, prone to warfare,
From the time that the hero puts on the harnefs of his fteed;
I will bear the pang ere I quit the fpot.

Gliding is the wave along the beach;
I perceive that the defign of that battle will be fruftrated;
It is ufual for the loquacious to run away.

(a) It was a maxim with the bards to admit nothing but truth into their compofitions, which may be an excufe for what he fays of himfelf: He is imitated by many—*Gwalçmai* is one:

Llaçar vy nghleddyv, lluç ydd ardwy glew,
Llewyçedig aur ar vy nghylçwy:
Cyvun-weftlawg dyvyr dydd neud gavwy
Cathyl o ar adar, awdyl offymwy.
   Gorvynig vy mhwyll yn mhell amgant
Heddyw wrth athreiddiaw tir tu Evyrnwy,
Gorwyn blaen avall blodau vagwy,
Balç caen coed, bryd pawb parth yd garwy.

   Vehement is my fword, like the lightning's glance to protect the brave,
Brightly glitters the gold on my round fhield:
The day I am foothed, when the murmuring waters harmonife
With a hymn from the birds, ftored with fweet mufic.
   My paffions inflamed with longing, wander far
This day, whilft roving through the vale to the banks of *Evyrnwy*
Brightly glare the branches of the apple-trees cluftered with bloffoms;
The woods difplay their proud robes; all look pleafed towards thofe they love.

Yſid ym a levarwyv,
Briwaw pelydyr parth y bwyv ; (a)
Ni levarav na fowyv. (b)

Meddal mignedd, caled rhiw, (c)
Rhag carn cawn tàl glan a vriw ; (d)
Eddewid ni wneler nid gwiw. (e)

Gwasgarawd naint am glawdd caer, (f)
A minnau a rinaäv (g)
Yſgwyd bryd briw cyn teçav.

Y corn a'th roddes di Urien,
A'r arweſt aur am ei ên,
Çwyth ynddo o'th daw angen.

Er ergryd angau rhag angwyr Lloegyr, (h)
Ni lygrav vy mawredd,
Ni ddyçanav rianedd ! (i)

(a) Neu, Briau pelydr parth y bwyf.
(b) Neu, Ny lafaraf na phowyf.
(c) Neu, Medal mi ened (miged) calet rhiw.
(d) Neu, Rac carn caun tal glan avriw.
(e) Neu, Edewit ny weether (ny wnel) nytiw (nid yw)
    Neu, Eddcwld ny wellaer nyd iw.
(f) Neu, Guas karaut (gwaſgarawſt) neint am glawd caer.
(g) Neu, A minneu armaif ys gwyd (yſguyt)
(h) Ll. Coç. Yr ergryt aghen rac aghywyr Lloegr.
    Neu, Er egryt angen rhag anghenwyr (anhepc/r) Lloegr.
(.) Neu, Ni ddyhunaf rianedd

What there is concerning me I fpeak of;
There is the breaking of fpears about the place where I am;
I will not fay but that I may retreat.

Soft is the bog, the cliff is hard,
With the hoof we fhall have the edge of the bank broken;
A promife not fulfilled is none at all.

As the ftream divides round the caftle-wall,
I alfo will prognofticate
A fhield with a fractured front, ere I run away.

The horn given to thee by *Urien*, (a)
With the wreathe of gold round its rim,
Blow in it if thou art in danger. (b)

For the terrour of death from the bafe men of *Lloegyr*,
I will not defile my honour,
I will not lampoon the young virgins.

(a) Prince of *Reged*, and the coufin-german of *Llywarç*.

(b) The horn was efteemed one of the moft precious articles poffeffed by a warrior; it ferved to give the fignal for war, and to circulate the chearful mead:

Dywallaw di'r Corn argynvelyn;
Anrhydeddus veddw o vedd gorewyn—
Hirlas buelin, braint uçel hen ariant,
Ai gortho nid gorthenau:
A dyddwg i Dudur, eryr aerau,
Gwirawd gyffevin o'r gwin gwinau.

Pour out the horn with the glittering yellow top,
Honourably drunk with frothy fparkling mead—
The *Hirlas* of the Buffalo, highly enriched with ancient filver,
And its cover, all pleafing to the lip:
And bear to Tudur, eagle of conflicts,
Some choice beverage of the deeply-blufhing wine.

Owein Cyudliawg, Prince of Powys

K

Tra vum i yn oed y gwâs draw,
A wifg, o aur ei ottoyw, (*a*)
Byddai re y rhuthrwn y wayw.

Diheu diwair dy waes, (*b*)
Ti yn vyw a'th dyft rhylâs:
Ni bu eiddil hen yn wâs.

Gwên wrth Lawen ydd wylwys neithwyr, (*c*)
Arthur ni theças: (*d*)
Aer a drawdd ar glawdd gorlas, (*e*)

Gwên wrth, Lawen ydd wylwys neithwyr,
A'r yfgwyd ar ei yfgwydd; (*f*)
A çan bu mab ym bu hywydd.

Gwên wrth Lawen ydd wyliis (*g*)
Neithwyr, a'r yfgwyd ar ygnis; (*h*)
Can bu mab i mi ni ddiengis. (*i*)

Gwên gygydd, goçawr vy mryd, (*k*)
I y lâs ys mawr cafnar:
Neud câr a'th levawr ! (*l*)

(*a*) Neu, A wifc o eur y ottew.
(*b*) Neu, Diheu diwair dy was (waes) di yn fyw.
    Ll. Du. Diau dywir dy was.
(*c*) Neu, Gwen, wrth lawen yd weles.
(*d*) Neu, A thuc ny techas (thechas)
(*e*) Neu, Aer (oer) adraud (a drawd) ar glawd (arglawdd) Gorlas.
(*f*) Neu, Ar yfguyt ar y yfguyd.
    Ll. Du. Aryfg ar ygnis (yfgwydd)
(*g*) Neu, Gwen wrth lawen yd wylwys.
(*h*) Neu, Ar yfgwyd ar y gwys.
(*i*) Neu, A chan bu mab im (imi) ny ddiengys (ddiengeis).
(*k*) Neu, Gwen gygyd (gwgydd) gochawn (gochawch) vy mryt.
(*l*) Neu, Nyt car ath lavawr (laddawr)

Whilst I was of the age of yonder youth,
That wears the golden spurs,
It was with velocity I pushed the spear.

Truly, thy young man is faithful,
Thou art alive, and thy witness is slain——
The old man that is now feeble was not so in his youth.

Gwên, by the *Llawen*, (*a*) watched last night—
Arthur did not retreat—
He darted through the slaughter on the green embankment.

Gwên, by the *Llawen*, watched last night, (*b*)
With the shield on his shoulder;
And as he was my son, he shewed himself bold.

Gwên, by the *Llawen* did he watch
Last night, with the shield uplifted;
As he was my son he did not retreat.

Gwên with the lowring look, irresolute is my mind,
Thy death greatly provokes my wrath—
Will not thy kindred mourn thee !

(*a*) A river, uncertain where; but perhaps the *Lune*, on which stands the present town of *Lancaster*.

(*b*) A similar description, by a bard of the twelfth century, has so much beauty as to need no apology for inserting it here—

> Gorwyliais nôs yn açadw fîn
> Gorloes rydau dwvyr Dygen Vreiddin;
> Gorlas gwellt didryv; dwvyr, neud iesin,
> Gwylain yn gware ar wely lliant,
> Lleithrion eu pluawr, pleidiau eddrin.

> I watched through the night with care, to guard the bounds,
> Where the pellucid waters plaintively murmur in the fords of *Breiddin*;
> The grass untrodden wears now a brighter green; how fair the stream,
> And sea-mews playful on their wavy beds,
> With polished plumage, gliding at their ease in love-united groupes.
>   GWALÇMAI AB MEILIR.

K 2

Gwên, vorddwyd tyllvra, (a) a wylias neithwyr
Yn ngoror rhyd Vorlas ;
A çan bu mab ym ni theças.

Gwên gwyddwn dy eiffillyd, (b)
Rhythr eryr yn ebyr oeddyd—
Betwn ddedwydd diangyd ! (c)

Tòn tyrvid, toïd ervid, (d)
Pan ânt cynrain yn ngovid ; (e)
Gwên, gwae ry hên o'th edlid !

Ton tyrvid, toïd açes, (f)
Pan ânt cyvrain yn ngnes : (g)
Gwên, gwae ry hên ryth-golles '

Oedd gwr vy mab, oedd ddyfgywen hawl ; (h)
Ac oedd nai i Urien ;
Ar ryd Vorlas y llâs Gwên !

Prenial dywal gâl yfgwn, (i)
Gorug ar Loegyr lu cyngrwn : (k)
Bedd Gwên vab Llywarç Hên hwn ! (l)

(a) Neu, Gwen vordwyt tyllvras.
(b) Neu, Gwen guydun (gwydn) dy eiffillut (eiffillydd.)
(c) Neu, Belun (Pi twn) dedwyd dianghut.
(d) Neu, Ton tyrfid coed erfid.
(e) Neu, Pan aut (nawd) cyvrein ygovid (y gofid, neu, yn ofid).
(f) Neu, Ton tyrfid caed aches.
(g) Neu, Pan aut (nawd) kyvrin ygnes (y gner.)
(h) Neu, Oed gwr vy mab oedifgwen haul (oedd is gwen haul.)
(i) Neu, Prennyal dywal gal yfcyn.
(k) Neu, Goruc ar Loegr lu (llu) Kyndrwyn.
(l) Neu, Yw hwn.

Gwén, with the brawny thigh, did watch laſt night
On the border of the ford of *Morlas*; (*a*)
And as he was my ſon he did not retreat.

Gwén, I knew well thy inherent diſpoſition,
In the aſſault like the eagle at the fall of rivers thou wert— (*b*)
If I were fortunate thou wouldeſt have eſcaped!

Let the face of the ground be turned up, let the aſſailants be covered,
When chiefs repair to the toil of war:
Gwén, woe to him that is over old, for thee he is indignant!

Let the face of the ground be turned up, and the plain be covered,
When the oppoſing ſpears are lifted up—
Gwén, woe to him that is over old, that he ſhould have loſt thee!

My ſon was a man, ſplendid was his fame;
And he was the nephew of *Urien*:
On the ford of *Morlas*, *Gwén* was ſlain!

The ſhrine of the fierce overbearing foe,
That vanquiſhed the circularly-compact army of *Lloegyr*:
The grave of *Gwén* the ſon of old *Llywarç* is this!

(*a*) There are ſeveral rivers of this name. One riſes in *Denbyſhire*, and falls into the *Ceiriaug* near *Chirk Caſtle:* But the *Morlas* mentioned here, moſt likely, was a river in, or contiguous to *Llywarç's* own principality, weſt of the foreſt of *Celyddon*, ſomewhere in the neighbourhood of *Lancaſter*. The name may poſſibly ſtill remain there; for the ancient *B-itiſh* names of rivers are ſurpriſingly retained in thoſe parts, where the language has been loſt for many ages; indeed moſt of the rivers of *Cumberland*, and adjacent parts, have kept the old names.

(*b*) Alluſions to the ſtrength, and fierceneſs of the eagle, are very common in the works of the ancients.   They generally repreſent him ſtationed at the mouths of rivers, or inlets, watching his prey; hence it muſt be underſtood, that they mean moſt commonly that ſort called the oſprey, or ſea eagle.

K 3

Teg yd gân yr aderyn ar berwydd bren,
Uç ben Gwên ; cyn ei olo dan dywarç :
Briwai galç Llywarç Hên !

Pedwar-meib arugaint a'm bu,
Eurdorçawg, tywyfawg llu ;
Oedd Gwên goreu o naddu !

Pedwar-meib arugaint a'm bwyad,
Eurdorçawg, tywyfawg câd :
Oedd Gwên goreu mab o'i dâd !

Pedwar-meib arugaint a'm buÿn (*a*)
Eurdorçawg tywyfawg unbyn ;
Wrth Wên gweifionain oeddyn'. (*b*)

Pedwar-meib arugaint yn nghenvaint Llywarç, (*c*)
O wyr glew galwythaint,
Rhull eu dyvod, clod tramaint. (*d*)

Pedwar-meib arugaint o veithiaint vy nghnawd, (*e*)
Drwy vy nhavawd lleddyfaint : (*f*)
Da dyvod vy nghod colledaint. (*g*)

(*a*) Neu, Pedwar mab ar hugaint am bwyn.
(*b*) Neu, Y wrth Wen gueiffyon ein oedyn.
(*c*) Neu, Yn cemieint Llywarch.
(*d*) Neu, Twll eu dyvot clot trameint.
    Ll. Du. Tulleu dyfod clod tra meint.
(*e*) Neu, A veithyant; neu, a weithieynt (*Ll. Du.* A neitheint.)
(*f*) Neu, Lledoffeint ; neu, lleddeffeint.
(*g*) Da dyvot uygeot colledeint (colleddeint.)

Sweetly fang the birds on the fragrant bloffomed apple tree,
Over the head of *Gwèn*, before he was covered over with fod.
He ufed to fracture the armour of old *Llywurç* !

Four and twenty fons I have had,
Wearing the golden chain, leaders of armies : (*a*)
Gwèn was the beft of them !

Four and twenty fons there were to me,
Wearing the golden chain, leaders of battle :
Gwèn was the beft fon of his father !

Four and twenty fons to me have been,
Wearing the golden chain, and leading princes ;
Compared with *Gwèn*, they were but ftriplings.

Four and twenty fons in the family of *Llywarç*,
Men that were valiant oppofers of the foe,
Liberal was the gift attended with boundlefs fame.

Four and twenty fons, the offspring of my body ;
By the means of my tongue they were flain :
Juftly come is my budget of misfortunes!

(*a*) The *Eurdorçogion*, or *wearers of the golden chain*, have been already mentioned ; but *Aneurin* may be quoted once more :

> Tri-wyr a thriügaint a thriçant eurdorçawl,
> O'r fawl yd gryfiafant u¬ gormant wirawd ;
> Ni ddiengai, namyn tri o wrhydri fofawd ¬
> Dau gadci Aeron, a Çynon daerawd,
> A minnau o'm gwaedfreu, gwerth vy ngwen-wawd !

> Three, threefcore, and three hundred heroes wearing the golden chain,
> There were of thofe that armed themfelves after too much beverage,
> There efcaped only three through the valorou¬ ufe of fwords ¬
> The two dogs of war from *Aeron*, and the ftubborn *Çynon* ;
> And I efcaped the fpilling of my blood faved by the facrednefs of the Loly mufe.

Pan lâs Pyll oedd tevyll briw, (*a*)
A gwaed ar wallt hyll,
Ac i am ddwylan Fraw frowyll! (*b*)

Dyçonad yftavell o efgyll yfgwydawr (*c*)
Tra vydded yn fevyll, (*d*)
A vriwed ar angad Pyll. (*e*)

Dyn dewis ar vv meibion, (*f*)
Pan gyrçai bawb ei alon,
Pyll wyn pwyll tân trwy livon! (*g*)

Mâd ddodes ei vorddwyd dros obell (*h*)
Ei orwydd, o wng ac o bell
Pyll pwyll tân trwy fawell!

Oedd llary llaw aergre, oedd aeleu eilwydd, (*i*)
Oedd dinas ar yftre:
Pyll wyn doed erçyll eudde. (*k*)

Pan favai yn ntws pebyll,
I ar orwydd erewyll,
Arddelwai o wr wraig Pyll!

(*a*) Neu, Oed tæuyll briw.
(*b*) Neu, Ac am dwylann ffraw ffrewyll.
(*c*) Neu, Dichonaf yftavell (yftevyll) o efgyll (oefgyll.)
(*d*) Neu, Tra uydaf yn fefyll.
(*e*) Neu, Afrifed ar angad Byll.
(*f*) Neu, Dyn deuis aruy meibion.
(*g*) Neu, Trwy linon; neu, liwon.
(*h*) Neu, Dros o bell.
(*i*) Neu, Aeleu eilvyd (aelaf eïlwyd.)
(*k*) Neu, Pyll wyn duet perchyll eurdde (eude.)
  Ll. Du. Pyll wyn oedd perchyll eurdde.

When *Pyll* (a) was flain gafhing was the wound,
And the blood on the hair feemed horrible,
And on each bank of the *Fraw* (b) rapid was the ftream !   .

A room might be formed from the wings of fhields,
Which would hold one ftanding upright,
That were broken on the grafp of *Pyll*.

The chofen man amongft my fons,
When each affaulted the foe,
Was fair *Pyll*, with a mind unreftrained, as flames up the chimney. (c)

Gracefully he placed his thigh over the faddle
Of his fteed, on the near and farther fide—
Pyll with a mind unreftrained as flames up the chimney.

He was gentle, with a hand eager for battle, he was mufic to the mourners,
He was a tower of ftrength on his fteed of war—
Fair *Pyll!* fearful is his covering of feparation !

Should he be at the door of his tent,
On the dark grey fteed,
At the fight, a hero would be conceived by the wife of *Pyll*.

(a) Another of the fons of *Llywarç*.

(b) There is a river of this name in *Anglefea*, on which was the ufual refidence of the princes of *North Wales*, thence called *Aberfraw*; but poffibly the *Fraw* mentioned here was in fome part of *Cumbria*.

(c) The original is *Llivon*, here rendered chimney; which fome have taken to mean a river; but the appellation may be given to one with as much propriety as to the other; for the word fimply means the *place of flowing*, or *paffing through*. There are a great many rivers called *Llivon*; but that the other fenfe is right here is plain from the fucceeding ftanza, where the laft line is the fame, except that *fawell*, or *air hole*, is ufed inftead of *Llivon*.

Briwyd rhag Pyll penglog fêr; (*o*)
Ys odid llwvyr yd llever (*b*)
Yn daw; eiddil heb ddim digoner. (*c*)

Pyll wyn, pellynig ei glôd, (*d*)
Handwyv nwyv erod o'th ddyvod, (*e*)
Yn vab o'th arab adnabod ! (*f*)

Goreu tridyn y dan nev,
A warçedwis eu haddev,
Pyll, a Selyv, a Sanddev.

Yſgwyd a roddais i Byll,
Cyn noi gyſgu neu bu doll,
Deiniaw i haddav ar wall. (*g*) ·

Cyd delai Gynmru, ac elyſlu o Loegyr, (*h*)
A llawer o bobtu,
Dangoſai Byll bwyll uddu. (*i*)

Na Phyll, na Madawg, ni byddynt hjroedlawg, (*k*)
Or ddevawd y gelwynt : (*l*)
" Rhoddyn !"—" na roddyn !"—cyngrair byth nis erçynt ! (*m*)

(*a*) Neu, Beriwyd rac Pyll pengloc ffer.
(*b*) Neu, Ys odid (ocddyt) llyfr (llwfr, lwfyr, neu llyfyr) yd lleuer.
    Neu, Ys odid llwfyr yd llecher.
(*c*) Neu, Yndaw (yn dan) ciddil heb ddim (daw) digoner.
(*d*) Neu, Pell cunic (cynnig) ei glod.
(*e*) Neu, Handdwyf nyyf yrot oth dyvod.
(*f*) Neu, Unfab a tharan (atharan) adnabot.
(*g*) Neu, Dciniau·y hadau, arvoll (ar wall.)
    Neu, Dimheu ei haddef ar wall.
(*h*) Neu, Ac elyſlu Lloegr (elydlu o Loegr.)
(*i*) Neu, Danghoſcis Byll bwyll ydu.
(*k*) Neu, Na Phwy l na Madauc ni bydynt hiraethauc.
(*l*) Neu, Or dewawt y (a) gelvynt (gehwynt.)
(*m*) Neu, Rodyn Uarodyn llygreir vyt nya erchynt.

There was fractured before *Pyll* a ftrong fkull;
Seldom was there before him a coward fniveller
That would be filent; the weak is fatisfied without any thing.

Fair *Pyll*, widely fpread his fame;
Am I not invigorated fince that thou haft exifted
As my fon, and joyful to have known thee!

The beft three men under heaven,
That guarded their habitation,
Pyll, and *Selyv*, and *Sanddev*. (*a*)

I gave a fhield to *Pyll*,
But before he flept was it not broken,
Going carelefsly to a dwelling?

Should *Cynmru* (*b*) come, and the predatory hoft of *Lloegyr*
With many on each fide,
Pyll would fhew them conduct.

Nor *Pyll*, nor *Madawg*, (*c*) would be long lived,
If according to cuftom there was a calling—   [fcorned.
" Surrender!"—" They would not furrender!" (*d*) quarters they ever

(*a*) *Selyv* and *Sanddev*, two other fons of *Llywarç.*

(*b*) *Wales*, according to common acceptation; but originally fo much of the ifland as was inhabited by the unmixt *Cynmry* This was the original name general to the whole people, and
howfoever feparated into tribes, or principalities with their appropriate names, they ftill retained
this remarkable appellation of *Cynmry*, or *Firft Generation.*

(*c*) Another fon of *Llywarç.*

(*d*) Surrender is not very clofe to the original; and as the literal meaning of the word is now
a popular phrafe that fhall be given likewife:——" *Would they give in?*"—" *They would not
" give in!*"

Llyma y mab oedd divai, tringar
I veirdd, ys ei glod lle nid elai,
Byll pei bellaç parhaäi. (*a*)

Maen, a Madawg, a Medel, dewrwyr,
Diyffig vroder,
Selyv, Heilyn, Llawr, Lliver. (*b*)

Bedd Gwell yn y Rhiw Velen,
Bedd Sawyl (*c*) yn Llan Gollen,
Gwarçeidw Llavyr (*d*) Bwlç Llorien.

Bedd rhudd neu's cudd tywarç,
Ni's evrydd gweryd Ammarç (*e*)
Bedd Llyngedwy vab Llywarç.

Goreu triwyr yn eu gwlad,
I amddifyn eu trevad (*f*)
Eithyr, ac Erthyr, ac Argad.

Tri meib Llywarç, tri anghymmen câd,
Tri çeimiad avlawen,
Llev, ac Arau, ac Urien.

(*a*) Neu, Llyma y mabed (ymabedd) divei tringar y
           Veird (ei eneid) ys y glod (Ni ferthynt ni fei eu clod.)
           Lle nid elei Byll pei bellach parei (parhaai.)
(*b*) Neu, Lliwer.
(*c*) Neu, Sawyll.
(*d*) Neu, Llamyr.
(*e*) Neu, Ni feirudd Gweryd Amarch.
    Neu, Nyfevryd gueryt ammarch.
    Ll. Du. Nis eiryd gweryd Cammarch.
(*f*) Neu, Y an diffyn eu treuad.

Behold my fon that was without a fault, and warlike;
With the bards his fame went, where would not have gone
Pyll, if longer he had continued.

Maen, and *Madawg*, and *Medel*, valient men,
And brothers not refractory,
Selyv, *Heilyn*, *Llawr*, and *Lliver*.

The grave of *Gwell* is in *Rhiw Velen*, (*a*)
The grave of *Sawyl* in *Llangollen*, (*b*)
And *Llavyr* guards in the pafs of *Llorien*.

The ruddy grave, is it not covered with fods?
The earth of *Ammarç* (*d*) will not be made lefs pure
By the grave of *Llyngedwy* the fon of *Llywarç*.

The beft three men in their country,
For protecting their habitation,
Eithyr, and *Erthyr*, and *Argad*.

Three fons of *Llywarç*, the three untractable ones in battle,
The three joylefs wanderers were
Llev, and *Arau*, and *Urien*.

(*a*) Not far from *Bala* in *Mârion*.
(*b*) In *Denbighfhire*.
(*c*) In *Montgomeryfhire*.
(*d*) There is a *Dôl Ammarç* in *Montgomeryfhire*.

Handid haws i amçwyſon, (*a*)
O'i adaw ar lan awon,
Y gyd â llu o wyr llwydion. (*b*)

Tarw trin rhyvel adwn,
Cledyr câd, canwyll yſgwn;
Rcën ncv l rhwy a endewid hwn. (*c*)

Y bore gan law y dydd,
Pan gyrçwyd Mwg-mawr-Drevydd,
Nid ocdd vagawd meirç Meçydd. (*d*)

Cyvarvan a'ın cavall, (*e*)
Celain ar wyar ar wall,
Cyvranc Rhun a'r drud arall.

Diaſbad a ddodir yn ngwarthav Llug Vynydd,
Odduç ben bedd Cynllug,
Mau gerydd, mi a'i gorug! (*f*)

Odid eiry toïd yſtrad,
Dyvryſiynt cedwyr i gâd:
Mi nid av, anav ni'm gad!

(*a*) Neu, Handid haus i amchuiſſon.
(*b*) Neu, Y gyd a llu ewyr llwydon.
(*c*) Tarv trin ryvel adun
    Cledir cad canvill o guuin
    Reıı new ruy a endeid hun.
(*d*) *Ll. Du.* Y bore gan lav ydit
    Ban girchuid Mug mawr brewit (*breniny Saeſen*)
    Nid oed vagaud meirch mechit.
(*e*) Neu, Kywarvan am cafall.
(*f*) Neu, Meugerit ıı̃i ae goruc.

May it be better for his conveniencies
That he be left on the banks of the river,
With a hoft of grey men. (a)

The bull of tumult, guider of the war,
And fupport of the battle, the bright elevated lamp—
Mover of heaven ! too long has he been liftened to.

The morning as the day appeared,
When the affault was made on the *Great Burner of Towns*. (b)
The fteeds of *Mefydd* (c) were not trained up.

Oppofite to my repofing cell,
There was the corpfe in blood expofed,
From the rencounter of *Rhun* and the other hero.

A cry of lamentation will be made on the top of the mount of *Llug*,
Over the grave of *Cynllug* ; (d)
The reproach belongs to me, I was the caufe !

Hardly has the fnow covered the vale,
When the warriors are haftening to the battle :
I do not go, I am hindered by infirmity.

(a) It feems that fome monaftery is alluded to.
(b) *Mwg-mawr-Dreuydd*, is an epithet, if my recollection is right, given to *Edwyn* king of the *Saxons* of *Deira*, in fome MSS.
(c) A fon of *Llywarç*.
(d) Another of his fons.
(e) Another fon of *Llywarç*.

Nid wyd ti yſgolhaig, nid wyd claig;
Unben ni'th elwir yn nydd rhaid—
Oç, Cynddilig, na buoſt wraig ! *(a)*

Pell oddyman Aber Llyw,
Pellaç ein dwy gyvedlyw :
Talan telais dy ddeigyr i mi heddyw. *(b*

Er yvais i win o gawg,
Ev a ragwan rai rheiniawg :
Eſgyll gwawr oedd waywawr Duawg ! *(c)*

Oedd edivar gènyv pan ymerçis, *(d)*
Nad gantu i ddewis ; *(e)*
Cynnydd y vai hael hoedyl mis ! *(f)*

Adwen leverydd cyni vrân ;
Pan ddiſgỳnai yn nghyvyrdy
Pen gwr, pan gwin a ddyly ! *(g)*

Meyrygawg marçawg maes,
Tra vynws Dovydd vy lles,
Nid yſwn vegis môç mês !

       (a) Nyduid ti yſgolheic nid vid eleis
             Unben nith eluir in dit reit
             Och Kindilic na buoſt gureic.
       (b) Neu, Talan telcis dy (te) deigyr hedyu.
       (c) Neu, Diwg ; neu, Dwg.
       (d) Neu, Ymercheis.
       (e) Neu, Nat gantu y diewis.
       (f) Neu, Cyn y dyfei hael hoedl mis.
       (g) Neu, Atuen leveryd kyni
               Fran (pan diſgynnei ygkyvrdy
               Pen (paen) gur pan guin a dyly.

Thou art no fcholar, thou art no hermit,
A prince thou wilt not be called in the day of confliÆt—
Oh! *Cynddilig*, (c) why wert thou not a woman!

Far from here is *Aber Llyw*, (a)
Farther apart are our two friendly tribes—
Talan, I have repaid thy tears to me this day!

Since I have drank wine from the goblet,
There has been a piercing rencounter of the men of fpears—
Like the wings of the dawn was the glancing of the lance of *Duawg*. (b)

I repented of the time that I intreated
That thou fhouldeft not have thy choice;
It would have been generous to have life prolonged a month.

I know the voice of the raven, omen of woe,
When it defcends on the council houfe—
Chief of men, a goblet of wine fhould be thy mead.

The viÆtorious knight of the field,
Whilft the Great Renovator permitted me profperity,
I did not then like the fwine, devour the acorns!

(a) Another fon of *Llywarç*.
(b) It is probable that this is the fame as is written *Aber Lleu*, in the Elegy on *Urien of Reged*, being the place where he was flain.
(c) One of the fons of *Llywarç*.

L.

Llywarç Hên, na vydd di wyl,
Trwydded a gefi di anwyl—
Tarn dy lygad, taw nag wyl !

Hen wyv vi, ni'th oddiweddav,
Rhodd am gyfful, (*a*) cwdd arçav—
Marw Urien, angen arnav !

A'i dy gyfful cyrçu brân, (*b*)
Can ddiwg ac argynan—
Marw meibion Urien açlan ?

Na çred vrân, na çred Ddunawd,
Na çai ganthudd yn fofawd,
Bugail lloi Llanvor llwybrawd. (*c*)

Yffydd Lanvor dra gweilgi,
Y gwna mor molud wrthi—
Llallogan ni wn a'i hi.

Yffydd Llanvor, tra bànawg (*d*)
Ydd aä Clwyd yn Nghlywedawg,
Ac ni wn ai hi llallawg.

Heïs Dyvyrdwy yn ei thervyn,
O Veloç hyd Traweryn,
Bugail lloi Llanvor llwybryn. (*e*)

(*a*) Neu, Rot am gyffut.
(*b*) Neu, Ai dy gyffut cyrchu bran.
(*c*) Neu, Llafnawg llwyprawd.
(*d*) Neu, Yffydd llafnfawr tra bannawg.
(*e*) Neu, Llafnawr llwybryn.

Old *Llywarç* be thou not abaſhed,
An aſylum thou ſhalt have, abounding with love—
Wipe thine eye, be ſilent, and ceaſe from weeping !

I am old, I do not recollect thee,
I want advice, it is that I aſk—
Urien is dead, and I am oppreſſed with trouble !

Is it for advice thou goeſt to the raven,
That ſings her harmleſs clamour—
Are all the ſons of *Urien* dead ?

Believe not the raven, believe not *Dunawd*,
That thou ſhalt not have from them one blow in thy cauſe,
Herdman of the calves wandering the paths of *Llanvor.* (a)   :

There is *Llanvor*, beyond the ſtream
From which the ſea augments its majeſty—
But I know not that it is an oracle.

There is *Llanvor*, and very loud
Doth the *Clwyd* (b) unite with the *Clywedawg* ;
But I do not know that it is ominous of other times.

The *Dyvyrdwy* (c) has ſpread over its bounds,
From *Meloç* as far as *Traweryn*,
Herdman of the calves ranging the paths of *Llanvor*.

(a) The church of *Llanvor* is ſituated on the banks of the *Dee*, about two miles below *Bala*, in *Meirion*. *Llywarç* ended his days in the neighbourhood, and was buried in that church.
(b) The *Clwyd* flows through the fine vale, to which it gives its name, in *Denbighſhire*, and falls into the ſea at *Rhuddlan*
(c) The river *Dee*.

Truan o dynged a dynged,
A dyngwyd i Lywarç y nos i ganed:
Hir gniv, heb efgor lludded !

Teneu vy yfgwyd, ar affwy vy nhu,
Cw bwyv hén, a's gallav,
Ar Rodwydd Vorlas gwyliav !

DIWEDD.

Wretched is the fate that has been fated,
That was fworn to *Llywarç* on the night of his birth :
Long pains without being delivered of his woes !

Thin is my fhield on my left fide,
Though I am old, if I can,
I will watch on the encampment of *Morlas!*

T H E   E N D.

NEW PUBLICATIONS.

POEMS,
LYRIC AND PASTORAL,
BY EDWARD WILLIAMS:

IN TWO VOLUMES, PRICE EIGHT SHILLINGS.

Sold by J. Owen, No. 168, Piccadilly ; E. Williams, Strand ; and J. John-
son, St. Paul's Church-Yard

By Subscription, some Time in 1793,
THE CELTIC REMAINS,
ORIGINALLY COLLECTED
BY THE LATE LEWIS MORRIS,
AUGMENTED AND ARRANGED
BY WALTER DAVIES, OF ALL SOUL's COLLEGE OXFORD.

The Work will be printed in One large Octavo Volume,
PRICE TWELVE SHILLINGS.

Subscribers' Names are received by the Editor, at Llanveçain, in Montgo-
meryshire ; J. Owen, Piccadilly ; and E. Williams, Strand.

IN ONE VOLUME OCTAVO, PRICE FIVE SHILLNIGS AND SIXPENCE,
THE
WORKS OF DAVYDD AB GWILYM,
A WELSH BARD OF THE FOURTEENTH CENTURY.

Sold by E. Williams, Strand ; and J. Owen, Piccadilly.

PRICE FOUR SHILLINGS,
THE FIRST AND SECOND PARTS OF
The First Discovery of America by the Europeans.
BY J. WILLIAMS, L. L. D. OF SYDENHAM.

Wherein the Expedition of Madog ab Owain Gwynedd, in the Twelfth
Century, is examined, and proved, by the present Existence of a Welsh Co-
lony on that Continent, under the Names of White Padoucas, Madawgwys,
White Indians, Civilized Indians, and Welsh Indians.

GWERTH 2 SWLLT,
TRAETHAWD AR RYDDYD,
O WAITH
Walter Davies ; ac i'w Cael Ganddo yn Llanveçain ; ac E. Williams, Strand.

In February, 1793, *will be publifhed,*
THE FIRST PART OF THE
WELSH AND ENGLISH DICTIONARY;
COMPILED FROM THE
LAWS, HISTORY, POETRY, MANNERS, &c. OF THE WELSH.
BY WILLIAM OWEN.

Many of the Patronizers of this Work having made inquiries after it, in confequence of a promife that it would be publifhed at a period now paft, the Compiler conceives himfelf under a neceffity to make known the caufe of delay.

The firft Propofals announced that this Dictionary would contain *Twenty Thoufand Words* more than any other of the Welfh Language. This was done on the fuppofition that the collections previoufly made by others, added to that by the compiler would be about that number. But after he had made fome progrefs in reading the Welfh Writings, for the purpofe of collecting words, he found what was previoufly done was but very partial, and he found his own additons fwelling to a bulk that he had no idea of. If he had been tolerably exact in his firft calculation, the work might have been publifhed a long time ago ; but, from the refult of his having examined regularly all the old manufcripts that fell in his way, the collection of additional words exceed the enormous number of ONE HUNDRED THOU-SAND, after throwing afide all the irregular and barbarous words. To thofe who have an idea of the labour attending the arrangement of fuch a mafs it is fufficient barely to mention the circumftance, to induce them to judge favourably of the delay that has happened.

GWERTH SWLLT.
Awdlau Yftyriaeth ar oes Dyn, Gwirionedd a Rhyddyd,
GAN
Davydd Thomas, o'r Waun Vawr, yn Arvon ; ac ar Werth Gantho.

ANCIENT BRITISH BARDS, VOL. II.
Towards the Clofe of the Year 1793, *will be publifhed,*
THE WORKS OF TALIESIN,
A BARD OF THE SIXTH CENTURY.
WITH
A LITERAL ENGLISH VERSION, AND NOTES,
BY WILLIAM OWEN.

Subfcribers' Names will be received by J. Owen, No. 168, Piccadilly ; and E. Williams, Strand.

www.ingramcontent.com/pod-product-compliance
Lightning Source LLC
Chambersburg PA
CBHW030106030726
47498CB00007B/2274